©Noboru Kannatuki

GOBLIN SLAYER

©Noboru Kannatuki

The party moved
forward… No.

Rather, that is
to say, they found
themselves cornered
at the tower's edge.

Contents

GOBLIN SLAYER

VOLUME 7

KUMO KAGYU

Illustration by
NOBORU KANNATUKI

YEN
ON
New York

GOBLIN SLAYER

KUMO KAGYU

Translation by Kevin Steinbach ✛ Cover art by Noboru Kannatuki

This book is a work of fiction. Names, characters, places, and incidents are the product of the author's imagination or are used fictitiously. Any resemblance to actual events, locales, or persons, living or dead, is coincidental.

GOBLIN SLAYER vol. 7
Copyright © 2018 Kumo Kagyu
Illustrations copyright © 2018 Noboru Kannatuki
All rights reserved.
Original Japanese edition published in 2018 by SB Creative Corp.
This English edition is published by arrangement with SB Creative Corp., Tokyo, in care of Tuttle-Mori Agency, Inc., Tokyo.

English translation © 2019 by Yen Press, LLC

Yen On
1290 Avenue of the Americas
New York, NY 10104

Visit us at yenpress.com ✛ facebook.com/yenpress ✛ twitter.com/yenpress
yenpress.tumblr.com ✛ instagram.com/yenpress

First Yen On Edition: May 2019

Yen On is an imprint of Yen Press, LLC.
The Yen On name and logo are trademarks of Yen Press, LLC.

The publisher is not responsible for websites (or their content) that are not owned by the publisher.

Library of Congress Cataloging-in-Publication Data
Names: Kagyū, Kumo, author. | Kannatuki, Noboru, illustrator.
Title: Goblin slayer / Kumo Kagyu ; illustration by Noboru Kannatuki.
Other titles: Goburin sureiyā. English
Description: New York, NY : Yen On, 2016–
Identifiers: LCCN 2016033529 | ISBN 9780316501590 (v. 1 : pbk.) | ISBN 9780316553223 (v. 2 : pbk.) |
    ISBN 9780316553230 (v. 3 : pbk.) | ISBN 9780316411882 (v. 4 : pbk.) | ISBN 9781975326487 (v. 5 : pbk.) |
    ISBN 9781975327842 (v. 6 : pbk.) | ISBN 9781975330781 (v. 7 : pbk.)
Subjects: LCSH: Goblins—Fiction. | GSAFD: Fantasy fiction.
Classification: LCC PL872.5.A367 G6313 2016 | DDC 895.63/6—dc23
LC record available at https://lccn.loc.gov/2016033529

ISBNs: 978-1-9753-3078-1 (paperback)
       978-1-9753-3079-8 (ebook)

10 9 8 7 6 5 4 3 2 1

LSC-C

Printed in the United States of America

GOBLIN SLAYER

❖ VOLUME 7 ❖

GOBLIN SLAYER

✝

Character PROFILES

"I am to goblins what goblins are to us."

GOBLIN SLAYER

A strange adventurer active on the frontier. He is famous for reaching Silver (3rd) rank hunting only goblins.

"Protect, heal, save."
—The Three Holy Tenets of the Earth Mother

PRIESTESS

Works with Goblin Slayer. A sweet young woman who must put up with her partner's antics.

"Ignorance is bliss, for learning is the highest joy." —Elven proverb

HIGH ELF ARCHER

An elf girl who adventures with Goblin Slayer. A ranger and a skilled archer.

The only things that matter to her are the weather, the animals, the crops…and him.

COW GIRL

A girl who works on the farm where Goblin Slayer lives. The two are old friends.

"How can you go adventuring without pen and paper?"

GUILD GIRL

A girl who works at the Adventurers Guild. Goblin Slayer's preference for goblin slaying always helps her out.

"Before they're polished, jewels and precious metals all look like rocks. No dwarf would judge a thing by its appearance alone."

DWARF SHAMAN

A dwarf spell caster who adventures with Goblin Slayer.

"A naga does not run."

LIZARD PRIEST

A lizardman priest who adventures with Goblin Slayer.

"Train yourself: kill with the blade. If blood flows, let it be the enemy's."— First of the "Secrets of Steel."

HEAVY WARRIOR

A Silver-ranked adventurer associated with the Guild in the frontier town. Along with Female Knight and his other companions, his party is one of the best on the frontier.

"Only a tangled skein awaits those who carelessly spin tales about love or the universe's mysteries...not to mention a woman's beauty."

WITCH

A Silver-ranked adventurer at the frontier town's Adventurers Guild.

"I won't make friends tomorrow with an enemy I respect. I'll do it today."

SPEARMAN

A Silver-ranked adventurer at the frontier town's Adventurers Guild.

"Love does not consist in gazing at each other, but in looking outward in the same direction."—A poet

SWORD MAIDEN

Archbishop of the Supreme God in the water town. Also a Gold-ranked adventurer who once fought with the Demon Lord.

©Noboru Kannatuki

Love is destiny

destiny is death

Even a knight who serves a
maiden

will one day fall into death's
clutches

Even the prince who befriends
a Sky Drake

must leave the woman he fancies
behind

The mercenary who loved a
cleric

will fall in battle pursuing his
dream

And the king who loved the
shrine maiden

controls all but the hour of their
separation

The end of life

is not the last chapter of an
heroic saga

So the adventure called life

will continue to the very end

Friendship and love

life and death

From these things

we cannot escape

Therefore what have we

to fear

Love is destiny

and our destiny is death

CHAPTER 1

A HANDOUT FOR HER

"I guess it's time to get married," High Elf Archer said, as if it hardly mattered to her. Her long ears jumped as she spoke.

The sunlight pouring through the window brought with it an oppressive afternoon heat.

It was summer.

This was not adventuring weather by anyone's standards. If there wasn't a pressing need to earn enough money to eat, nobody would have willingly gone out in the scorching heat.

Being in the tavern, however, wasn't much better. Several dozen people were still wearing their gear, something they felt compelled to do given their status as adventurers. The collective body heat was stifling, hot enough to give the sunlight a run for its money.

The lingering humidity left drinks tepid; people took dainty sips to make them last. No one in their right mind had any interest in moving.

That was when one adventurer came bursting in, sweat dripping down her forehead and a bag at her side.

"Hello, everyone! Postal delivery!"

This was not unusual. The delivery of urgent letters was a common form of employment for adventurers. From her place at the front desk, Guild Girl signaled several of the tavern's occupants, who came rushing up.

Each letter carried its own tidings.

"Ugh! They're foreclosing... Gimme a break already!"

"That's because you went into debt just to buy your equipment, idiot."

"Hah! My little sister had a kid! I'll have to go see her after one more adventure."

"Whoa, take that back! You know saying a line like that is a sure way to die, right?"

"Huh, a personal summons from the capital. Awesome. This is a good sign."

"So, another...date. A trip. It's...been a while."

Demands for repayment, letters from home, urgent quests, and so on. Perhaps it was the heat that made everyone overlook High Elf Archer's words in the midst of all this chatting and trading of information.

A single piece of paper is sometimes called a leaf, but the letter High Elf Archer had received was literally written on an actual leaf. It was covered in a beautiful, flowing script in the elf language; High Elf Archer looked it over and then nodded to herself.

"I guess it's time to get married," High Elf Archer said, as if it hardly mattered to her. Her long ears twitched as she spoke.

"......"

There was a moment of silence where all the occupants of the room looked at everyone else, trying to comprehend what they'd just heard.

The chatter in the Adventurers Guild exploded with the force of a bomb.

Dwarf Shaman spat out his wine; Lizard Priest stuck out his long tongue and hissed, "Oh-ho!"

"Say again?" Guild Girl asked, while beside her, Inspector's eyes were agleam.

"Time for *what*?!" Female Knight demanded, rising to her feet. "Hey," Heavy Warrior said, a look of resignation on his face as he pulled on her sleeve.

Rookie Warrior and Apprentice Cleric pretended to pay no attention, but it was obvious they were listening.

"Wha— Wha—" Priestess kept repeating, her hand to her mouth and her face growing red—and her eyes sparkling.

In all of this commotion, three words could be heard:

"Is that so?"

Goblin Slayer spoke with his usual indifference.

"To whom?"

"An older male cousin of mine," High Elf Archer responded, still completely calm. She waved her hand and smiled. "Talk about a shock. I never would've imagined it'd be with someone as straitlaced as him!"

"Hmm," Goblin Slayer said, nodding. "So—"

"Congratulations!" Priestess, her voice full of emotion and her face wreathed in a smile, leaned out toward High Elf Archer. She grasped the elf's hands, speaking from the bottom of her heart. "Um, do elves have wedding ceremonies like we do? If it's all right—"

"Of course! And it's for a member of the chieftain's family, so this is gonna be a big one. By all means, come!"

"Sheesh," Dwarf Shaman said, shooting a sidelong glance at the gabbing girls. He had finally managed to mop up the wine he'd spit out, wring out his beard, and pour himself a new cup. "And here I thought the twilight of the elves had come early, what with her being the chieftain's daughter."

"Ha! Ha! Ha! Ha!" Lizard Priest slapped his tail happily against the floor. "Thus have the elder ever thought of the younger."

"Bah! I'm sure I'm actually younger than she is."

So...was getting married at two thousand years old considered early or late for the elves?

Ignoring the dwarf's perplexed expression, Lizard Priest took a regretful bite of his cheese. "I suppose this means bidding farewell to our mistress ranger. Ah, a lonely day that shall be..."

"? Why would you bid me farewell?"

"Mm. Will you not become rather busy?"

"There won't be any kids coming along for at least another two or three hundred years." *Who gets pregnant during their first couple of decades?* High Elf Archer looked a little pouty.

"Gracious, elves do measure time on a grand scale, don't they?" Lizard Priest muttered when he heard her speak of spans almost beyond his imagining.

"Well, we're practically immortal. What, aren't lizardmen?"

"Princes, in fact, are allowed only one egg, but for us the pattern is be born, multiply, live, kill, then die."

"The cycle's important, isn't it?" *Spin, spin.* High Elf Archer drew a circle in the air with a slender finger. In this respect, the elves and the lizards, who both abided strictly by nature, had something in common. One might love battle and the other not, and one might be immortal and the other mortal, but life and death came to them just the same.

"Huh..." Priestess made a noise, apparently still a bit confused. Souls went up to heaven, where the gods resided, and where they received many comforts. Once in a while, such a soul might return to the board, but this was somewhat outside the cycle of nature.

"But," Priestess asked, tilting her head, "do elf husbands normally let their wives go all over and do dangerous things after they get married?"

"Uh-uh! No way my cousin would permit that." High Elf Archer laughed and waved her hand. "He was in love at first sight, I'm sure. Even though he's so serious and hardheaded... Actually, maybe that's exactly the reason."

"Er... Come again?" Priestess put a finger to her lip. "Hmm." Something about this conversation wasn't making sense.

It feels a little...off. Like we're talking past one another.

"So," Goblin Slayer said, coming back into the discussion so suddenly that High Elf Archer found herself blinking. "Who is getting married?"

"Oh, my older sister."

"Coulda said that a li'l sooner, ya Anvil!" Dwarf Shaman gave her a scolding slap on the behind.

"Wha?!" High Elf Archer went from flummoxed to angry, her ears pointing straight back. Tears brimmed in her eyes. "Just *what* do you think you're doing?!"

"What's this? First I've ever heard of an anvil that can't stand being hit!"

"You're the worst!" By this point, she had completely abandoned anything resembling the dignity normally associated with a high elf. "This is why I hate dwarves! You... You beer barrel!"

"I thought I told you—it's called being full-bodied, and we appreciate it!"

And they were off. Priestess was used to these sudden explosions of bickering by now. She held her mug in both hands, taking little sips of her lemon water, which was practically a tepid drink by now.

"If we're going to be guests...we'll have to get her a gift or something."

"Is that so?" Goblin Slayer nodded. He crossed his arms and fell silent for a moment, then he grunted and finally, with some difficulty, said, "I think I—"

"*No*," Priestess said, although she was smiling. She was pointing one finger squarely at Goblin Slayer, who swallowed what he had been about to say. "We've been specially invited to a wonderful celebration. You can't not go."

"That..." Goblin Slayer broke off for a moment. "...may be so, but—"

"We can ask the receptionist to make sure other people take care of the goblin slaying."

"Hrk..."

It was like having Protection, a miracle that had come to be something of her specialty. Her smile deflected any and every attack.

Goblin Slayer made no further sound; Lizard Priest rolled his eyes in his head.

It seems milady receptionist and the farm daughter have taught him well.

"Heh-heh-heh. Well, perhaps I and master spell caster will come up with an appropriate gift." He made a solemn and important-looking gesture then brought his palms together in a strange way. "But my dear cleric," he added, "it seems you've become rather assertive!"

"Of course I have!" Priestess puffed out her small chest so as to look as strong as she could. "I learned from Goblin Slayer, after all!"

§

Now, then.

Members of the Guild staff are often enjoined to be calm and even at all times.

After all, it's the men and women of the Guild who are the first to provide information to those embarking on an adventure. When a quest giver comes to them with a crisis, they are the first face that person sees.

It would be unseemly for a staff member to appear rushed or disinterested. Instead, their clothes must be without a wrinkle, their shirt or blouse starched, and their makeup just so.

Bed head and yawning are, of course, totally unacceptable. The moment one becomes a civil servant, one takes on the responsibility of representing one's country.

"...But then again, when it's hot, it's hot." *Ah-ha-ha-ha.*

With a laugh, Guild Girl poured Goblin Slayer and the others cups of cold black tea. There were one, two, three, four glasses on the desk in her little part of the reception counter. High Elf Archer and Priestess had dragged Goblin Slayer over between them. Lastly, Guild Girl set a glass down in front of herself, putting a hand to her cheek and letting out a breath.

"A wedding, though... How wonderful."

"Yeah, I'm thrilled," High Elf Archer said, nodding with a serious, knowing look. "Thank goodness my sister wasn't too old for marriage."

"How old is she?"

"Hmm..." The archer counted on her fingers, shaking her head briefly. "About eight thousand or so, I guess."

Guild Girl, thinking that "or so" could probably represent another three zeros, smiled dryly. "Listening to elves makes you realize how silly it is to worry about your age."

Another sigh. She wouldn't get anywhere rhetorically digging her own grave.

Priestess offered several "Ahems" and "Ums." The girl had only just turned sixteen and didn't seem to know how to address the older woman, even though she herself was a cleric. If nothing else, Priestess didn't think that Guild Girl's appearance gave her any reason to be worried about how old she was.

"But being as pretty as you are... Do you really need to be concerned about it?"

"Hee-hee. Well, thank you very much." Guild Girl smiled at the polite question Priestess finally came up with.

High Elf Archer gave a jovial wave of her hand and drained her glass in a single swig. "That's right. When it comes to age, you can't compare a dragon to an elephant, or an elephant to a mouse. It just doesn't work."

"Elephant." Unexpectedly, Goblin Slayer's helmet tilted in confusion. "What is that?"

"...You don't know about elephants?" High Elf Archer's ears wiggled, pleased to have a chance to educate the warrior. She spread her arms wide as she described the mysterious creature. "It has legs like pillars, a tail like a rope, ears like fans, a body like a wall, tusks like spears, a back like a throne, and a nose like a vine. Plus, it's huge."

"...A beast?"

"Oh, and it's colored gray."

"I don't understand at all," Goblin Slayer said with a grunt then gulped down his tea.

Guild Girl watched them happily then let out a bit of a chuckle. "Maybe I can show you the entry in the Monster Manual under *Elephant* some time. Now..." Her gaze moved around her desk, and she flipped through some papers. "You wanted me to assign those goblin quests, right?"

"Uh-huh. We'd like to bring our friend Goblin Slayer along," Priestess said calmly. Her smile, like a flower in bloom, never wavered.

"Personally, I don't particularly want to miss it." Goblin Slayer set his empty glass down on the countertop with a clack. "I simply do not want to leave the goblins to their own devices."

"Yes, yes, obviously not," Guild Girl said with a soft smile. He was as dispassionate and decisive as ever. Some people took him for a simple obsessive, while others saw him as trustworthy and reliable. Guild Girl, needless to say, was in the latter group.

"From early spring into summer, the goblins are at their strongest. Perhaps it is because they are angry."

"Is there any season when the goblins aren't scary?" High Elf Archer asked.

"Hrm..." Goblin Slayer crossed his arms and grunted.

Guild Girl listened to the two of them with some pleasure. "All the same," she said quietly, "there isn't that much goblin slaying in summer, is there?"

"Is that true?" Priestess asked with evident surprise.

"Yes," Guild Girl said. *At least, there aren't that many quests.* Then, rather than explain further, she shuffled through her papers for no particular reason. It would be rude to speak of such inauspicious things when someone had just received a wedding invitation.

Summer: to goblins, the most salient thing about this season was that it was not autumn. The crops in the fields were still young, and of course, harvest was a long way off. No matter how much the goblins might want food, there was simply not much to gain from attacking villages. So instead, they shifted their focus to travelers, wandering shepherds, and itinerant healers during the hottest time of year.

What did summer mean for goblins? Spring was all well and good, but in summer, the rains got heavier, and the accursed sunlight grew ever more intense. Living in a hole became quite unpleasant. Granted, one didn't imagine goblins to be overly concerned about their living situation, but they were always angry about something. And more reasons to get angry naturally meant a greater incidence of violence.

Woe to the traveler who was set upon by goblins on the road in summer. Goblins didn't have the wisdom to store up food, although even if they had, it would soon have spoiled. After they'd had their fill of making sport of their victim, they would immediately eat whatever they could of the unfortunate soul, thinking nothing of the future.

Man or woman, in the end, not even the bones would remain.

Sadly, it's an all too common story.

Travelers losing their lives on the road, of course, was hardly a phenomenon that only occurred in summer. Goblins and Non-Prayers were by no means the only ones who were hungry. Bandits, brigands, and mercenaries turned to raiding—among others—were all out there.

The point is, every corner of the world was full of danger. Some took this as a reason to criticize the king or the country's administration, but such people simply didn't know their history. In all of time and memory, there has never been an age without an element of danger.

Similarly, resources have always been limited. As far as Guild Girl knew, the current king was doing a perfectly decent job... Or at least, so she thought. He didn't start unnecessary wars, and he had faced off with the Dark Gods' followers to keep the country safe.

We've got peace now, as far as it goes.

Even if the definition of peace was merely the lull between wars.

But to repeat, resources were limited and danger was ever present. The Guild wouldn't necessarily receive a quest simply because one traveler had gone missing. For one thing, if nobody knew that the person had disappeared, nothing would be done. It was a sad situation, and a flaw in the Adventurers Guild. Adventurers moved on these sorts of problems only when a traveler's relation filed a quest...

...Or when the adventurers themselves have very good hearts.

"But there *are* still goblins out there," Goblin Slayer said, with no heed for what was going on in Guild Girl's mind. "That will not change."

"But," said Priestess, shrewdly pretending to ask a question while actually cutting in, "you can't defeat them all by yourself, can you? And you don't have to, right?"

"..."

Goblin Slayer was silent. After so many years with him, Guild Girl knew that this was how he acted when he had been backed into a corner.

In some ways, he's not that difficult a person to understand.

An involuntary giggle escaped her lips, and Goblin Slayer's steel helmet turned toward her. She waved a hand as if to say *Nothing, nothing.*

"Honestly," she said, "it won't do for us to be troubling you with every single goblin quest that comes along, Mr. Goblin Slayer."

"Well, there you have it," Priestess said with a sweet but pointed cough. "Will you handle this for us?"

"Oh, certainly. I know this man would never take a vacation if we left him to his own devices."

"Sounds a lot like you."

Someone gave Guild Girl an unexpected rap on the head, provoking a little *ow!* It was her seatmate and colleague, Inspector, standing behind her with a sheaf of papers in hand.

Inspector sighed as if to suggest that this served Guild Girl right, and she followed up by gently tapping her papers against the other woman's shoulder. "Remind me how long it's been since you last took a day off?"

Guild Girl clutched her head and protested weakly, "I—I take them..."

Inspector produced another exasperated sigh. "So then you're going to this wedding, too, right? That's what these kids are here for, isn't it? To invite you?"

Before Guild Girl had a chance to answer, High Elf Archer was leaning in over the desk. "Of course!" she said, nodding vigorously. Without any need to pretend, she added, "We're friends, after all!"

Seeing this display of genuine eagerness, Guild Girl responded with an ambiguous expression and a scratch of her cheek. Then her fingers played through her hair, twirling her braids. Yes, she was aware it wasn't very polite.

"Er... Well, I certainly appreciate the sentiment, but..."

No, stop. If I turn down this invitation...

How could she explain herself to High Elf Archer, let alone Priestess or Goblin Slayer? She took a quick glance at his helmet, even though, as ever, it hid his expression.

"Just take a couple days off already!"

"Yipe!" Another blow from the papers.

As Guild Girl sat there groaning quietly, Inspector put on her best smile and said, "Now, Mister, uh... Goblin Slayer."

"What is it?"

Guild Girl made a little squeak, but Inspector ignored her, pulling the papers right out of her hands. They were, of course, a collection of the nearest goblin-slaying quests.

"It'll be best for both of us if we get some of this work out of the way," Inspector said, rolling up the papers like a scroll and handing the lot to Goblin Slayer. "Maybe you could help my friend here relax by taking care of two or three goblin nests."

"Naturally."

There was no argument, no hesitation as Goblin Slayer took the quest papers in one decisive motion. Silently, he unrolled them and considered the descriptions. He never so much as glanced at the rewards. What he wanted was information, knowledge about the goblins' fighting strength.

After a long moment, he asked softly, "Is it all right?"

High Elf Archer was frowning as hard as she could, her long ears back against her head, but she answered, "I can't speak for the dwarf… But me, I'm not gonna say no."

"You're sure? I don't much mind either way."

"Excuse me very much, Goblin Slayer, sir," Priestess said, furrowing her shapely eyebrows. She raised a pale pointer finger and, in a tone suggesting they'd had this conversation more than once before, said, "When we don't have a choice, it doesn't count as a *discussion*, remember?"

§

"Hrr—gyaaaaaahhhhhh!"

The woman's scream, like the gibbering of a chicken having its neck wrung, echoed throughout the twilit chapel.

However many tried to push their way closer, there was a physical limit to how many goblins one person could accommodate at a time. Yes, goblins were small, but even counting both arms, her mouth, and perhaps her hair, there was room for maybe just five or six at a time.

There were easily more than a dozen monsters surrounding the woman bound to the altar at that moment, though. The violation of her chastity was horrific enough, but this victim was subject to all their cruel desires at once, truly a pitiful position.

The woman whose agonized scream had sounded in the worship hall was now dressed in nothing more than the rags of what had once been a traveling outfit. Her limbs, which could just be seen through the press of goblin bodies, were tan and fairly muscular.

She had been a traveler lodging in this convent, in a small library dedicated to the God of Knowledge.

Now there was no way to know where she had meant to go or why she had stayed in this place. The texts, the gems of wisdom stored here, were no longer in a fit state to be read. All the knowledge gathered by the maidens—who had left their homes and shut themselves up in this place for any number of reasons—had been trampled underfoot. The goblins had taken these precious records of knowledge and torn them apart, defiled them, even set fire to a few at random.

The pillaged library now held only the nuns, their spirits broken by unimaginable predations. The traveler saw what the goblins had done to them, and yet, she chose to fight—good, strong prey for the little devils.

Had she been fighting to protect the nuns or to open a way for her own escape? The goblins assumed it must be the latter. The more honorable reading, however, was that the traveler had wielded her sword bravely, with no concern for herself.

At least until the goblins pulled her to the ground, beat her mercilessly, and broke her arm.

It had been several days since then, and the remaining goblins were still busy getting their revenge for the ones she had killed. They had left the traveler for last so that they could enjoy seeing her terror build as she witnessed the fates they devised for the nuns.

They never once thought that she might try to escape. Or rather, they assumed there was no possible way she could.

Goblins habitually demonstrate extreme overconfidence despite the absence of proof. They never imagine anything they attempt might fail. And even on the off chance that anything should happen—

"GOORRIRRROG!!"

"Urgh! Aggh—gah—y—you bas—taaaghh!"

—it would always be because some idiot like this had gotten in their way.

The goblins fully believed that everyone in this little library was a complete and utter fool. They kept this room full of incomprehensible, boring papers, and there was so little food. Humans, the goblins chuckled, did so much that made so little sense.

The goblins, of course, could have never understood the meaning of the tomes held within this library. It was just off a road, standing quietly in a forest where it had been built with the conviction that while knowledge and wisdom were born of the profane world, it was important to avoid becoming sullied by that same world.

Just because it was a small library didn't mean it lacked any defenses against monsters or bandits. It had stone walls, and occasionally, traveling adventurers or mercenaries would stay there. But prolonged exposure to the elements could wear away a part of a wall. And there were those times when no armed visitor was lodging with them.

Was that why the goblins had targeted them? Why had they been attacked by the goblins?

One could ask, but the God of Knowledge was unlikely ever to lead one to an answer.

Goblins were like a natural disaster; they came from nowhere at all. They had simply happened to appear here, at this moment.

"Hrrraaaaghhhh!"

The library was now a place of debauchery. And over in one corner of the God of Knowledge's worship hall, a single goblin rested his chin in his hands, enjoying the sound of the woman's screams in his ears.

Once they'd had their fun with her, would they keep her alive to bear their young, or immediately kill and eat her?

Most likely, she would become food, the goblin thought. The other young-bearers needed something to eat, and anyway, it would be boring not to kill her. Unsatisfying.

"Gyaaaaaaahhhh!"

A high-pitched scream. Some impatient goblin must have applied a hatchet to her broken arm or something.

"GROB! GOOROORB!!"

"GOORROB!"

Somebody complained to the hatcheteer, he responded, and their cruel cackling at the thrashing woman filled the chapel.

This wouldn't do. There were several ways to enjoy a dead woman, but now was the only moment to seize the pleasures of a live one.

The goblin licked his chops, his tiny brain straining. Maybe he could find a good opportunity to cut in line, get a chance to enjoy the woman while she was still alive. This was his only concern; he had no interest in the other goblins he would be cutting ahead of, much less the young woman herself.

Goblins had a sense of solidarity, recognized one another as fellows. But their first loyalty was always and ever to themselves. How could they gain, have pleasure, achieve the best position, kill people who were evil—or at least people they didn't like?

The death of other goblins made a perfect excuse to enjoy their victim until they killed off the unfortunate thing.

"GROOROB!"

"GRO! GOORB!!"

The goblin picked one of the others almost at random and lit into him.

I've been on guard all this time! You all need to do some guarding, too! It's not fair for goblins who haven't been on guard duty to have all the fun, you greedy bastards.

The goblin made his case (in which he highlighted only those details that were convenient) then gave the thoughtless creature a shove on the shoulder.

"Er—ergaahh! Y— Y-you're…killing…me…!"

"GROB! GOOROBB!"

This was a monster who cared nothing for either other goblins or how the pitiful woman tried to resist him. The cruelties by which he enjoyed himself don't bear speaking of.

Here's the important point: absorbed in his enjoyment, *he never noticed.*

"GRRRRR…"

He didn't notice the arm reach out of the darkness and grab the goblin who stood grumbling about the unfairness of it all. The eerily silent appendage wrapped itself around the goblin's neck like a snake and squeezed hard.

"…B—?!"

Before the creature could even cry out, a knife had slit his throat.

A hand covered the goblin's mouth as he choked on his own blood, resting there for several seconds until he had stopped breathing.

The goblin's corpse was readily rolled behind one of the pews, and then the owner of the arm waved toward the shadows.

That owner was a man, wearing grimy leather armor, a cheap-looking steel helmet, a sword of a strange length, and a small, round shield on his arm.

It was Goblin Slayer.

At his gesture, Lizard Priest came forward, his tail tucked in. High
Elf Archer followed him, then Priestess, and then Dwarf Shaman.
None of them made a sound as they moved: not a footstep, not a rustle
of their clothes.

The reason they could pull off such a feat was thanks to the girl who
was praying with her eyes shut, her hands wrapped around a sounding staff.

"O Earth Mother, abounding in mercy, grant us peace to accept all things."

They were ensconced in the absolute quiet granted by Priestess's
Silence miracle.

Her vestments were covered in dark stains, evidence of the several
goblins they had already dealt with. The cruor-smeared marks didn't
seem to bother her, though; she only knelt and continued to pray. Her
faithful heart helped to protect the adventurers with this soundless
bubble.

High Elf Archer was much the opposite; she looked like she might
burst into tears at any moment. "Ugghh…"

She may have been using a perfume pouch, but even so, the stench
of goblin waste, and of the juices of their innards, assaulted her sharp
senses. She couldn't keep the disgusting stuff from getting on her
cloak, leaving her outfit smelling rather unpleasant.

Why can't the gods block out smells, too? High Elf Archer looked up
reproachfully at the statue standing in the worship hall.

It was an image of the sage who had charted the movements of the
stars.

There was, of course, no answer to High Elf Archer's impertinent
question.

*I'm here saving your followers because apparently you can't do it yourself. I'd
appreciate a little gratitude.*

Okay, maybe that was a bit too close to sacrilege. Her ears twitched,
and she set an arrow into her bow.

The adventurers' party had made it to the chapel without undue difficulty. And now they were faced with twenty or so goblins, absorbed
in their fun. They weren't going to let this chance go.

The members of Goblin Slayer's party nodded to one another, followed by a series of quick signals.

" . . . . . "

" . . . . . "

It was Dwarf Shaman who acted first. He took a mouthful of fire wine from the flask at his hip and immediately spat it out. The mist settled over the room as he chanted, *"Drink deep, sing loud, let the spirits lead you! Sing loud, step quick, and when to sleep they see you, may a jar of fire wine be in your dreams to greet you!"*

The goblins, afflicted by Stupor, began to loll on their feet, where-upon Goblin Slayer jumped into action. He vaulted over the pew, running along the stone floor and sending his sword flying. The blade traveled noiselessly through the air until the moment it left the area of Silence's effect, when it made a soft whistling sound.

Even goblins, as stupid as they are, wouldn't miss that.

"GOOROB! GOROOOB!!"

"GRRORB!!"

Several of the monsters pointed and shouted, but it was too late. The goblin who stood thrusting his hips felt something enter the back of his head and pierce him clean through to his mouth. Did he even understand what it was?

The goblin, his spine sheared clean through, foamed at the mouth, his dirty golden eyes rolling in his head.

"GOOROOROOOB?!"

"One."

Goblin Slayer practically lunged forward, using his shield to lash out at one of the nearby goblins. In the same motion, he grabbed a sickle from the hip of the first writhing monster, using it to cut the throat of the second.

"Two."

Using his shield to stop the blood from spattering on them, he pulled out the blade then tossed the goblin down so it was covering the young woman.

"You are alive, correct?"

He glanced down at the twitching, blood-covered woman beneath the corpse.

He knew how the goblins worked. It would be more than a little troublesome if they were able to use the woman as a shield against him.

The motions he was seeing, though, were probably shock from pain and blood loss. She was still alive, but she didn't have long. As usual, time was of the essence.

The goblins made their hostility toward the invaders plain. Goblin Slayer watched them vigilantly.

"Hurry!"

"Let us be on our way, then."

"R-right!"

Lizard Priest swept Priestess up in his arms then set off at a run, his claws digging into the stone floor. He leaned forward at an angle that would have been untenable for a human, but his long tail allowed him to maintain his balance.

"GOROOOB! GROBB!"

"GGOOORB!"

The goblins, needless to say, would not let them get away with this. They may not have been very intelligent, but they weren't going to let these women slip through their fingers all at once. And Lizard Priest literally had his hands full with Priestess...

"Krrraaahhhhhhaaaa!"

"GOOROB?!"

Then again, as long as he had his claws and fangs and tail, who cared about his hands? Dragons and nagas certainly didn't need weapons.

"GROOB?!"

"GOBORB?!"

An old proverb said to let sleeping dragons lie. But what did goblins know about proverbs?

Lizard Priest's tail and the claws of his feet each struck a goblin, sending them flying. The wounds would not be fatal, but all he needed right now was to get Priestess up to the altar.

"Shall I remain on the front row?" he asked.

"Yes, please."

In the middle of this brief conversation, Goblin Slayer let go of the sickle blade, which was lodged in the skull of a goblin.

"GROBBB...?!"

As his victim collapsed, he grabbed the rough-hewn club out of the creature's hand. It would be enough; he didn't need to be precise right now.

"Well then, milady Priestess. I leave this to you."

"Sure thing. Good luck!"

Lizard Priest set her down gently, using his tail to keep the goblins at bay, then made his strange palms-together gesture.

"O sickle wings of Velociraptor, rip and tear, fly and hunt!"

The fang between his palms grew into a Swordclaw before their eyes, and Lizard Priest set upon the enemy, howling.

"Krrraaaaaaaahaaaaahhhhaaaa!"

"GOORBGG?!?!"

He was a cleric, yes, but a fighting one, the kind that might be called a warrior-priest. Had he been born to another race, he might have made an excellent knight.

In contrast to Goblin Slayer, who made quick, precise jabs at vital points, Lizard Priest was a whirlwind of violence. The chapel, already besmirched with the blood of the nuns and the filth of the goblins, was now further dirtied with the goblins' blood.

"Okay…!"

Priestess, for her part, still clutched her sounding staff. She nodded energetically and turned to face her own battlefield.

The young woman's breathing was ragged; Priestess knelt beside her, heedless of the gore and filth that got on her in the process. The scene was beyond awful, but she swallowed her disgust, along with whatever it was that had come back up from her stomach.

No matter how many times I see things like this, I never get used to them. But…

She must never get used to them, she thought forcefully. And each time she repeated this to herself, her faith became stronger.

"O Earth Mother, abounding in mercy, lay your revered hand upon this child's wounds."

She gripped her staff imploringly, lifting up her heart to the Earth Mother in heaven.

Please, be so gracious as to heal this person's wounds. Save her life. Save her.

And so at long last, she had the chance to cast Minor Heal again.

And the munificent Earth Mother responded to the heartfelt prayer of her dear follower. A pale light bubbled forth, leaping toward the young woman's injuries, starting to staunch the flow of blood.

The miracle would not, of course, restore lost vitality. Even a divine miracle could not easily undo wounds of the body and mind.

But neither would she die immediately.

"Goblin Slayer, sir, we're okay over here…!"

"Good." Without pausing, Goblin Slayer reached into the item pouch on his hip, pulled out an egg, and flung it at the goblins.

"GOOROOROB?!"

"GOOOROBOROOB?!?!"

An unpleasant smoke sprang up, prompting a chorus of shouts. Several of those goblins who had been enjoying torturing the woman now thrashed about in pain, tears in their little eyes. The egg had been a shell filled with Goblin Slayer's homemade tear gas. He hadn't been able to use it at first for fear that the gas might get into the wounds of the hostage girl, but that was no longer a concern.

"Eight— Nine!"

He tossed his club at one goblin, then brought down another with a rusty sword he had stolen. He slashed the creature's throat, not caring whether he destroyed the weapon in the process. There was a whistling from the monster's windpipe, along with a geyser of blood, and then the goblins collapsed one on top of the other.

"GBBB…!"

"GORBG! GGOOBBG!"

Half the goblin number had been annihilated in the space of a moment, and now the monsters were afraid. As scared as they were, though, they hated to let their hard-won prey escape. Not to mention the ugly part of their minds that longed to add the new young woman and the elf girl to their collection.

However, it was difficult to get past the human warrior and the lizard monk out in front.

Well, then…

"GROOB!"

"GORB!"

Immediately, several of the goblins dropped their weapons and charged blindly. Were they trying to form up, or run away, or—? No.

"They're going for shields!" Goblin Slayer sized up the situation in an instant and issued orders.

The fleeing creatures were heading for drop lids on the ground. They were going to bring up the women they had captured to bear their young. They would use them as meat shields.

"I hate that about goblins. If they think I'm just gonna stand here— Hah!"

The creatures suddenly found arrows protruding from their hips. From the shadow of the pews, High Elf Archer had let loose a merciless hail of arrows.

"GROB! GROOORB?!"

"GOOROB?!"

Three shots without a moment's pause. Three goblins fell to the ground, screeching.

It was easy to aim for the head, but there was always the possibility of a fumble. At the moment, immobilizing the monsters was more important; they could be dealt with after that.

High Elf Archer took just an instant to aim, then planted a bud-tipped bolt in a goblin's eyeball.

"Orcbolg! I've got things covered over here!"

"Well then, shall I take the stairs?"

Dwarf Shaman's work as a spell caster completed, what remained was physical labor. With surprising agility for such a large frame, he bounded toward the staircase. He drew his hand ax almost faster than the eye could see and assumed a fighting stance; he was clearly no amateur.

"GOOROOB!"

"GRRRRORB!"

This was where the goblin advance would stop.

The creatures had originally gotten in through a crack in the paltry defensive wall, but now they were the ones who were surrounded. Just like many new adventurers, the goblins had never imagined this might happen. They believed that it was theirs to kill, and not to be killed. This was an absolute; yet, here they were in the opposite situation.

Goblin Slayer understood this well. He himself had been that way once.

"Fourteen... Fifteen!"

"Krrraahhhh!"

Goblin Slayer smashed one creature's head with his club then grabbed a hand spear and stabbed another in the throat.

Lizard Priest struck out with claws and fangs and tail, rendering goblins into clouds of blood.

This was a party with four Silver-ranked adventurers and one Steel-ranked adventurer.

More importantly, one of those adventurers was Goblin Slayer.

There had never been any question of whether he would defeat twenty-odd goblins holed up in a church building. For him, the question was always how to do so quickly, how to kill precisely, and how to rescue any hostages.

§

"Twenty and three, is it?"

The battle had ended some time later. The sun was sinking, and the library was submerged in darkness. The only light came from lanterns flickering here and there.

Goblin Slayer did his work nonchalantly in the pale illumination: he went from one goblin corpse to the next, stabbing each with his weapon to make sure it was dead, then piling them up in a corner of the chapel.

The worship hall, now reeking of blood, rot, and refuse, and stained a gruesome crimson, no longer bore any sign of its former sacred purity. Whether or not it had been the goblins' objective, they had succeeded in utterly desecrating this place.

Just over twenty nuns had worked in the library. Roughly half of them were still alive. The rest remained only as the meat and bones in a stew pot.

Lizard Priest was in the process of bringing each of the nuns upstairs into the chapel from the basement storehouse.

"Stay strong, now. When dawn breaks, we can take you somewhere less upsetting."

"Thank you... Truly..."

"Think nothing of it. We may revere different deities, but monkeys came from lizards, in the end. That makes us cousins."

"Heh-heh… You lizardmen…say the strangest…things…"

The women chuckled among themselves. They were wrapped in cloth, although nothing could hide how filthy and emaciated they were. One look at the bandages wrapped around their ankles made it clear that they were not going to be walking anywhere.

Priestess found herself biting her lip. If there was one pain she did not yet know, it was that of a rusty dagger cutting her Achilles tendon.

"…It's all right now," she said. "We'll get you back to town soon."

"Tha…nk…y…ou…"

"Don't try to talk. Right now, you just need to rest."

Priestess moved conscientiously among the pews, administering first aid to the nuns and the traveler.

Everyone avoided asking what would become of them now.

There are quite a few, Goblin Slayer mused. So many of them who had maintained their sanity, and had neither committed suicide nor been used up then killed. *This library could be considered lucky.*

Thanks to the traveler, who had no doubt been prepared to fight to the death, one of the nuns had been spared this horror. She had been sent to another temple with a message and on her return discovered what was going on. She had gone back up the road to file a quest at the Adventurers Guild, but it had taken several days for adventurers to be dispatched.

It was thanks to the traveler that Goblin Slayer and his party had made it here. The hours she had bought with her blood gave them the time they needed to arrive.

If the traveler had decided instead to abandon the temple, or to throw down her weapon after only a token resistance, the nun would never have been able to escape, and the situation probably would not have been discovered until things were far worse.

"…Twenty-three, then," he murmured as if he himself almost didn't believe it. Then he tossed aside his bloody spear. It rolled noisily over to a corner of the chapel where there rested a pot with what remained of the food. In place of the spear, he took up a sword from a convenient goblin corpse, putting it in the scabbard at his hip.

It was only after doing all this that Goblin Slayer sat down in one of the pews.

"If it had not been for the books and the hostages, it would've been quicker to set fire to the place." He sighed deeply.

"…Hmph. What a thing to say," Priestess chided, pattering over to him. He looked at her without moving his helmet.

She must have finished providing first aid. Her blood-spattered cheeks softened, and then she managed a full-faced smile. She was trying not to show what must have been considerable fatigue from using two miracles.

"You want her to get angry at you again? *No fire!* she'll say." Priestess put her pointer fingers up by her head and flicked them up and down.

She was trying to joke—maybe forcing herself to. Goblin Slayer didn't know one way or the other. The shadows cast by the thin candlelight, combined with the visor of his helmet, kept him from reading the subtleties of her expression.

Finally, he simply said, "Indeed," and then closed his eyes.

He didn't intend to rest for very long, of course. He steadied his breathing, relaxed his awareness just for an instant, and then focused it again.

After all, there were still goblins around. Perhaps not here, but somewhere. There was nowhere he could let down his guard.

"…It took some work, though."

"Well, that…" Priestess's eyes flitted here and there as she tried to pick her words. "…happens sometimes, I think."

"…I see."

"Even the gods aren't all-powerful."

Then, almost hesitantly, she sat down next to Goblin Slayer. She was close enough that he might have felt the heat from her body, if he hadn't been wearing his armor. Goblin Slayer's eyes widened ever so slightly at the faint sound of breath he could detect past his metal helmet.

"How is the traveler girl?" he asked.

"Asleep, finally… She's okay in the short term. But she doesn't have enough blood."

"Tomorrow, then."

Priestess immediately grasped what Goblin Slayer meant by this brief response.

They would act the next day. In other words, they would spend the night here. They certainly couldn't ask the rescued women to walk. They would need a carriage or cart of some sort. Moreover, moving this many people at night would be dangerous. Especially without a plan.

"Make sure you rest a bit in the meantime."

"...Right." Priestess nodded. Her eyes drifted shut. She entertained no notion that she might actually sleep, but just closing her eyes was enough to relax a little. Goblin Slayer had been willing to take on a bit of the weight on her shoulders.

"But..." She heard Lizard Priest's footsteps approaching softly. He looked around somberly then continued in a quiet voice, "I feel the little devils have been...rather more clever of late."

"You think so?"

"It's only a feeling, but..." And then he went on quickly, with the special excitement that lizardmen seemed to have for matters of battle. "Ever since the goblin paladin, I have noticed it."

"I agree," Goblin Slayer said with a nod. "Perhaps they've gotten smarter...?"

Although, he added, he had labored to kill them precisely so that they might not learn.

Or perhaps my enemies to this point have been only puppets?

No. He dismissed the notion with a shake of his head. In some cases, one could chop off the head to destroy the body, but this was nothing nearly so simple. Was that not a lesson he had learned fully a decade ago?

"We will need some new plans ourselves."

"Pfah! The little monsters wouldn't know the value of a gem if it hit them in the eye." Dwarf Shaman bustled up, carrying an armful of cargo. The copious dust around him indicated that he must have been in the storehouse or somewhere similar.

None of them, of course, would stoop so low as to steal from these nuns. The point was to make sure everything was safe.

All the same, Lizard Priest rolled his eyes in his head with great interest. "Were any of the texts safe?" he asked.

"Just the ones they didn't take for trash," Dwarf Shaman replied. There was a clatter as he piled several objects onto the pew: stone tablets—no, perhaps clay. Such items were not as convenient as paper, but they were proof that records from the Age of the Gods and the Elder Days still existed.

"I doubt they could tell these from flagstones," Lizard Priest said, brushing the surface of one of the tablets gently so as not to scratch it with his claws.

The form of the letters appeared quite old; even Lizard Priest could not read them. The assiduously nongeometric characters formed patterns that threatened to make the reader dizzy.

"In our ignorance of what they say, perhaps we are not so different from the goblins. But let us be grateful that something survived."

"We'll have to figure out exactly what they are when we have a chance. But that can wait."

"Yes." Goblin Slayer nodded. "How are things outside?"

"Long-Ears is having a look around. She's got good night vision, and a ranger's agility."

If there's any left, she'll find them. The dwarf pulled out his wine jug. Goblin Slayer accepted it and took a swig, drinking lustily through the visor of his helmet. The spirits burned on the way down, calling his attention to how his focus had been dulled by fatigue.

"...You've both used spells. You need rest."

"And so do you... But maybe that's a luxury we can't afford. We need to make sure we have enough for a front row." Then the dwarf took a mouthful of wine himself, before passing the jug to Lizard Priest.

"Oh-ho," the lizard said, squinting, and took a big mouthful of wine. His long tongue slid out to lick the droplets from his jaws, and he coughed once. "It makes one wish for cheese."

"When we get back," Dwarf Shaman reassured his companion, pounding him on the shoulder. "Can't let ourselves get distracted just 'cause we're heading home."

"True, but I think we're okay for tonight." The clear voice came from the direction of the door, which creaked as it opened. A silhouette slipped into the chapel, like a cat making its way along the road at night. The woman shook slightly, her long ears twitching—it was High Elf Archer.

"I did a circuit of the area, but I didn't see any footprints from any escaped goblins."

"You're sure?" Goblin Slayer asked softly, to which she replied, "I'm sure."

High Elf Archer frowned and scratched at some dried blood on her cheek. "So as far as heading home, if we don't spot any goblins between here and there, I think this is the end of it."

"I see." Goblin Slayer nodded shortly, looking at the pile of corpses in the corner of the chapel.

Twenty-odd goblins. Twenty-odd goblins they had dealt with and killed themselves.

Then there were the injured women sleeping on the pews.

Is this the end of it?

"......I see." He nodded again and shifted slightly. Then he gently shook Priestess, who was leaning against him. "Wake up. She's back."

"...Mm? Ah. Oh, r-right." Priestess sat up with a start. She gave a few quick shakes of her head and rubbed her eyes, forcing her drifting attention to focus.

"Okay, I'll clean up, then. We're all..."

The words *very dirty* never quite reached her lips; she swallowed them instead. She grabbed her sounding staff and began walking among the women sleeping on the pews, High Elf Archer following her. Priestess emerged into the center of the room, and there she knelt, clutching her staff in both hands. A posture of prayer.

"O Earth Mother, abounding in mercy, please, by your revered hand, cleanse us of our corruption."

Moved by the devotion of her precious follower, an unseen hand reached down from heaven to touch the girls' skin. There was a pleasant feeling accompanied by a sensation of touch as soft as that of a feather.

And behold: before their very eyes, the filth sloughed off the girls and flew away—all the dirt, the streaks of blood, the gore stuck to their clothes. Somehow, their faces seemed to relax, transforming to show expressions of repose.

"Mm," High Elf Archer said, squinting like a cat. She opened her arms wide. "That's really something. It's almost like they were washed with water. Is that the newest miracle you got?"

She would have to apologize to the gods for her earlier complaints.

"Yes," Priestess replied with a hint of happiness. "When I told the head of the temple that I had been promoted to Steel, they asked me to perform the ceremony."

"Kind of a restrained miracle, though, don'cha think? Didn't they have anything flashier?"

"...I had to go with what I needed," Priestess murmured, averting her eyes.

"Ahh," High Elf Archer frowned, understanding.

In general it was said to be the gods who decided what miracle a supplicant would receive, but sometimes a fervent wish could gain one a particular ability.

This was the Purify miracle. It invoked an act of the gods to remove impurity. That was, as it were, all it did. And to use an all-too-valuable miracle on something like that...

Yet, at the same time, the idea of being able to clean off her clothes and body once a day while on adventure gladdened her girlish heart. In addition, the miracle could also purify water or air to a certain extent, so it couldn't hurt to have around.

There was also the issue that to measure the worth of divine intervention merely in terms of how much it benefited the user was the worst kind of sacrilege.

"......"

Priestess put a hand to her small chest and took a deep breath. Her eyelids fluttered and she bit her lip.

I've become used to it, haven't I?

After all the talk of weddings, they came here and saw what these goblins had done, what an awful state they had left these young women in. And although her heart ached, she still found herself able to have a little chat. Even if it was partly for show.

It would have been unimaginable a year before.

"It's a good miracle."

A heavy hand fell easily on her shoulder. She jumped and looked up to see a grimy metal helmet. Those few words were enough to make her heart pound.

"There are uses for it."

And then Priestess's brow drooped, an ambivalent expression on her face.

§

The crimson of twilight spread to every corner of the plaza.

It was sunset in summer. The west wind blew in to carry off the heat of the day, spreading ripples through the sea of grass in the pasture.

"Okay, everyone, time to go home!"

The cows, which had been munching contentedly on grass, raised their heads with a bevy of lowing. Slowly but surely, they started walking, forming a herd that made for the barn.

Cows were generally obedient like this. There was little need for Cow Girl to get too involved with them, but that didn't mean she had no work to do. It was important to count the cattle, making sure all the animals got back to the barn safely. Yes, *he* checked the fence diligently every morning, but that didn't mean there might never be a problem. Foxes and wolves were trouble enough, but it was also possible simply to miss an animal out in the fields.

And once the cows were all in the barn, then she would have to feed them. Livestock like cows and horses were precious assets. It was impossible to pay too much attention to them.

"…Good, you're all here." Cow Girl, crooking her fingers as the cattle walked by, counted off the last one then gave an energetic nod of her head.

It had been two days now since he, her longtime friend, had set off on an adventure.

It was only natural that he might be out adventuring some days. He was an adventurer.

There were days he didn't come home. Days she was simply waiting.

Eventually, there might even come a day when the waiting never ended.

He was an adventurer, and it was only natural.

Heh. Can't go down that road, or I'll never come back.

"Let's just focus on work. Work!"

There was another gust of wind.

The summer breeze brought with it a bounty of aromas: the smell of fresh grass, the distant odors of the many dinners in town, even the smell of the cows.

"Hmm…"

And then there was a smell like rusted metal. It was an odor that, to her chagrin, she had become much acquainted with over the past several years.

Cow Girl stopped in the process of following the cows to the barn, turning on her heel. Far away, she could see a figure coming from the direction of town, approaching at a bold, nonchalant stride.

Clad in a grimy metal helmet and cheap-looking leather armor while a sword of a strange length swung at the hip, and a small, round shield rested on an arm.

Cow Girl squinted. And then, as always, she smiled. "Welcome home. You tired?"

"Yes," he replied with a nod. "I'm home."

She came up to him at a jog. She took a short breath in, then out. His movements looked normal. She felt her cheeks relax.

"You're not hurt. Good, I'm glad."

"Yes." He nodded assiduously then started walking again; he had slowed somewhat from earlier. Cow Girl fell into step beside him.

"Hrm…" Her face pinched slightly. If she could smell him, could he smell her sweating? She took a little sniff of her sleeve, but she couldn't tell.

Eh, I guess it's a little late for that.

"Hey, what do adventurers do about dirt and stuff, anyway?"

"We change when we can. Wipe our bodies. Some even use spells or miracles."

"Huh!"

"Sometimes body odor can alert goblins to your presence. It's foolish to be upwind of them."

I guess that makes sense. Cow Girl nodded then swooped around to stand on his other side.

"What is it?" he asked, but she simply waved the question away and said, "Don't worry about it. Do you want dinner tonight? Or did you eat already?"

"No."

"Okay, I'll cook for you, then. Stew okay?"

"Yes." Then the helmet nodded gently up and down. The soft voice, too, sounded more lighthearted than usual. That alone was enough to make Cow Girl glad she had taken the time to prepare this meal.

Look at me. I'm so easy.

Well, she didn't exactly feel bad about it. Things were fine this way.

"You must be tired though, huh?"

"…"

There was no answer. He still had the bad habit of clamming up when he didn't have a good response.

Cow Girl giggled a little and leaned forward, as if she might be able to see inside the helmet from underneath. From the other side of the steel visor, she couldn't see his expression, but she had a pretty good idea what it was.

"Rough time?"

"…There are no easy jobs."

"True enough."

Their shadows stretched out in the summer twilight.

The cows were back in the barn. All that was left was to go home.

They had walked the path home together so often since they were little. How many times did this make it now?

She didn't feel that much had changed since the old days, although his shadow was now a little longer than hers.

"By the way…"

"Hmm?" She kept her eyes on their silhouettes as she answered. She changed her stride a little bit, trying to get their shadows to overlap.

Not for any special reason. It was just something she suddenly remembered doing as children.

"It seems there is a wedding."

"Wedding…?"

Well, now. She found she couldn't help glancing at him. He spoke the word as if it were unfamiliar to him, like it came from a foreign language.

Wedding. A wedding. To join together with someone. To spend your lives together.

"A wedding, huh? And were you invited?" she said quietly.

"Yes," he replied with his usual brevity. "My..." And then he paused for a moment. "In my party, there is an elf."

"Oh," Cow Girl said, squinting. The cheerful, upbeat ranger girl. "Her."

"Her older sister and cousin, it seems."

"That's nice."

"I was told to invite you as well."

"...Are you sure?"

"That is not for me to decide."

Hrm, Cow Girl grunted.

There was the farm. There was work. Could she really leave it all behind for days on end?

Summer was a busy time. So was autumn. So were spring and winter. All year long, she had to worry about the weather and the crops and the animals.

But then... Oh yes, but then.

An elf wedding!

The phrase resonated within the deepest reaches of her heart. She had dreamed of such things when she was little, all the while certain she would never see one: The faeries dancing around, clothes more beautiful than anything she had ever seen, and music such as she had never heard. The bride and groom resplendent.

She had heard of such things in bedtime stories but had always assumed they were nothing more than that.

What's more, she had never been away very long from either her hometown (now gone), or the farm where she currently lived. It seemed like a desperately long time since she had imagined going anywhere.

"I wonder... Is it really okay?" she murmured, as if it might be a genuinely bad thing.

"I will speak to your uncle."

"…Okay." Perhaps the blunt kindness in his tone was a response to her own vague mumbling.

That had to be it, she decided. *I'm sure it is. I like that better.*

She moved ever so slightly, so that their shadows stopped overlapping. So that only the hands of their silhouettes seemed to be intertwined as the dark figures stretched out over the red field.

"A marriage, huh…?"

They were almost back to the house.

It was a short distance to walk together. Enough to share what they thought. To share a few words…

"Do you ever think about that sort of thing?"

"…"

He was silent for a moment. His usual behavior when he didn't know the right thing to say.

"It is difficult."

"Maybe so," she murmured, spinning around on her heel. She started walking backward, hands clasped behind her. "In that case," she continued, looking toward him, "what about…when we were little? You promised to marry me when we grew up."

"…"

Cow Girl heard a slight sigh from inside the helmet. "I remember no such promise."

"Oops… Saw right through me, huh?"

She laughed out loud, spinning around again as she did so, and kept walking.

Their shadows separated. Their shadows' hands separated. Now… Yes, it was too late now.

But we should have made that promise.

Somehow the twilight sun found its way into her eyes, and she blinked rapidly.

Of How the Girls' Slow Reactions Are to Blame

"Huff... Puff... Pant... Ahh!"

Huffing and panting, she tumbled through the hellish greenery.

Her bare feet were torn by rocks and scratched from the thorns and branches of the forest plants, none of which she recognized, and all four of the limbs visible under her short clothing were slick with blood.

The trees blocked out the sunlight, yet the dim world under the canopy was brutally humid, and she sweat profusely. Running made her throat burn, but she had no idea where there might be safe water.

It was the same with food. She saw berries and bugs and grass but couldn't begin to guess which were edible.

At this point, in fact, she had no sense of which direction she was even going. The sun was hidden, depriving her of any way to determine where she was running. Her path didn't seem to be headed north, but she couldn't be sure.

In the rain forest, the sounds of animals and birds, the rustling of trees, all came together to envelop her in a cocoon of noise. She had never really been able to detect anything as ambiguous as "presence," but...

If I'd known this was going to happen, I would've taken some ranger training.

"Oww, ow..."

She hated the way her hair clung to her skin; she tried to brush the sweat from her forehead but immediately regretted it. She only succeeded in making her wounds there hurt worse.

How did this even happen?

There was no answer. There was no one left to answer. She had lost all her companions.

It would have been easy to sneer at them for being naive.

Another possibility was that they had simply been unlucky, but that was cold comfort.

This was the reality: she and her companions had attempted an adventure, they had failed, and they had been routed. That was all.

"If only...I at least...had a weapon...!"

Their raft had capsized, and by the time she'd come to on the riverbank, it had been too late. Her equipment was gone, along with her friends.

Why did she continue to run rather than give up? Because she was an adventurer.

And adventurers didn't give up.

It was their right to complain about whatever was happening, but they never backed down from it.

Above all, even when the situation looked hopeless, it wasn't over.

She didn't know where her companions were. That meant there was a possibility she might still find them again.

My sister... I'm sure she's all right... She's gotta be.

The thought of her older sister, with whom she had been working, brought a smile to her face.

The last she had seen of her was a hand reaching down from the leaning raft to pull her out of the river where she had fallen in.

Her sister, the leader of their party and the object of everyone's respect, had been a druid.

A person who was one with nature—surely she was all right.

Or so the girl kept telling herself as she ran desperately through the forest.

That's it! I can follow the river.

It might have been a dangerous gambit in light of her pursuers, but it was better than barreling aimlessly among the trees.

Yes. She was running away. Desperately, in order to survive. And *they* would fully understand that.

"——Eeek?!"

Following the sound of water, she broke through the trees to arrive at the river again—and quickly suppressed a scream.

She was confronted with a bizarre object.

It looked like something that had fallen prey to a butcherbird—impaled on a twig, stored to be eaten later. Or like a frog that some children had been tormenting for fun. Or a marionette tangled up in its own strings.

It was a person.

A corpse. This person had died in an awful way: a spike pounded from the anus through to the mouth, the body impaled upon it.

It brought to her mind a series of comical images from shadow-puppet plays she had seen.

"Wha— Urr... Ackk..."

It hardly seemed real. But she felt herself twitch reflexively, the contents of her stomach rising up toward her mouth.

She tasted something bitter. A simple fact flashed through her memory: the last thing she had eaten had been grilled fish. Skewered and burnt.

"Oh... Ugh..."

She couldn't stop herself from dropping to her knees. It was the wrong thing to do, but she realized that too late.

They could be sensed moving nearby. It wasn't that they were trying to hide themselves. They weren't really capable of that.

It was simply that she wasn't paying attention.

"Ee... No—ahh—ahhh!"

When, in a panic, she tried to react, scads of the tiny shadows were already upon her. Overwhelmed, she fell backward, her bottom sinking into the mud.

I'm gonna drown...!!

Her reaction was instinctive; she began to flail her arms and legs, windmilling, kicking.

Against this many opponents, of course, such resistance was futile. All present knew how this would end.

"Hrk?!"

There was a cackle and something caught her feet. She gave a strangled cry as she felt her legs being forced open.

A crudely sharpened stick was driven in with a dramatic flair, and she felt herself go pale.

"No... N-no, no, no, no, nooo! How can—I don't wanna—die... like this...!!"

Why did things have to end up like this?

She didn't know.

It would be all too easy to sneer and say she was too stupid to know.

Another possibility was that she had been unlucky; but that was cold comfort.

Whatever the case, she never registered that it had been her sister on that spike.

She didn't even think of it as one of her party members.

All she knew was how they were going to kill her.

CHAPTER 2

BEARD-CUTTER GOES TO THE SOUTHERN RIVER

The moment they disembarked from their carriage, the heat of summer assaulted the party, along with an earsplitting racket. People coming and going on the flagstones. Conversations of every type. The river burbling its way through the town. The wind blowing.

For a moment, the overwhelming sense of activity left Cow Girl thinking there must have been a festival or something.

"W-wow..."

"Are you all right?"

She felt a gentle hand support her, guarding against a sudden dizzy spell.

"Er... Yeah... Fine," she replied, nodding to someone. That someone happened to be a person she'd become fast friends with over the past year: the receptionist from the Adventurers Guild. She was impeccably dressed, as ever. Today, she was wearing a pure white summer dress that reminded Cow Girl that this girl was a public official—in other words, part of the nobility. It wasn't what she normally wore, but even so—in fact, just for that reason—it left a strong impression.

"I just got a little lightheaded with all the people..."

"You haven't seen anything yet. The capital is even more crowded."

"I can't believe you can even breathe there..." *I don't think I could manage.*

Guild Girl snickered at Cow Girl's assessment, stepping down from the carriage as if she did it every day.

You know, when she holds those braids down against the wind, she really does look like a city girl. She couldn't look more different from me.

Cow Girl gave a private sigh, overcome by what a bumpkin she felt like. She had attempted to wear something a little different from usual, but she'd had nothing like the success of Guild Girl.

She was embarrassed, though, to wear her mother's dress again, so this was what she had been left with. And yet, she couldn't quite settle into herself.

Cow Girl wandered around behind the carriage to where the bags were stacked. They would have to unload the luggage.

A leather-gloved hand slid out and stopped her. "I'll do it." The hand grabbed some luggage as soon as she heard the short sentence.

She looked over and saw Goblin Slayer in his characteristic grimy helmet.

"You rest a bit."

"Oh, I'm fine," Cow Girl said, waving off her old friend. "I can ride a horse all day. A carriage is no problem. I know what I look like, but I'm pretty strong!"

"Perhaps so, but this trunk has to do with my business."

Hmm, Cow Girl grumbled. That was fair. Personal business was important.

"All right, well, let me handle my own luggage, at least."

"Okay." For some reason, his brusque nod made her smile. She didn't hide the grin as she grabbed her bag.

She had never seen Goblin Slayer at work before. And doing something other than slaying goblins, no less. This wasn't really different in kind from when she asked him to help around the farm, but still, it seemed new.

She went over and stood in a corner of the station so that she would be out of the way; Guild Girl stood beside her, smiling. Cow Girl had learned enough in the six years of their acquaintance to know that this was not a pasted-on smile.

"I'm guessing you haven't seen him at work too often, either."

"Yeah. I'm usually behind a desk at the Guild."

"Oh yeah? …I guess that makes sense."

"Well, there was one time…" *I thought I might have a heart attack.*

"Huh!" Cow Girl said, her lips pursed.

As the two of them stood talking, work progressed apace.

"Gods above. We haven't seen this place in a year, and it looks like we left yesterday. Doesn't anything ever change around here?" Dwarf Shaman said, casually grabbing trunks as Goblin Slayer hefted them down from the luggage rack.

Like most of his kind, Dwarf Shaman was as strong as he was short. He piled up the cargo, one piece after another, without so much as breathing hard.

"They say three's a crowd, but we've got four in women alone. How are us men going to relax?"

"Ha! Ha! Ha! Ha! Ha! Are they not beautiful and sprightly? That is enough." Lizard Priest was taking the bags from Dwarf Shaman and putting them onto a luggage cart. Lizardmen were naturally brawny, but on top of that, he had the muscular build of a warrior-priest. He tossed the baggage onto the cart faster than Goblin Slayer could unload it.

"And one cannot make light of a woman's meticulous nature, either. Is that not so, milady Priestess?"

"I really don't think it's anything special…"

Priestess scratched her cheek with embarrassment, but Lizard Priest only laid on more praise. "Ah, but careful packing is so important. What if the clay tablets were to break?"

Priestess looked at the ground. "It's really nothing special… I just packed them with some reeds and moss."

The luggage in question was the clay tablets they had recovered from the library some days before. According to the nuns they had rescued, the tablets had been discovered at some ancient ruin or other, and the letters had not yet been decoded.

That being the case, there was no point leaving them in some frontier burg with no resources. They could carry some kind of prophecy; or ancient, secret magics; or the hidden truth of all history; or…

Old, indecipherable texts had been the cause of no small strife of late. The adventurers logically came to the conclusion that the safest thing they could do would be to leave the tablets at the Temple of the God of Law in the water town.

"Heh-heh. That's right, earn your keep, dwarf." High Elf Archer jumped down from the carriage with balletic grace and a smirk that stretched from ear to ear. She gave Dwarf Shaman a hearty smack on the shoulder. "I'm gonna go pick up some gifts for my sister."

"Yes, fine. Gods... If we weren't here to celebrate, I'd smack you right back on that flat little bottom!"

"Why, you—!" High Elf Archer jumped backward, covering her modest behind with her hands and glaring at the dwarf.

She was able to clown around like this because they were in the safety of the water town.

A year ago, it had been different.

Priestess closed her eyes for a second, with an emotion that mixed nostalgia with fear but was not quite either one. That summer, this area had been attacked by goblins, and hardly anyone realized it. The memories were still fresh for her. After all, the whole party had almost died fighting that enemy.

"..."

Goblin Slayer, who had been as close to death as any of them that time, slowly looked from one side of town to the other.

"...I don't sense any goblins here."

She found it rather satisfying to be able to come back and see what their work had achieved.

They had been away for a year—yes, a whole year already.

From what she could see, the water town looked almost exactly as they had last left it, everything still clicking along in peace. Merchants and travelers passed by, clerics in the service of the Supreme God hurried about, and children walked alongside their parents. Wizards and knights-errant queried passersby as to whether they didn't need bodyguards to protect their belongings, boasting of their achievements in battle.

The clattering of horse hooves mingled with the quick talking of merchants making deals with one another; a very important-looking woman worked her way down the street.

But there were no goblins.

For Goblin Slayer, that was enough.

And insofar as there were no goblins, there was nothing for him to do here.

And yet, I am here.

He wondered what he should make of this.

Even if he'd had any interest in a non-goblin-slaying quest, he would never have had the time to look at it. He had certainly never imagined he would take up a courier quest like this one.

Follow the river that ran through the city upstream, to the south, and as quick as walking, you would find yourself at the elves' forest.

As such, the party had been asked to accompany the clay tablets; there was some kind of talk of the job covering traveling expenses. Because it was a Guild quest, they were allowed to use a Guild carriage to reach the water town. When they received the reward, it would be enough to cover their expenses in town, as well.

Finally, there was the fact that they would be protecting clay tablets that the goblins might have some interest in. This was the aspect that finally got Goblin Slayer on board.

"Okay, everyone, I'm going to go to the local guild to say hello and report that we completed the quest."

Everything had been arranged by the good offices of Guild Girl, with her fine sense of timing and her unflappable smile. Who better than a bureaucrat to orchestrate something like this? Any time plans for a quest involved more than simply going to a location, looking around, and killing some monsters, there was a way she could help.

"After that, there's the luggage, the inn, securing a boat... Oh, and gifts. Do we know what the couple likes?"

"Best learn about the elves from an elf, I'd say. Got an opinion, Long-Ears?"

"Naturally," High Elf Archer replied, nodding confidently. Her ears gave a surprisingly majestic twitch, and she added, "Besides, I haven't been back home in ages. I'll need something to bring my clan."

"Er, uh, then maybe I can, too...?" Cow Girl edged her way into the conversation, putting a hand to her generous bosom. "I mean... I don't get a lot of chances to come to places like this, and I kind of wanted to try a little shopping..." She sounded uncharacteristically hesitant, her eyes flitting from one place to another.

High Elf Archer blinked several times. "Just come with me!" she exclaimed, smacking herself on the chest. "As a matter of fact, I've been to this town before. I can show you around!"

"Well then," Dwarf Shaman said, looking dubious about this display of confidence, "once we've found the inn and the boat, maybe we'll tag along." He stroked the white beard of which he was so proud. "Otherwise, who knows what Anvil might get up to on her own?"

"Ooh, how about you come over here and say that!" High Elf Archer exclaimed. Dwarf Shaman said something laughingly in return, and off they went again, arguing hard enough to sound noisy even over the hubbub of the water town streets.

Lizard Priest rolled his eyes in amusement when he saw people watching the pair with surprise.

"Well, just think of us as porters," he said. "We do have the strength."

"Sorry. I know how much trouble you're going to…" Cow Girl bowed her head apologetically, but the lizardman monk put his palms together.

"What's to apologize for? Consider it an act of gratitude for your plentiful supply of wonderful cheese. Think naught of it."

Cow Girl felt a hand on her shoulder. "Hee-hee. Well then, maybe I'll join the rest of you after I finish everything that needs doing."

She didn't know when Guild Girl had come up behind her. Her braid gave off a faint, sweet aroma; maybe she was wearing a bit of perfume. Just a dab, not so much as to be anything but tasteful. It felt a world away from Cow Girl.

Must be nice…

The thought passed in an instant, but it must have shown on her face.

"A girl likes to dress up from time to time, doesn't she?" Guild Girl was smiling almost mischievously.

Cow Girl put up her hands. "Heh, yeah. Ha-ha… Think you could help me out?"

Of course. Guild Girl smiled and nodded, and soon her gaze had moved along to something else.

What was that something? You should be able to guess by now.

It was Priestess, who stood looking rather uncomfortable, as if she wanted to say something but couldn't.

"And what about you?" Guild Girl asked. "That festival outfit of yours was awfully cute."

"Eurgh?!" Priestess made a sort of choking sound and flailed her arms, spluttering. "That wasn't—," and "I-it's not for me!" in between gasps.

Cow Girl, however, had already circled around to cut off her escape. The farm girl boxed Priestess in with her generous chest, hugging her close.

"Not so fast! I don't know how that sort of stuff will look on me, either, but I'm still going. So you're not getting away."

"Ohh... Please just...don't be too hard on me...okay?" She was shaking like a small animal. Cow Girl nodded at her as if at a little sister.

Well, Cow Girl herself wasn't exactly a fashion maven. She would have to let Guild Girl take the lead...

"......"

Goblin Slayer was silently watching the girls banter with each other. Cow Girl had always been outgoing, but it was still good to see her become part of the group like this. Bright and laughing, zipping around and having fun.

He let out a breath. A sort of relieved *phew*.

"...I do not know much about either gifts or clothes," he said flatly, grabbing on to the crossbeam of the luggage cart.

"Ho," Lizard Priest said at this, his tail wagging. "Porterage, then? Perhaps it could wait until all else is finished?"

"There is a slight chance that goblins want these tablets." Rather unusually for him, the words carried the ring of an excuse. "We ought to move them sooner rather than later."

"...You're quite sure?"

"I think so," he said, the helmet moving. "I'm certain of it."

"Hmm...," Lizard Priest mused, letting out a hissing breath. After a moment, though, his tail swayed gently. "Very well," he said. "Once we have settled on an inn, we'll dispatch someone to the temple."

"Please do."

Then Goblin Slayer began to walk off, pulling the cart behind him.

By the time Priestess noticed the creaking of the wheels, he was already far away, a figure growing smaller in the distance.

§

He focused on nothing but the sound of the running river as he pulled the cart along.

The people milling about him stared at the pathetic-looking adventurer then quickly passed him by. Admittedly, his outfit was somewhat shocking. People probably assumed he was some beginner.

Why else would an adventurer, bedecked in full armor as if ready to delve into a dungeon, be pulling a cart through the middle of town? He didn't quite look like he belonged among the rivers and boats of this city, whose elegance flowed from the old capital where it was built. People snickered at him behind their hands.

None of this mattered to Goblin Slayer.

He kept walking along the route that he had pounded into his memory, and eventually, he arrived at a resplendent building standing by the waterside, supported by marble columns. People dressed in clerics' robes and clutching law texts came and went busily through the front entrance. There were others among them who looked very serious; these were people who had come for some suit and who now approached the temple with trepidation.

The sun had passed its zenith already, its clear, bright rays reflecting off the image of the sword and scales. This was the great Temple of the Supreme God, who gave this world law and justice and order and light.

There was probably no safer place on all the frontier than this. Goblin Slayer, however, continued to scan the area vigilantly as he strode with his cart into the temple.

In the waiting area, people shot him anxious glances as they marked time until their cases would be heard. He went farther into the building.

"Excuse me, sir, please stop there!" Naturally, he had been noticed. A sandals-clad young cleric came rushing up.

Goblin Slayer halted with a "*hrm*," and then he noticed the young man appeared to be praying something softly. He assumed it was something like Sense Lie. Things were so complicated these days.

The adventurer brought the cart to a creaking halt.

"I've come to complete a quest," he said.

"Sir?"

"A quest," he repeated, pulling up the silver tag around his neck. "Perhaps it will help if I say Goblin Slayer is here."

Unfortunately, it didn't help.

"Please wait just a moment, sir," the cleric said, rushing back inside and leaving the adventurer by himself.

Goblin Slayer crossed his arms and, as he had been told, he waited. He felt that he had often seen such rushing about lately.

Perhaps young clerics are all alike...

At length, the young man returned with an older woman and, for the third time, Goblin Slayer explained, "I have come to complete a quest. The transport of some texts."

"Yes, of course, sir, I understand," the woman said with a friendly smile. She nodded at him several times. "The archbishop is waiting for you. Please, come this way."

"All right." Goblin Slayer grasped the crossbar of the cart again and began walking.

"My apologies for delaying you," the priest said, but Goblin Slayer merely gave a slight shake of his head as he went by.

The woman—the acolyte—who went ahead of him swayed her hips in a way that caused her behind to wiggle each time she walked. Not enough to be unseemly, however; in fact, her movements were very graceful.

The Supreme God was the master of law. But it was said that it was Pray-ers who should make official legal judgments. Perhaps, then, this acolyte was simply trying to act appropriately for a place of judgment. And for Goblin Slayer, there was no higher praise than to recognize something as the fruit of much practice.

"If only you had come around the back way, you wouldn't have had to wait," she said, clearly implying his status as a personal friend of the head of this temple.

"I did not know that," he said. He didn't sound at all reproachful. "I've caused you trouble," he added.

"Not at all, sir, it's quite all right. I'm sure the archbishop will be overjoyed." She smiled widely at him.

Goblin Slayer tilted his head slightly in her direction. "...I believe I remember meeting you before."

"Yes, sir. And may I thank you for all the good you did our archbishop at the time."

"I only slew the goblins."

This woman was an attendant, one of those who served Sword Maiden closely. He worked this over in his mind. "Hmm. Does she sleep now?"

"Indeed, and very well, at that." The acolyte looked as if she were talking about her own child as she smiled. "She's slept like a baby this past year. I'm sure she feels much safer now."

Ah, but don't tell her I told you. It would only make her pout.

He nodded. "I see." And then he added, once more under his voice, "Well and good, then."

They proceeded farther into the temple, past the courtrooms where cases were heard, through hallways full of shelves. Toward the innermost sanctum, a place of marble pillars and silence.

He had taken this path before, and it led to the same place as before.

Several great, round pillars surrounded the room, sunlight the color of honey drifting between them.

At the far end of this farthest room stood a statue of the Supreme God, like the sun, an altar set before it. And at the altar was someone with perfect posture clasping the sword and scales, a beautiful woman offering prayers...

"...Ahh," she said, the joy unmistakable in her voice. "You've come. It is you, isn't it...?"

There was the faintest rustle as the woman, her buxom body covered in just a single thin piece of cloth, stood from her prayers.

Behind her blindfold—which served only to highlight her beauty—her gaze shifted, and a breath escaped her rich lips.

It might seem like seduction, or perhaps a certain devilishness. But her aura was, without question, that of a pure priestess.

"It seems things are well."

"Yes… Thanks to you." The archbishop, Sword Maiden, smiled like an innocent little girl, her red lips softening. She made a motion with her hand, almost like a bit of a dance; the acolyte bowed her head and retreated soundlessly.

Goblin Slayer watched her go, the steel helmet concealing his expression. Sword Maiden looked at him with great warmth.

"I'm afraid I troubled you for that girl's sake…"

"It was nothing," Goblin Slayer said, shaking his head. "My duty."

The previous winter was still fresh in his memory, when he had done battle with some goblins on the snowy mountain in order to rescue a noble girl. The young woman had tried very hard to appear brave. Goblin Slayer didn't know what had happened to her after her rescue. Apparently, she was in contact by letter with Priestess and High Elf Archer, but it didn't occur to him to ask them about her.

"…I can't say she's completely better," Sword Maiden said gently, as if she sensed what Goblin Slayer was wondering. "Her wounds are deep and pain her greatly." Her lips pursed slightly. "But she has stood back on her feet. She's doing all that she can, to the extent of her ability."

"I see."

"…And what about me?"

Goblin Slayer *hmph*ed and said, "I heard on the way here." Then he let go of the cart's crossbeam with a clatter. "I brought the ancient texts."

"So you have. I've heard the story." Her lips pursed again, perhaps in annoyance at not being able to ask him personally. But at the very least, there seemed to be no change in the fact that he was looking out for her.

She moved along the marble floor almost as if she were skating across it, approaching the cart with no evident concern. Her pale, delicate hand reached out and brushed the surface of the wooden chest.

"Perhaps you'd be so kind as to open it for me?"

"Yes."

Goblin Slayer took the sword at his hip and used the tip to pry open the chest. It wasn't something a normal adventurer would do, risking their beloved weapon.

But this was Goblin Slayer. Sword Maiden knew that, so she wasn't surprised by what she noticed.

The chest opened with a screech of protest. Inside were the clay tablets, buried in soft detritus. Sword Maiden ran her hand along the profusion of characters engraved into their surface, as gently as a lover.

"This writing is old... Very, very old. I think the words might pertain to magic... Perhaps."

Maybe all this would have been surprising to someone who didn't know who Sword Maiden was. But as the archbishop of the Supreme God, ruler of law, she would certainly have a miracle of appraisal.

"Does it say anything about goblins?"

"I'm not sure," Sword Maiden replied with a sad shake of her head that caused her golden hair to ripple soundlessly. "I'm afraid I can't quite say. I would have to read a little more closely..."

"I see." Goblin Slayer nodded. "In that case, I'm not interested. I will leave them with you."

"And I will keep them. Thank you." Sword Maiden put a hand to her bountiful bosom and gave a deep bow. It was not the way an archbishop would normally behave toward a mere adventurer—even if she had once been an adventurer herself.

She raised her head slowly, then her sightless eyes looked at the clay tablets as if they were a gift.

"I'll take them to the library later."

"...You yourself?"

"The responsibility has been passed to me, hasn't it? I'd better see it through." Before Goblin Slayer could say anything else, she added an emphatic "Right?"

She looked like she was dancing as she moved closer to the man in his crude leather armor. A faint, sweet smell tickled his nose, perhaps the perfume she was wearing.

"Will you be back again soon?"

"No." This caused Sword Maiden to squeeze the sword and scales. "We will head south immediately."

"Is that so...? ...I see." The strength went out of the hand that held the symbol. "How unkind," she murmured. "I don't believe this trip involves goblins..."

©Noboru Kannatuki

"My friend…," Goblin Slayer started. "My friend…invited me. I could not refuse."

"You've got that kind heart…"

Her words were not a reproach, exactly, but there was a barb in them.

Goblin Slayer, however, responded, "One never knows when or where goblins may appear."

"That's certainly true." She laughed, and it was like the sound of a bell; it hung in the air as she backed away.

She straightened her clothes (though they didn't really need it), adjusted her grip on the sword and scales, and gave a quiet cough.

"Be careful, if you're going to travel the river."

"Careful of goblins?"

She ignored the question, saying quietly, "There have been reports of boats sinking."

I wish you safety in your travels.

Goblin Slayer let her make the holy sign over him with her fingers. Then he nodded and set off at a bold pace. He didn't look back.

Just as she had hoped.

§

"I, uh… I bought what they said, but… Am I really supposed to wear this?"

"It's something, isn't it? Humans think of the most interesting things. I just thought it might look good."

"This is cutting-edge fashion even for the capital. It's only recently that having your arms and legs so exposed has become popular."

"I've got a sneaking suspicion this is going to be a little too small…"

There was a spray of water, and the four girls' voices flew prettily around the riverbank.

It was the next day, and the five adventurers and two tagalongs were riding a raft. The water vessel had a white sail, and the wind pushed it gently upriver.

Trade wasn't especially frequent between the elves' village and the water town. The forest dwellers were quite proud, with little interest in money and even less in whatever baubles humans might produce. And when two sides could not fulfill mutual needs, then trade could not flourish.

Rather, most of the boats on the river were bound for the pioneer villages that stood along its banks. Very few of them went farther south, to the forest of the elves.

There were, of course, exceptions...

"If I'd known we were going to be traveling by raft, I might've stayed home!"

"We were able to borrow it, and that is enough."

They had already drifted past several villages, and the sun was climbing to its height. They had just bought some bread from the farmers at the last of the riverbank settlements marked on their map, and Dwarf Shaman was busy complaining.

As he took one of the pieces of buttered bread being passed around, Goblin Slayer said, "What is there to complain about?"

"You're a surprisingly even-keeled man, Beard-cutter."

"Is that so?"

"I should say so... Here, Scaly."

"Ah, many thanks."

Lizard Priest was piloting the raft with deft strokes of a pole. He settled the vessel in the lock, then let out a hissing breath.

Locks are devices designed to regulate the difference in water level between a canal and a natural river. When heading from the upstream to the downstream, the water in the lock would be gradually lowered to the downstream height. This meant that regardless of what you were riding on, there was bound to be a bit of a wait. A perfect time for a bite to eat.

Lizard Priest stuffed the bread into his jaws, his eyes rolling. "Mmm. But to think, it seems my tongue has become accustomed to the products of that farm so that now I wish for them."

"Ha-ha-ha-ha-ha-ha! Well, look who's become a gourmand! How about it, Beard-cutter? What about you?"

"If it is edible, that is enough," Goblin Slayer said softly, glancing around. He was looking at Cow Girl, who was sitting over by the other women, tearing off pieces of bread and eating them. She glanced in his direction, too, and their eyes briefly met.

"...Perhaps I do not quite mean that," Goblin Slayer added then looked down at his hands. He was whittling some wood with a knife, preparing something. Somethings, rather. One was a short club with a strange groove carved into it; the other looked more like a sharpened spear. When he finished with the grooved thing, Goblin Slayer put his blade to the tip of the longer object.

As he worked, he took the bread that he held in one hand and jammed it lazily into his visor.

"Hey, mind your manners!" Cow Girl exclaimed. "Chew your food properly."

"Sorry," he replied, sparing a glance in her direction and shoving the bread in a little more slowly. Then he looked down and resumed his work.

"Sheesh," Cow Girl grumbled, but Dwarf Shaman grinned and looked at what Goblin Slayer was doing.

"Got a spear there?" He picked up one of the objects with interest.

It was a simple wooden spear, nothing special. It didn't even have a proper tip.

"I am not skilled enough for my arrows to penetrate water. And a raft has no stones to pick up and throw. I need a ranged weapon." Goblin Slayer grabbed one of the weapons and held it up to the light, inspecting the work. Apparently, he found it unsatisfactory, because he resumed shaving away at it.

"One must be prepared," he said brusquely. "More so than usual."

"Ahh. I know what you mean. I heard the same rumors." Dwarf Shaman set the spear down with a sour look then sat on the raft. He pulled the stopper from the jar at his hip, pulled a cup from his bag, and offered Goblin Slayer a pour of fire wine. A rich aroma of alcohol wafted from the cup. Goblin Slayer shook a hand in refusal, so Dwarf Shaman drank the thing down in a single gulp.

"Sunken ships... You don't think they're just accidents?"

"It would be best not to assume so. As in everything."

There were only so many ships that traveled upriver. Most of them were adventurers, or the handful of merchants who had found favor with the elves. Hunters, perhaps, or medicine people. Some came seeking caves or ruins, or to collect rare herbs or animal parts with the indulgence of the forest's masters.

They had gone up the river on rafts, and they hadn't come back down. That in itself wasn't necessarily surprising. The only reason anyone knew the boats had sunk was because the elves, as a sign of goodwill, had sent the washed-up remains of the vessels back.

There were some who said, under their voices and without real proof, that maybe the elves had sunk those boats.

"It could be goblins," Goblin Slayer said confidently, with a glance at High Elf Archer. She was stuffing buttered bread (not the most refined meal) into her face, her long ears bouncing up and down. "Mmm. Eating somewhere new is the greatest." She puffed out her cheeks squirrelishly, a gesture Priestess couldn't help but laugh at.

"True. I lived in the Temple myself, so I know what you mean."

"Last time I was here, I walked along the banks. Going by boat is a new thing for me."

Or rather...by raft. She twirled her pointer finger in a circle in space.

"Right," Priestess agreed, putting some bread in her mouth, chewing delicately, and swallowing. "Is this that bank?"

"Yeah, it sure is."

It had been more than six months now since the two of them had bathed in that hot spring, looking up at the stars.

"Well now, is there a story here?" Guild Girl asked solicitously, leaning over.

Priestess and High Elf Archer looked at each other with exaggerated expressions of thought.

"A story? Hmm."

"What story could she be talking about?"

It wasn't precisely a secret to keep to themselves, but it was a valuable enough memory to act important about.

High Elf Archer's ears flopped happily. Guild Girl shot her a suspicious look. "I'll have to make sure to question you *thoroughly* about this at your next interview."

"Hey, that's abuse of authority, isn't it?"

Guild Girl had dealt with far too many people like High Elf Archer for this little quip to upset her mask. "How tragic, to serve so loyally and yet have adventurers keep secrets from me!"

Being two thousand years old (that's twice a thousand), High Elf Archer should have been equally poker-faced, but instead, she ground her teeth in frustration.

"Aww, but I wanna hear, too," Cow Girl said, clapping her hands. "I want to hear all kinds of things about life outside town!"

"Huh. Well, in that case… This was back before I met Orcbolg…"

And thus, Cow Girl's interjection became the pretext for a story of adventure.

Out of the corner of his eye, Goblin Slayer could see the women chatting amiably. High Elf Archer's ears flounced and she gesticulated frequently; Cow Girl listened with a smile. Guild Girl whispered about backroom secrets of the Guild, Priestess's eyes wide.

Goblin Slayer gathered up the ten or so sharpened sticks he had prepared, putting his woodworking tools back at his belt.

"When the lock opens, I will take over from you."

"Very well," Lizard Priest replied, slapping his tail down. The resulting jostling of the raft provoked cries from the women.

When the lock finally did open, the raft flowed with the water out into a valley.

"W-wow…"

How many moons could it have taken to carve out a piece of land like this? The river was itself like a scar left by time. The ravine was almost like one giant slab of rock, now in several layers. The mountain must have existed from the Age of the Gods, and the river would have been working away at this place for just as long.

The rocks were so large as to block out the sun at times, casting their shadows before them; among them, the burbling of the river and the blowing of the wind could be heard.

This explained it. This was why the village of the elves was sometimes called a land apart, "the country of shadows." It didn't feel like part of the mortal realm.

"This is incredible…!" Cow Girl exclaimed, looking at the massive stones as the raft wove its way through them. Everyone understood how she felt. There were a great many things in the world that were beyond any fantasy of hers.

"My home is just through here," High Elf Archer said, standing on the raft with no apparent sense of danger and puffing out her slender chest. "How about it? Even the dwarves never built something like this!"

"You're right, Long-Ears, we don't seek to compete with the work of the gods. Mastery of the hammer and chisel is our goal." He stroked his beard then added with a smirk, "And I'm guessing the elves didn't build these, either."

"Hrrrmn!" High Elf Archer's ears went straight back, and she lit into the dwarf as usual.

Everyone around them was used to this, and no one let it distract them from the scenery. Priestess made a variety of inarticulate noises, blinking rapidly. "This is amazing…"

"I've read about this in Guild paperwork, but seeing it firsthand is really something," Guild Girl said.

"No kidding." Cow Girl nodded. "Takes your breath away, huh? Hey…"

What do you think? she was about to say, but the words never left her lips.

When she turned around to ask, she found him standing at the back of the raft, staring far beyond the edges of the valley.

"How does it look?" Goblin Slayer asked softly, his hand on the tiller.

Lizard Priest considered, making his strange palms-together gesture, his eyes scanning the area constantly.

"Hmm. Above or below, perhaps."

"I agree."

"This is no ocean. On a river, we're unlikely to encounter a kraken."

"Kraken," Goblin Slayer repeated. "What's that?"

Lizard Priest's eyes rolled in his head. "More likely than not, I would guess above."

"Understood."

This was a side of him she had never seen. He looked just like he always did, and yet somehow different. Cow Girl put a hand to her bulging chest to calm her heart.

"Ah—"

She swallowed some saliva. But just as she was about to try again to say something, High Elf Archer's clear voice cut her off.

"Hold on!"

The ranger already had an arrow in her bow. The adventurers glanced at one another once then sprang into action.

Priestess clutched her sounding staff firmly, while Dwarf Shaman began rooting through his bag of catalysts. Lizard Priest grasped a dragon fang in his hand, and Goblin Slayer, one hand still on the rudder, lowered his hips.

"Think we'd best take down the sail. Give me a hand," Dwarf Shaman said, squinting against the sun.

"Oh yes, be right there...," Priestess said, going over to him.

Goblin Slayer, diligently working the pole, looked at the two young women. "Get down and cover your heads with cloths." His voice was sharp.

"Oh, uh, r-right, sure...!" Cow Girl nodded quickly. She rifled through her belongings, pulling out a rag.

"Over here, quickly!" Guild Girl looked equally nervous with her own cloth.

The two of them huddled together under the coverings, trying to make themselves as small as possible. Each thought she could feel the other shaking, but maybe it was herself.

They didn't know. That ignorance was their companion as they sat holding hands tightly.

Lizard Priest stood above them to protect them.

"...From the banks?" he asked.

"Probably," High Elf Archer answered. "Something's coming. A...a lot of somethings!" She drew back her bowstring, her ears working quickly up and down to catch any sound.

An instant later, there came the howling of wolves, and a hail of stones rained down into the valley.

§

"O Earth Mother, abounding in mercy, by the power of the land grant safety to we who are weak!"

First, Priestess invoked a miracle, clinging to her sounding staff.

How could the Earth Mother fail to protect her devoted disciple? An invisible barrier sprang up around the raft. The incoming rocks and sticks bounced off it, *bump, bump, bump,* making little splashes as they fell into the water.

Sweat was running down Priestess's brow. "I-if it doesn't get any worse, maybe we can…"

No sooner had the murmur escaped her, though, than the whistling sound of an arrow chilled her heart. Whatever was up on the banks, it was clearly something intelligent.

Figures approached the ridgeline. High Elf Archer knelt down, her bow ready and her gaze hard.

Animalistic howls. Groans. The noise of feet, not hooves. Her long ears twitched up and down, collecting every bit of sound.

She had seen these enemies before. Knew the sound. She had confronted them in the past. These were…

"Goblins…?!"

Goblin riders.

She cried out when she caught a glimpse of the cruel faces.

"I thought we were supposed to be in your homeland!" Dwarf Shaman shouted.

"Well, *sor*-ry!"

"So it *was* goblins," Goblin Slayer said calmly, tossing the pole to Lizard Priest. "Take the rudder."

"Understood!" With his strength, Lizard Priest would be able to push the craft a little bit. There wasn't likely to be any close-quarters fighting for him, anyway.

Lizard Priest punted the pole against the bottom of the river, and the raft pushed forward, although it complained.

"Stinking sons of—!" High Elf Archer drew her bow smoothly despite the quaking vessel, firing off an arrow almost instantly. It passed through the divine barrier around them, slowed, and then dropped toward the ridgeline.

"GORRB?!"

There was a muffled scream as one of the goblins was unhorsed—or unwolfed—and fell to the ground. The corpse bounced twice on its way down, colliding with the raft and setting it shaking.

"Eeek?!"

"Eep...!"

Guild Girl and Cow Girl both fought to suppress their screams under the blanket.

It wasn't enough that the silent corpse should have an arrow in it; its head was split open and it was gushing dark blood. No matter how many adventure stories one might have heard or read, seeing such a brutal death up close was something else again.

"What's wrong?" Goblin Slayer asked. He pulled the arrow out of the body, then gave the remains a ruthless kick into the river. There was a loud splash and the corpse sank out of view.

Cow Girl watched it disappear. Then, her hand still firmly in Guild Girl's, she said in a slightly shrill voice, "W-we're fine..."

"Good, then." Goblin Slayer glanced briefly at them then tossed the arrow to High Elf Archer. "I don't know if we can finish them off. Loosen the heads of your bolts."

"Crafty as ever," High Elf Archer said wearily, tugging at the head of the arrow he tossed her. Even though the head was not made of metal, if it stayed lodged in the body, it would encourage the wound to rot and spread sickness in the nest. It was a classic Goblin Slayer trick, but the kind of thing High Elf Archer wasn't very fond of.

"...Yah! Hah!"

Even so, her bowstring sang out again and again, sending arrows raining down on the ridgeline. Three shots, two screams. No falls. High Elf Archer clicked her tongue. Beside her, Goblin Slayer picked up one of the spears and attached a stone object to the wooden shaft.

Lizard Priest breathed a sound of admiration. "A spear launcher," he said. "What a familiar thing you have."

"You know it?"

"It was quite common among warriors of my village."

The lizard people prized close combat most of all; they found even simple ranged weapons distasteful. And throwing, anyway, was something humans excelled at. Rhea rock-slingers were nothing to sniff at, either, but rheas generally disliked combat. And yes, Dwarf Shaman used a sling, but his magic and his ax were his main weapons.

"Will it reach?" Dwarf Shaman asked.

"Easily," Goblin Slayer replied, just the one word.

"Right, then…!" Dwarf Shaman pulled a bottle of some kind of liquid out of his bag. He popped the cap and poured something like peach juice into the river. Meanwhile, he let his consciousness twist.

"Come, undines, the banquet's laid; come and sing and dance and play!"

The spray of water took on the form of a beautiful maiden, and behold, the river began to flow backward.

No… Not the whole river. Only the water where the raft rested had begun to turn. This was Control Spirit.

"Maybe I don't quite see eye to eye with this one!" Dwarf Shaman shouted, glaring into the water. "I can't get much speed out of it!"

"It's enough," Goblin Slayer said, and then he sent his spear flying.

It raced toward the sky with unnatural speed. This was followed by a terrible scream—not from a goblin, but from one of the wolves they were riding on.

"We have little but luck to help us here," Goblin Slayer spat, readying the next spear. "I do not know how many goblins there are. We can't kill them all."

"May I say, we *do* have one option," Lizard Priest said. He was still both manning the tiller and standing guard over Cow Girl and Guild Girl. "Milord Goblin Slayer, might we consider escaping the enemy rather than slaughtering them?"

"I do not like it. But…" Goblin Slayer loaded the next bolt into his launcher and sent it flying toward the ridgeline with a motion of his arm. It disappeared out of sight, and then a moment later, there was a scream.

"GOORARB…?!"

The goblin tumbled off the back of his wolf and fell from the cliff. The corpse flipped about as it hit the water with a huge splash.

"…We will have to settle this after we escape." That made two. Goblin Slayer picked up the next spear. "How is our defense?"

"Holding… Somehow!" Priestess responded, raising her staff and standing as boldly as she dared upon the raft. The entire defense of their party currently rested on her narrow, delicate shoulders. The gods had provided the miracle of the invisible barrier, but it was Priestess's prayer that maintained it.

The attacks came relentlessly, and as they did, her breathing grew harder and her legs threatened to give out. It was thoroughly impressive that she could perform three of these soul-enervating supplications to the heavens in a single day.

"Uhh…!"

Even so, she was approaching her limit. The barrier weakened as the gasp escaped her. She drew in a harsh breath and forced herself to breathe evenly. She forced strength into her feet on the raft and her hands on the staff.

"I'm going to add another one…! Give me some time!"

"Please do." Goblin Slayer brought up his shield to block a stone that came through the barrier.

Branches, stones, rocks, and even some arrows. The motley collection of projectiles tapped and clattered on the raft, causing it to yaw this way and that.

"Hrm…!" Lizard Priest gave a shove with the pole, sending the raft back slightly, but the current was like a rushing wave that washed across the vessel.

"Wah?! *Pfft!*"

"Ah, oh no…!"

The water soaked the cloths under which Cow Girl and Guild Girl were hiding, provoking more shouts. They were in danger of being flooded out from under their protection, but they clung to each other and held on.

Guild Girl gave a quick wave to Goblin Slayer, who had glanced in their direction, then she blinked several times. Suddenly, there was a considerable amount of detritus—branches and pebbles and other flotsam—on the raft. Had the goblins flung all this at them? No, it couldn't be.

A look at the water around them revealed a copious number of chips and splinters of wood floating by, even entire barrels drifting along.

"Hrrgh… Ah!"

Lizard Priest fought mightily to control the raft's direction, but the pole collided with a barrel, causing the craft to shake violently.

Another wave crashed down on the adventurers, soaking them and inundating their vessel.

"Oh..."

That was when Guild Girl saw something glistening white: a human skull drifting right past her.

She tried to pick it up with a trembling hand, but even as she reached out, the skull was sucked down under the water, and it disappeared.

She watched it disappear mutely. Soon, it was replaced in her view by several floating piles of trash, restrained with ropes.

"This m-might be bad," she said with a quiver in her voice. "I think they mean to sink the raft!"

The terrible cackling of goblins filled the valley, echoing crazily.

"GRRROB! GOORRB!"

"GROBR!! GOOORRRB!!"

There was no need for the goblins to face the adventurers personally in order to kill them. They could simply capsize the boat, or weigh it down with junk until it sank.

Yes, flipping the raft over would do the trick. The goblins could point and laugh as the foolish people drowned; if anyone survived, then they could enjoy attacking from the high ground.

It was now clear what had happened to the boats that had come this way and not returned.

"Gah! Noisy *and* in the way...!" High Elf Archer gave one of the piles of rubble a frustrated sweep with her leg, kicking up a spray of water but otherwise having no discernible effect.

The goblins simply had to keep throwing rocks and rubble from above.

Dwarf Shaman, equally frustrated, made a series of arcane gestures. "I'm going to have my undine get that stuff off the raft," he said, "so take some potshots with your bow or something!"

"'Or something'?! What do you mean, 'or something'?!"

The gorgeous spirit danced upon the raft. Her sensuous movements swept away the rocks and other debris, pushing it into the running river.

By this point, everyone was soaked from head to foot, but the raft was still somehow stable. That did not, however, mean they could relax. Much damage had been done, and the debris was piled up underwater, making it all too easy to capsize.

"...So they learned from the lock," Goblin Slayer muttered, firing off yet a third spear.

He didn't bother to watch what happened. There would be a scream, or there wouldn't.

The goblins were hiding themselves cannily along the edge of the cliff, following on wolfback to keep up the attack. The river wound its way among the towering spires. There was no ceiling, but this...

"It is as if we've wandered into their nest," Goblin Slayer said quietly. He used one of his spears to break off an arrow lodged in his shield.

"O Earth Mother, abounding in mercy..."

All this was happening in front of Priestess's eyes. Her knees were shaking still, and not only because of the difficult prayers.

She was finding it hard to breathe. Her tongue seemed to stumble over words her throat could barely summon forth. Her head spun and her vision grew hazy. Her fingers could hardly move; it was all she could do to hold on to her staff.

How am I supposed to...?

How was she supposed to invoke Protection and keep everyone safe? That was the only question for her. It was the only thing she could do.

What else could she do? How could she see them safely out of this place?

Her teeth chattered; she set her jaw to stop them. Memory after memory came back to her. She closed her eyes and pushed them away.

"Oh..."

At that moment, a light glimmered in her mind like a premonition from heaven.

Priestess opened her eyes. Her trembling lips formed a prayer as if guided by something other than herself. She raised her staff.

"O Earth Mother, abounding in mercy, please, by your revered hand, cleanse us of our corruption!"

The gods were great.

The Earth Mother reached down from the heavens, her hand sweeping through the water and making it clean.

Everywhere the light touched, the water ran clear, all the filth in it disappearing. Moreover, the great many dirty things in the river were cleansed away and vanished.

"...Wow!" High Elf Archer blinked, her ears twitching. She was justifiably impressed to see the effects of the Purify miracle with her own eyes. "You really do have your moments, huh?"

"I don't. The Earth Mother does... Although she can be a little harsh." Priestess groaned, the strain of connecting directly to the divine having given her a splitting headache. "Please... Do it now!"

"GRR?!"

"GOORB?!"

The goblins were naturally agitated by this turn of events. The trap they'd laid so carefully had been undone by something they didn't even understand.

Their ugly voices echoed as the confusion ran among them.

Far be it from Goblin Slayer to miss such an opportunity.

One goblin had leaned over to get a closer look at the river; a spear ran him through from his jaw right out the back of his head. He tumbled into the water in a spray of blood—and then his corpse vanished, purified away by the Earth Mother.

"Eventually, we will have to find and destroy their nest," Goblin Slayer said. "You're up."

"Gladly!" Even as he poled the raft along the undine's current, Lizard Priest opened his mouth wide. He filled his lungs with a great breath, the breath of the wyrm that rules over all things. *"Bao Long, honored ancestor, Cretaceous ruler, I borrow now the terror of thee!"*

Dragon's Roar echoed through the valley.

Goblins aren't the only ones frightened by dragons; every living thing fears them.

"GOORBGROB?!"

"GRORB!!"

The goblins' gibbering mixed with the frightened yelps of their wolves. Goblin riders were still goblins. They were not even especially accomplished riders.

They tried and failed to calm their mounts; the wolves literally ran away with their tails between their legs. Some of the goblins were thrown to the ground; others clung desperately to the fleeing animals. All of them beat a pitiful retreat.

The adventurers continued to watch the ridgeline vigilantly for a few minutes. Over against the sound of the stream, they used the pole to keep the raft moving.

At last an hour passed, then two, and at length, the wind that blew through the valley grew warmer.

They were floating toward a great, dark wood, a forest of old trees that had stood for thousands or perhaps tens of thousands of years.

Priestess clung to her sounding staff, praying to the Earth Mother to relieve her anxiety.

They were nearly out of the valley. That meant they would soon be in the realm of the elves.

§

The firecrackers danced into the sky with a series of pops, leaving little traces of light behind them. The sky was quite red now, now that it had caught hold of the salamander's tail.

It was not long after they had chased off the goblins and left the valley. The sun was well past its zenith and was sinking to the west, settling behind the trees.

The adventurers entered the massive forest, landing the raft on the riverside at a place indicated by High Elf Archer. She said the village was still a ways off. In that case, they figured a night's rest would be better than a forced march.

"I sure didn't expect we'd be wearing these so soon…"

"If we'd known we were going to get so wet, we should have put them on to begin with!"

"Heh-heh. We wouldn't have had a chance to wear them otherwise. Oh, do you know how to put it on?"

"Oh yeah, I'm fine. The only thing I don't understand is why you'd bother wearing one at all. Like this, right?"

A rope had been strung between some tree roots and towels draped over it. From the other side, the women could be heard having an animated conversation. There were four of them, after all; it was bound to get a little noisy.

After a few minutes, the towels were pulled down from the inside. Four women in swimsuits appeared like a vision.

"I just don't get why you would put on clothes specifically to get wet. Can't you just go without?" High Elf Archer looked very uncomfortable, playing with her hair in an uncharacteristic gesture of embarrassment.

"Why worry?" Lizard Priest responded promptly. He had stopped working to roll his eyes. He opened his mouth importantly. "I admit I little appreciate skin with no scales, but my judgment is that this outfit rather suits you."

"You think?" *Well all right, then.* High Elf Archer gave a little nod as if she now accepted the situation.

Dwarf Shaman looked like he was about to make one of his usual smart remarks, but it turned into more of a sneeze, and then he shut his mouth. Perhaps he figured there was no need to deliberately sour the elf's mood right when they were going back to her home.

"...I s'pose our opinions on the looks of Long-Ears and friends are well established by now."

"I guess. I'm honestly a little jealous..." Guild Girl put a hand to her cheek, though she had no cause to be embarrassed.

Of course, she came from a part of society where people were taught not to show too much skin. It wouldn't be quite true to say she wasn't embarrassed, but it was what it was. The work she did each day couldn't be undervalued. She wasn't especially afraid to be seen this way—which made her quite different from Priestess, who was hiding behind her.

"Oh... Ohhh..."

The cleric's face was bright red, and she was trying to make herself as small as possible. She was much ashamed of her own small, youthful body. What she was wearing now wasn't so different from the outfit she had worn for the dance at the harvest festival, but having others beside her for immediate comparison was not easy. At least Witch, with whom she was discreetly (she thought) infatuated and with whom she certainly couldn't compare, wasn't present. She wished she could be like that sorceress someday, but that was only a sign of how far she still had to go.

"Oh, you're fine," Cow Girl laughed, patting Priestess on the shoulder. Cow Girl thought of her as sort of like a little sister and found her willowy body adorable. She also felt that she herself had gotten a little muscular from all the work she did. She twisted her hips around for a look, a dubious expression on her face. "Good enough... Maybe?"

"That is not a question I can answer," Goblin Slayer said. He had taken four of the sharpened sticks from earlier and set them in the ground, describing a square. His helmet was pointed toward the group of women; he wasn't so uncouth as to fail to spare them even a glance. Still, his appraisal may or may not have made them very happy... "But personally, I think they look good on you."

Sheesh. Cow Girl sighed. Somehow she knew that after taking a quick glance, he had immediately looked away again.

Her cheeks softened into a smile. It was just how he was.

"I think you could stand to learn a little more about girls' feelings."

"Is that so?"

Guild Girl giggled beside her. "I think our dear Goblin Slayer is fine the way he is." Yes, she might wish he were a little more attentive, but there was something about him being him that made her heart dance.

He thinks they look good on us. Personally.

The brief sentence was as good as a sonnet from him.

"I would be...embarrassed if anyone looked at me too long..."

So this is good by me. Priestess was trying to make herself even smaller. Her cheeks were red, and it wasn't just because of the sunset.

High Elf Archer leaned forward as if hoping to get Priestess to unwind a bit. "So I just have to duck in the river and scare up some fish, right?"

"Yes."

"Although I won't eat them," she said with a glance around. "But no choice." She almost looked upset, but her ears fluttered happily, and she ran into the water, kicking up little splashes.

Lizard Priest watched the girls chat and play on the riverbank from the corner of his eye. He nodded solemnly. "Now, perhaps these leaves will do for your purposes." The huge armful of leaves he was carrying rustled as he shook them. His long tongue slipped out and touched the tip of his nose. "I apologize I could not gather more. It will soon be dark."

"I know," Goblin Slayer said, standing up. "Let's get the crossbeams set, then."

It was straightforward work. They just needed to affix upper and lower crossbeams, eight in total, to the wood poles Goblin Slayer had put in the ground. Then sticks would be laid on the lower level to make a crude floor, while leaves would be spread on top as a roof. A nice, simple shelter.

Considering the presence of poisonous snakes and insects in the forest, it would be foolishness itself to put up a roof but then sleep on the bare ground.

They built two shelters: one for the men and one for the women. Normally, they had only five people, but today it was three men and four women.

"Gracious me," Dwarf Shaman said, looking away from the ongoing work to check on the girls in the water. He was on fire duty; he wasn't tall enough for anything else. Dwarves were unrivaled for their handling of fire, but as a keeper of spirits, it wasn't his strong suit. Dwarf Shaman quickly gave up on trying to strike a spark and instead produced a flat stone from his bag.

"Dancing flame, salamander's fame. Grant us a share of the very same."

He pressed the stone between his hands and incanted Kindle, producing a firestone. He tossed the glowing rock from hand to hand ("Hot, hot!") and surrounded it with some other stones. It would do in lieu of a fire.

The glow from this makeshift "bonfire" shone on the party. At the moment, it was being used to dry out their sopping clothes, but no doubt the garments would soon be replaced by fish.

"Don't you think it's a bit...unguarded, letting the girls play like that?"

"I will keep guard enough for all of us." Goblin Slayer had finished laying the floor and had started on the next step. "And I want to give them a chance to relax." As he stood sticks up in the earth, his helmet inclined ever so slightly toward Cow Girl and Guild Girl.

Then it turned to High Elf Archer, who had dragged Priestess in to help hunt for fish.

"Perhaps it's 'cause this is her homeland," he grunted softly.

"Ho-ho! She had no time to show this side before. Ah, hold! My skill does not match yours." Lizard Priest laughed, showing his fangs, draping leaves on the wooden beams as soon as they were up. "But why, milord Goblin Slayer, do you display the compassion of Maiasaura?"

"...What do you mean?"

"That you are rather a more considerate person than your appearance would suggest."

"Is that so impressive?" Goblin Slayer let out a breath. "Am *I* so impressive?"

"I would call it a quality more valuable than mithril," Dwarf Shaman said, tossing a small stick onto the fire. The dancing salamander opened its jaws and took a bite and, with a crackle, grew hotter.

"Just look at that long-eared lass," Dwarf Shaman went on. He indicated the river with one heated branch. High Elf Archer was there, reaching into the water with both hands as if to catch a fish. But she missed and, instead, sent up a great splash straight at Priestess.

That caused Cow Girl to burst out laughing, whereupon Guild Girl splashed her, too.

Maybe High Elf Archer had grown tired of the fruitless fishing expedition, or maybe she had just decided to forget it, but in any event, she had dragged Priestess into it...

"I don't believe she thinks of herself as a high elf at all." Dwarf Shaman chuckled, his smile almost hidden by his beard.

"Whatsoever the case, we are already in the land of the elves," Lizard Priest said, plopping himself down by the fire and rubbing his scaled hands together.

Once they had somewhere to sleep, all that remained was to wait for dinner. And he did love both meat and fish.

"I don't believe the little devils will easily reach us here."

"You don't?" Goblin Slayer took his cue from Lizard Priest, sitting down as well. He clapped his hands to get some dust off then muttered, "I thought the same."

"...That right?" Dwarf Shaman shrugged, his eyes half-shut, and he grabbed the flask at his hip. He uncorked it and began pouring spirits into a cup from his bag. He offered the drink around.

"Anyway, start with a drink," he said. "Not enough to get drunk, of course."

"..."

Goblin Slayer looked silently from the drink to Dwarf Shaman, then at the girls playing in the river.

Cow Girl noticed him and gave a big wave. Goblin Slayer nodded.

"Very well."

Shortly thereafter, there came a cry of "We got some!" and the fellowship was able to proceed to dinner. Perhaps unwilling to be left out, High Elf Archer had helped catch seven separate fish. Dwarf Shaman snorted softly but skewered and grilled the catch without complaint.

The seven of them (including the girls) sat in a circle and waited for the fish to cook. Though they'd been so shy earlier, playing around seemed to have helped the girls relax, and now they sat there with just a single blanket over them. Their clothes, which hung over the firestone, were not yet dry, and they couldn't put on any of their other clothes because their supply of outfits had to last until they reached town.

Instead, they dried off their bodies, mopped their sopping hair, and waited eagerly for dinner.

"Well, looks like everyone's having a good time." Dwarf Shaman pulled a variety of small bottles from his bag of catalysts. He opened each one, taking a whiff to check the smell, then distributed pinches onto the food.

When at last they could hear the crackle of melting fat, he announced, "That should do it," and distributed a skewer to each of them.

Despite the simplicity of the meal, an enticing aroma wafted from it, no doubt thanks to Dwarf Shaman's spices.

High Elf Archer brought the food up to her nose, giving it an experimental sniff, after which she glared at the dwarf. "...You know I can't eat this."

"I just wanted you to feel included. Patience. If you won't have it, I'm sure someone will."

"Hmph…" High Elf Archer's long ears drooped as she looked the fish in its dead white eye, before tossing it to Priestess.

"O-oh! I can't possibly eat two of them…"

High Elf Archer smirked. "What's the matter? There's a feast tomorrow, you might as well get some practice eating. I'll have some dried beans."

"…All the more reason to make sure my stomach's empty, then." She grimaced at High Elf Archer, but the ranger ignored her. Priestess blew on her fish to cool it, starting in with little nibbles.

The fat melted in her mouth with a slight bitterness, then a salty flavor spread across her palate. "Mm!" she exclaimed, her cheeks softening into a smile. Then, "Are we close?"

Uh-huh. High Elf Archer nodded, popping open the beans she had retrieved from the luggage. "We're probably right on the border between the forest and the village. They might even find us before we find them."

"So your older sister is going to be a bride," Cow Girl said, taking a generous bite of her own fish and murmuring, "Mm, that's good." Then she said more loudly, "I'll bet elf brides are gorgeous…"

"Well, obviously!" High Elf Archer chuckled and puffed out her chest as if Cow Girl were talking about her. She spread her arms and elaborated: "My older sister is especially beautiful! She's a high elf, after all!"

Dwarf Shaman looked up from his meal long enough to interject, "You're walking evidence of how that doesn't prove anything." But in her current mood, High Elf Archer was able to ignore even this slight against her.

"Ho-ho-ho. I hope they will be welcoming toward a lizardman," Lizard Priest said. He had taken a round of cheese from his luggage and was slicing away at it with his claws. He stuck pieces on his skewer, where he cooked them over the fire. His scaled hands hissed as they rubbed together in anticipation while he waited for the cheese to melt.

"You really like cheese, don't you?" Guild Girl said as she watched him. She was taking dainty bites of her own fish. "It seemed like you were something of a coordinator in that battle earlier. At least from what I could hear…?"

"Administration has its own trials."

"Spare me the details. It's all trouble."

So many things to think about. Guild Girl smiled ambiguously; no doubt she had more than enough concerns of her own.

In fact, neither adventurers nor staff knew that much about the day-to-day work of the other. There were so few opportunities to experience either the danger of adventure or the brutality of desk work.

"I've had some really informative experiences on this trip. Even if they were a little scary."

Sorry, High Elf Archer seemed to say, her ears drooping again. "When we get to the village, I'll be sure someone gets a piece of my mind. 'What are your guards doing?!' That sort of thing."

"I'll have to be sure to greet your sister properly, though," Guild Girl said. "I need to let her know how much I appreciate all you do for us."

High Elf Archer scratched her cheek as if embarrassed. "Going to my sister with that sort of thing is all well and good. But as for my older brother…"

"You have an older brother?" Goblin Slayer asked quietly, in between stuffing pieces of fish into his visor.

Well, I mean cousin. High Elf Archer answered shortly, her pointer finger drawing circles in the air. "I can't quite remember what you humans call it. A brother-in-law-to-be?"

"You mean the groom?"

"Yeah, that's it," she said with a nod. She popped more food into her mouth and looked at the sky. It was already nearly black, a medley of stars just visible through the leaves of the trees. With a cadence like music, High Elf Archer explained that the elves called this the "rain gate."

"My cousin," she said, "he's been crazy about my sister for ages, acting all big about it!"

"Well, pride is certainly the one thing everyone associates with elves!" Dwarf Shaman quipped.

"Exactly!" High Elf Archer replied. "He's a real elf's elf."

"But if they're getting married…," Priestess said, putting a finger to her chin in thought. Then she smiled as the answer came to her. "Your sister must have figured out that he cared about her!"

"He wasn't exactly subtle about it. Not that I know what she sees in him. It all seems like a lot of trouble to me." Then came that tinkling laughter. High Elf Archer hugged her knees. "You know what elves do when they want to get someone's attention? They sing to them." Her voice was quiet, as if she was revealing a secret, and carried just a hint of mischief. "He went around singing this epic ballad about all his great martial achievements, until he got beat up."

"Ah. Some bandits got him?" Lizard Priest asked with amusement.

"No—my sister did!"

The entire party laughed.

High Elf Archer shared one story of old times after another, tales she could never have told at a wedding reception. Like the time her cousin had wanted to catch a deer as a gift but failed. Or the time he had gotten sick, and her sister had been so worried about him that she couldn't sleep and ended up catching cold herself. There was the time her sister had overcooked some baked treats (an uncharacteristic lapse), but her cousin had eaten them all with a straight face.

There was the fact that High Elf Archer had learned everything she knew about herbs, fruits, and more from her sister, while her cousin had taught her archery and how to cross a field in a hurry.

Or when she'd said she was going to leave their village, her sister was opposed, but her cousin supported her...

She had spent two thousand years in these woods. There were so many memories scattered throughout those changeless, ever-turning days.

In the middle of this flood of stories, Goblin Slayer said, "So this is your home."

"That's right."

"That's good."

"Well—" High Elf Archer's eyes narrowed like a smiling cat's. "It's where my heart is."

Goblin Slayer nodded. Cow Girl blinked at him for a moment.

Then he said, "And there are goblins near it."

The note of anger in his voice was unmistakable.

CHAPTER 3

THE FOREST OF THE ELF KING

The place was strange, eerie.

The sun was just rising, a hint of light coming from just beyond the horizon. The sky, where it was visible through the branches, was a deep blue.

Goblin Slayer rifled through his item bag in the predawn light. From the simple sleeping area behind him, beyond some bug netting, came soft groans and gentle snoring.

It was Lizard Priest and Dwarf Shaman, both of whom were still asleep. The dwarf might not get up until breakfast, but the lizardman would awaken come dawn.

As for the women, Priestess would already be up and at her prayers beside her bed. Guild Girl woke up at the same time each day, which was before breakfast; she said it was most convenient for her work. Cow Girl would soon be awake as well.

High Elf Archer had taken an early shift of guard duty as she planned to sleep until someone roused her.

A party that didn't let its spell casters get sufficient rest was a party that would soon be destroyed. For that reason, High Elf Archer and Goblin Slayer traded off turns on the watch. As it happened, Goblin Slayer was quite happy to take the later shift.

From midnight until dawn, he had no desire to sleep. The chance to let someone else watch from evening until the dark of the night, while he rested, was something new this year, a small—

"Luxury, perhaps." He put some fragrant herbs through the visor of his helmet and chewed on them. A bitter flavor spread from his throat up to his brain, stimulating his focus. He crunched down on the tough leaves a second time.

Yes, the place was eerie.

Goblin Slayer adjusted his grip on his sword so that he could draw it at any time.

Would the goblins gang up and attack us in the middle of the day?

Attack a group of armed adventurers, perhaps assuming that the element of surprise overcame any disparity in armament.

Was it possible?

Above all, there was the wolf pack to consider. Goblins were bad enough, but they had a contingent of riders. Imagine the resources that must take to support.

And yet they are able to do it.

Food. Stables. Equipment. And amusements—yes, amusements.

Was that why they were attacking the boats?

They were located directly beside the elf village. Why had they built such an elaborate operation?

What for? What were they planning?

Goblin Slayer chewed the leaf once, twice, three times more.

His thoughts came in a flurry of disconnected ideas, bubbling up and then disappearing.

Suddenly, a voice called out.

"Awaken, on your feet! Where do you varlets think you are?"

A gust of wind through the woods carried the interrogation to them.

Goblin Slayer whipped out his sword and jumped to his feet. He found himself, however, met with an obsidian blade.

With great annoyance, he looked up at the weapon's owner.

Someone was standing on the raised floor, having torn aside the bug netting. The sun was at his back, but it was clear he was—

"An elf?"

"Indeed. And this is our territory."

The one who spoke so proudly was an elf warrior, young and beautiful—as all elves are. He wore leather armor, carried a bow, and had a quiver of bud-tipped arrows at his hip.

More striking than anything, though, was the armor protecting his head. It was a shining headpiece made of mithril.

The elf with the shimmering headpiece regarded Goblin Slayer balefully, his expression suspicious.

"...Do you really fight with that sword?" the elf asked.

"Against goblins, yes," Goblin Slayer replied evenly.

The elf's sharp gaze moved from the sword with its strange length to the round shield, then the grimy leather armor, then the cheap-looking metal helmet.

"Some barbarian warrior, are you? And a dwarf..."

"...And a lizardman, at your service." Lizard Priest, who had sat up in the meantime, brought his palms together in a strange gesture. Dwarf Shaman, who had just gotten up, was sitting there and making no attempt to hide his displeasure. To be attacked by elves while sleeping was the ultimate humiliation for a dwarf.

The elf looked at each of the three of them in turn, having more or less gathered who and what they were.

"So. Adventurers..."

"Roughly."

"...Indeed. Was it you who did battle with the goblins yesterday?"

Goblin Slayer nodded his grimy helmet.

"I see," the elf said, his eyes narrowing and his hand sliding on his sword. "We finished off the ones you left behind."

At that, Goblin Slayer grunted. That meant his attempt to spread disease in the nest had been thwarted. On the other hand, the escaped goblins had been killed. Perhaps it was well and good, then.

The elf seemed uncertain what to say in the face of this unintimidated attitude.

"...I have just one question to ask you," he said gruffly.

"What is it?"

"The arrow that pierced one of the goblins appeared to belong to a fellow of ours."

The elf with the shining helmet produced the projectile in question. It had a bud tip. It was covered in dark goblin blood, but the tip was faulty, hanging at an angle.

"We know, however, that this girl would never use such a crude bolt."

"......"

"Tell me what you did to her. Your answer may decide your fate at my hands—"

Goblin Slayer didn't say a word, but Lizard Priest and Dwarf Shaman looked at each other and shrugged.

"You must be the one who sang an epic poem instead of a love song."

"Indeed, it seems it was that very love who set you straight."

"...Wha?!" The elf with the shining helmet was thrown for a loop. He grasped his sword tighter, as if ready to raise it at any time. His pale countenance, the pride of his people, was instantly ruby red, and he shook violently.

"Y-you filthy vermin...! Where in the world did you...?!"

"The girl you're seeking," Goblin Slayer said with an uncharacteristic sigh. "That's her over there, isn't it?"

"Hrk...!"

In the blink of an eye, the elf was off like a shot.

"Starwind's daughter, are you there?!"

He jumped several meters in a single graceful bound; when he found the shelter, he tore away the bug netting without hesitation.

"Yes?"

"Huh?"

"...Ah."

He was soon frowning. Before him were three young women—young women who, awoken by the commotion outside, had quickly made themselves up to see what was going on.

Three people, six eyes, opened wide to gaze at the intruding elf.

They were in the middle of an adventure, of course, and no one in that position would deliberately change into pajamas to sleep. But that didn't mean they were happy to have some stranger see them at their rest.

And there was one other thing.

Over in a corner of the sleeping area, a ball of blankets shifted and squirmed.

"...What's going *on*? The sun's barely up..."

High Elf Archer yawned, stretched like a cat, and crawled out from under her covers. She rubbed her eyes, scratched her head, and looked around vacantly.

"Buh? Elder brother? What, did you come to get me?"

"......"

Priestess looked like she was about to cry, Cow Girl was frowning, and Guild Girl had a soft smile on her face.

The elf with the shining helmet swallowed heavily.

Then he darted back, as if dragged by string, as the girls began to shout noisily.

"...Fine bodyguard work," he said when he landed, coughing once. "I appreciate your bringing my sister-in-law here. Compensation will be readied for you. May your honors travel a safe road home."

"These are my *friends*, brother." High Elf Archer stuck her head out of the shelter and glared at him, but the other elf only gave an elegant shrug.

"...That's elves for you, they just..."

But whatever crude comment was destined to end that sentence, even Dwarf Shaman had sense enough to keep to himself.

§

"I do apologize, calling you back when you've only just left on your journey."

"Only just? It's been years already. In fact, it's been a long time, brother."

"...You reek of human." The elf with the shining headpiece frowned as he walked beside High Elf Archer, who strode confidently through the forest.

The look may have been inspired in part by his sister-in-law's flippant attitude, but it was probably mostly because of the glares he was getting from behind as he guided the party along. Specifically, from the three women.

"I understand what is in your heart," Lizard Priest said to the elf, sticking his tongue out. "My people live in a great forest of their own, but the realm of the elves is indeed striking."

"It has been growing since the Age of the Gods. A mortal who entered could not expect to find his way out again in his lifetime."

The elf couldn't be blamed for the note of pride in his voice. The forest was indeed like a great green labyrinth. There was a profusion of vines, huge trees that blocked the road, and paths so narrow even wild beasts couldn't traverse them. The underbrush seemed to reach out to catch one by the foot. It was hard enough for the adventurers; it must have been a tremendous effort for Guild Girl and Cow Girl.

The fact that they still proceeded relatively unhindered toward the interior was itself a sign of the elves' hospitality. It partly explained why the women settled for glaring rather than complaining aloud.

"But," said the elf with a dubious glance behind him, "to think that Orcbolg, of whose name I have heard, should turn out to be...like this."

"I don't know what people say about me," Goblin Slayer said nonchalantly, prompting a snort from the elf.

"Your manner of speech," he said, "leaves much to be desired."

"More importantly, tell me about those goblins."

"They weren't especially unusual, as goblins go." *They matter little. Sometimes there are more of them, sometimes less.* "It's been hot recently. Don't such creatures multiply in the heat?"

"'Recently'?"

"The past ten years or so. It's been like this ever since that furor over the Dark Gods began."

"Is that so?" Goblin Slayer said softly. "Just lately..."

"If the goblins are not threat enough to force us to build fortresses, then they are not worth fussing over."

"You don't have to act all aloof," High Elf Archer piped up. "Just tell him that a wedding is *not* the time for goblin talk."

"Children should be seen and not heard," the elf with the shining headpiece snapped at his younger cousin.

"I'm not a child," High Elf Archer said. Her lips folded into a pout, but it was clear from the bouncing of her long ears that she was still in a perfectly good mood.

Priestess, making up the back of the party, whispered softly to Guild Girl, "…So I guess the elves really don't bother themselves about goblins?"

"What, you too?" Guild Girl replied with a wink. "If that's the first thing you think of in this situation, you might want to be careful he doesn't rub off any more on you."

"Errr, heh-heh…"

Priestess scratched her cheek and laughed as if to pass the subject off, causing Guild Girl to murmur, "Gracious me."

Then she went on, "Actually, even a lot of elvish adventurers act like that, especially if they've just left the forest." *It's not that they have no sense of danger, just a poor grasp of scale.*

The most basic fact about goblins was that they had the intelligence and physical strength of human children, that they were the weakest of monsters. Elves might well be frightened only of things much larger and more powerful.

"After all, they do have those eyewitness accounts."

"…? Of what?"

"The battles of the gods."

Oh. Priestess gasped then quickly covered her mouth. It wasn't impossible that some of the elvish elders were in fact that old.

This would have been a time back before all things were decided by the roll of the dice. An age hardly known even to myth and legend.

"Evil spirits, dragons, dark gods, demon lords, and all manner of awful creatures came from another plane."

It made sense, then, that the elves would regard goblins as barely a nuisance in comparison.

Yes, occasionally some unlucky soul would die at their hands. But to those destined for so short a life already, what was a few years either way? Compare that to the sort of cataclysm that comes only once every decade, or century, or millennium…

"No matter what goblins do, they aren't going to cause something like that," Guild Girl explained.

"…Huh," Cow Girl said softly. "You see?" Guild Girl replied.

Priestess, however, cast her eyes to the ground with an inexpressible sadness.

Goblins didn't matter. They were hardly worth taking note of. "Yeah, you're right," she said as nonchalantly as she could, but with a glance at *him*.

He was near the head of the line, as the one who stood on the party's front row, sandwiching the rest of them between him and her. She wanted to say something to him, but hesitated.

Then she found her chance stolen by the elf with the shining headpiece.

"There is, in fact, something even more on my mind than the wedding," he said.

"Oh! I'm gonna tell Sis you said that!" High Elf Archer exclaimed. Dwarf Shaman told her not to blather, but she waved him away.

"It seems the One That Stops the Waters is getting closer to the village of late."

"What thing are you talking about?"

"An ancient thing that lives in the forest. We have always been instructed not to lay a hand on it," the elf told Goblin Slayer.

"Oh-ho," Lizard Priest said quietly. "And how long, if I may ask, has this ancient thing been living?"

"I don't know," he replied, "but it was already called old even when I was young."

"The Triassic, then? Or the Carboniferous, or Cretaceous..." Lizard Priest started mumbling important-sounding things to himself, before finally, he nodded somberly. "Mmm, most intriguing."

"Whatever it may be, its territory is separate from ours. It emerges only rarely, but..."

"Truth is, I've never even seen it, although people keep telling me it's there," High Elf Archer said, her ears twitching in thought. She turned to her cousin. "Does it really exist?"

"I've seen tracks several times. My grandfather claims he once saw the creature itself."

"How many Ages ago was that?" High Elf Archer laughed.

At that moment, the wind gusted. It was a fresh wind, sweet and summery, full of the aromas of leaves and grass.

It blew through the trees as if it might go on forever. And where did it come from?

The source yawned in the middle of the forest, a great space that stretched from heaven to earth.

Was it a village shaped like a forest? Or was it a forest that looked like a village?

The canopy stretched to heights unfathomable, the houses made from massive, hollowed-out trees. Pathways woven from vines and leaves stretched among them.

And elves, beautiful elves in flawless attire, walked those pathways as if dancing through the air.

The patterns that adorned the bark of the trees were many and various, and the sibilance of the leaves filled the air with its music.

Layer upon layer stretched up and up, the village sprawling so high it threatened to scrape the sky.

"W-wow…" Cow Girl blinked, her eyes shining, as the sound of amazement escaped her. She had never seen such a thing in all her life, had never imagined she might experience anything like this as long as she lived.

This was the sort of place she had imagined when her old friend had talked about wanting to become an adventurer. She took a step forward, then two. She was standing beside him, and ahead of them was a great spiral gallery that ran up and around the exterior of the village. She found herself wanting to lean out and look, but he cautioned her, "It's dangerous. You'll fall."

"Oh yeah. But look… This is incredible…!"

Still holding on to her arm, Goblin Slayer said only, "Yes."

Cow Girl puffed out her cheeks in annoyance, but there were less petty things to attend to. Leaning on him, she looked around the elf village as if set on burning it into her memory.

"Gracious. You elves do know how to build," Dwarf Shaman remarked with a hint of disappointment—indeed, of defeat—in his voice.

"They do at that," Lizard Priest said. "My own village is in a forest as well, but it does not look anything like this."

Dwarf Shaman looked up at the elf with the shining headpiece. "…I don't suppose y'had help?"

"The fae helped us, dwarf," the elf replied. "Naturally."

"Heh! That's really something. So y'don't do it with your own hands?"

The party's collective shock was no doubt expected. High Elf Archer chuckled, sticking out her small chest, and gently elbowed Priestess, who was holding on to her sounding staff. "Pretty neat, huh?"

"Yes, very much so!" She nodded at the archer, who was winking mischievously. "I never knew such a wonderful place existed in this world."

"Heh-heh-heh! You think so? Aw, gee...!"

High Elf Archer stuck out her chest as she swelled further and further with pride. Guild Girl started to giggle. "The capital was quite an impressive place, but this..."

The human capital was lovely, but surely the timescale on which it had been built was different. This place had not been made by the hands of any people but rather had been built up by nature itself, truly a work of the gods.

High Elf Archer ran to the front of the line with little mincing hops like a bird. When she opened her lips, the words she wove were in the melodic language of the elves.

"Good morn and good night, by a sun and two moons' light, from Starwind's daughter to her friends—"

She turned back to them and spread her arms wide. Her hair streamed out behind her like a comet.

"Welcome to my home!"

She smiled as wide as a flower in bloom.

§

They went through a corridor woven of branches and found that their room was the hollow of a great zelkova tree. A vine curtain hung down over the entrance to the large chamber.

A carpet of long mosses was spread over the floor, and there were a desk and chairs that seemed to be extended knots of the tree itself. Almost translucent leaves were clustered in front of the window, admitting the afternoon light with its gentle warmth. The vine drapes here and there must have been the entryways to sleeping quarters.

The only thing in the room that suggested the work of anything other than nature was an elven tapestry that seemed to be woven from strands of morning dew. The delicate, fluid illustrations depicted a series of stories that stretched back to the Age of the Gods. Unlike the myths and legends humans told, chances were that the elves had observed this history with their own eyes.

There was no fireplace, for obvious reasons, but the warmth of the tree itself, tempered by the breeze, was perfectly comfortable.

Even better, the entire room was suffused with the aroma of the wood.

Cow Girl took a deep breath, savoring the smell, and then let it out slowly.

"This is incredible! I've only ever heard of anything like it in stories."

She felt wrong, somehow, entering the room wearing her dirty leather boots. She crept in as quietly as she could, one step, then two.

As she got closer to one of the chairs, she discovered that mushrooms were growing on it like a cushion.

She smiled: it really was like some old fairy tale. She tried sitting down gently. The cushion felt soft and puffy beneath her bottom as she sank into it. She found herself exhaling in admiration.

"Wow... This is great."

"Um, okay... Let me try...!"

Clutching her sounding staff nervously, Priestess dropped onto one of the chairs. The mushrooms supported her light frame capably.

"Eek! Ack!" she exclaimed, like a little girl, getting a chuckle out of Guild Girl.

That cleric was like a child trying to act grown-up. She always took the opportunity to have some fun when it presented itself.

"I've known some elf adventurers, but I've never been invited to their home," she said, looking studiously around the room. She ran her hand along the tapestry on the wall. It showed a half-elf hero and their companions fighting for the Dragon Lance. It must have been a scene out of some military epic.

"How was this made?" Guild Girl asked. "Is this something else the fae did?"

"It was not made, but your conjecture isn't wholly wrong," the elf with the shining headpiece answered, with a touch of courtesy toward this knowledgeable human woman. "The forest bestows its affection upon us and creates the form of these things, an expression of its power."

"They say one goes to the dwarves for sturdy dwellings, to the rheas for comfort, and to the lizardmen for fortresses," Lizard Priest said, sweeping his tail with great interest along the moss carpeting. He let out a breath, apparently relieved to find that even the long, heavy appendage left no mark on the floor covering. "But my, elven houses are deeply intriguing in their own right."

"To hear such from a child of the nagas is compliment indeed," the male elf said with an elegant gesture. A show of respect, one supposed, for the courageous and ancient lizardmen who knew so much of the circle of life. He added self-deprecatingly, "I'm afraid that, busy as I am with the preparations for this joyous occasion, I have lacked the time to make your dwellings suitably inviting..."

High Elf Archer, however, gave him a merciless jab with her elbow and said with lidded eyes, "Now, brother, don't fish for compliments."

"Erk..."

"I don't care how busy you were, I'll bet this took months."

She sniffed and then jumped clear over the moss and into one of the chairs.

"Dibs on this one!" she exclaimed, landing on the mushroom cushion of the seat with the best view of the window.

High Elf Archer looked like she might kick up her feet right then and there. "Most uncouth," her cousin frowned. "If *she* were to see this, I think you would get a piece of her mind."

"Did you hear that? Not even married yet, and he's already saying '*she* this' and '*she* that' like she's his wife!" She chortled with a sound like a ringing bell, completely ignoring her cousin's rebuke. "So. What's next?"

"Hrm. You're no doubt tired from your long journey, so we've readied a bath and laid out a midday meal for you."

The elf with the shining helmet rubbed his brow as if fighting a headache but retained his people's natural dignity. Maybe he was used to being nettled by his sister-in-law-to-be like this. They had, after all, spent two thousand years together before she left.

"What would you like to do?" he asked.

"I will unload the luggage," Goblin Slayer answered immediately. "Goblins may yet come."

By this time, we need hardly record the reactions of his companions to this remark.

The elf with the shining headpiece found himself staring in some amazement. High Elf Archer pressed one hand to her cheek and waved with the other. "I'll stay here, too, then. You never know when Big Sis might drop by." She gave a bit of a resigned laugh, which the others were used to. Hence, they all nodded together.

"I think I'll get m'self some food while the ladies make their toilette."

"I believe I agree with that plan."

"Are—are you sure?" Guild Girl asked, blinking. For as often as she took care of adventurers, there had been few opportunities for adventurers to show care for her. An ambiguous expression came over her face at this unaccustomed situation, and she nodded hesitantly. "If you're quite sure it's all right for us to go first…"

"We shall be going first in our own way. Should women not be given priority in attending to their appearance?"

"Well then, thank you very much. I'll be happy to go wash off the dust and sweat." Guild Girl nodded once more, this time apologetically, but she had no actual objection.

Priestess had gotten off her mushroom chair and now pattered over to Goblin Slayer.

"What is it?" the helmet asked, turning to her. She fixed it with a pale finger.

"Goblin Slayer, sir, you have to be sure to eat and bathe, okay?"

"Yes."

He didn't sound very happy about it, but Priestess was satisfied. She puffed out her little chest triumphantly.

Cow Girl smiled helplessly. "Hey, don't go grabbing us girls' stuff, especially the changes of clothes." She conscientiously made the point. So long as she warned him, she knew he would be careful, but if she didn't say anything, well, he was capable of being totally clueless.

"…Which are those?" He sounded a bit concerned now.

Cow Girl nodded. "We'll grab some clothes for after our bath, so try to remember which bags we get them from."

"Okay."

"But don't look in them!"

"…Perhaps someone other than me should handle those bags."

"What?" came High Elf Archer's voice, her ears flapping and a smile crossing her face. She was thoroughly confident that letting Orcbolg handle *all* the luggage would be vastly more entertaining than having anyone else do it.

"I suppose if two thousand years didn't change you, a few more weren't going to do it," the male elf said with a sigh. He felt someone slap him on the back, although strangely low down.

He turned to see Dwarf Shaman's bearded face, with a very knowing look on it.

"Well, lead on, Sir Groom," the dwarf said. "I'm sure the ladies are eager for their bath." He gave the elf another encouraging smack and laughed uproariously. "Unlike the elves, we mere mortals can't linger over every little thing."

§

"You want to know why we elves do not eat meat?"

"'Sright. I just want to understand why I'm being fed nothing but leaves and fruit."

"It's a question of balance, O friend who dwells in the earth."

"You mean an issue of numbers, then, of the creatures that live in the forest? …Oh-ho, this banana is delicious."

"Taste then this drink as well, Honored Scaled Priest. It uses tapioca."

"Ah, the cassava root. My people have been known to boil and eat it. Perhaps this is the truth behind those grilled candies."

"Now, then. For one animal to grow to adulthood takes many years, but for fruit to ripen on the tree takes a year at most, and the supply is plentiful."

"Hmm… Well, I suppose it must be nice not having to worry about your food supply."

"What is more, we need not fear being eaten by the animals, nor need we leave the forest."

"You mean the ecosystem would be threatened if you had to hunt for your daily sustenance. Aha! Indeed, indeed."

"Yes, hence we help ourselves only to grasses, fruits, and berries. Do you see now, dwarf?"

"I get it, but I don't have to like it."

Dwarf Shaman looked at the plate of mushrooms in front of him, blowing out his cheeks with something less than tact.

The great hall built under the sprawling roots of a towering tree doubled as the elves' dining area. In place of lamps, several closed buds full of sea sparkles hung around the room, and the tables were piled with food.

There were grapes and bananas, tapioca, and salads featuring a medley of herbs and vegetables, along with grape wine and a drink also made from tapioca. When it came to elegance and atmosphere, and both quality and quantity of food, even Dwarf Shaman could find nothing to complain about.

And yet...

"I just can't ever envision m'self eating bugs..."

"They're quick to reproduce, and there are a great many varieties of them. And to top it all off, they're delicious."

On the huge plate in front of the dwarf was a pile of large beetles, stripped of their shells and boiled. He pulled a leg off one and dipped it in sauce; when he bit down, he found it crunchy and responsive in the mouth.

He had to admit, it *was* good.

For dwarves, food was no less important and no less to be honored than gems and jewels. And as a dwarf, Dwarf Shaman, by his beard, would not deny when something was delicious.

But—but still.

"They're still *bugs*, aren't they?"

"I myself find them delectable."

"Hrmph! A jungle cousin of this lot, you are...!" Dwarf Shaman glared at Lizard Priest, who was smacking his lips as he crunched down on an insect, shell and all.

Maybe they could keep the things from *looking* like bugs. Or at least add a little salt.

The dish had a light flavor of good ingredients, but it was so obvious that one was eating insects. That was enough to make even Dwarf Shaman lose his appetite.

"Oh, fine! I guess this leaves me with the grilled sweets."

"Oh, not eating yours? I suppose then, ahem, I might just help myself to one of these legs…"

"You fool," he said, slapping away the scaly, outstretched hand. "A dwarf never shares his meal with another!" He began ferrying the grilled sweets to his mouth.

The treat's moist center had a distinct sweetness; it was said to be the elves' secret recipe. Perhaps there was honey worked into it; in any case, it was nourishing, and he never seemed to tire of it no matter how much he ate.

Dwarf Shaman had been stuffing food into his mouth, crumbs flying into his beard, for some time when he froze, suddenly having had a thought.

"Don't tell me. Do these treats have bugs in them, too…?"

"We shall leave that to your honored imagination," the elf with the shining headpiece said, at which an expression difficult to describe passed over Dwarf Shaman's face. He looked at the half-eaten sweet in his hand then tossed it into his mouth as if to say *ah, well,* and swallowed it noisily.

As Lizard Priest watched the dwarf, he somberly touched the tip of his nose with his tongue and opened his jaws.

"So long as we reside at your fortress—er, is that word appropriate in the case of the elves?"

"This is not a place prepared against battle, but insofar as the chieftain lives here, you aren't wrong."

"Then I should certainly wish to greet your chieftain."

This caused a faint smile to play over the lips of the elf with the shining headpiece. "An audience is already planned for you. Indeed, all who visit this forest are as if they were already before the chieftain."

"………Ahh."

Lizard Priest squinted and craned his neck. The ceiling, which was in fact the bottom of the massive tree above them, was far away, illuminated by the gentle glow of the sea sparkles.

There was a quiet rustling of the leaves in the wind, accompanied by the sound of water flowing by the roots.

So long as an elf was not killed and did not wish for death themselves, they would go on living.

So what, then, happened if one did desire death…?

"I see."

All was part of the forest. Part of nature. Part of the cycle. One simply faded away and joined all that was already here.

The chieftain lived here. This very place *was* the chieftain.

Looking up in wonderment, Lizard Priest put his palms together in a strange gesture. Though they envisioned it differently, the lizardmen also saw returning to the circle as one kind of ideal death.

"I offer my most heartfelt thanks that we have been granted to touch even the hem of the dress of the one who oversees this great forest."

"Your thanks is accepted," the elf said, glancing over at Dwarf Shaman, who had puffed out his cheeks as if to ask what all the fuss was about. "To know there is one from beyond our wood who understands this is a joy unlooked for. May I ask—what do you think of this place?"

"Oh, my brief look around suggests how busy everyone is."

And indeed they were.

The great hall was decorated with many weavings in preparation for the wedding, along with harps strung with spider's silk. But with the exception of a few serving girls, there was no sign of anyone there at all, let alone any entertainers.

"Has it all to do with the wedding?"

"Not all of it," the elf responded, taking a sip from his tapioca drink as if to join his words together. The cup he drank from was the polished horn of a deer, and nothing more, yet it was a work of art. "There have been many whispers in the woods of late. Many have gone to see."

"To see the One That Stops the Waters, you mean?"

"So there're things in the forest that even the elves don't understand," Dwarf Shaman said with a nasty grin.

Never letting his elegant smile slip, the elf replied, "Then let me ask you, O dwarf: do you know all things that sleep in the depths of the earth?"

"...I take your point," Dwarf Shaman grunted. "You have me there."

"Heh-heh-heh! Milord Goblin Slayer would surely ask whether those things were the work of goblins," Lizard Priest said, chuckling merrily and grabbing another insect leg. He let slip the thought that he would have no complaint if there were some cheese around.

"On that point," the elf said.

Lizard Priest nodded soberly. "Mm. Cheese is the milk of a cow or a sheep or the like, fermented, as they say—"

"That is not what I meant... Is he really the famous Orcbolg, the Goblin Slayer? The kindest man on the frontier?"

"Indeed, he is."

"He very little looks it."

Lizard Priest rolled his eyes in his head. "I know he can appear rather unimpressive at first glance. But what makes you say that?"

"My cousin seems to have taken a liking to him," the elf said wryly, sounding like an older brother concerned about his little sister. "She has a rather...*unique* personality, much like someone else I know... Erm, I suppose there's no need to hide it from you. I should say, much like me."

"Ho! That's just it, er, eh, Sir Groom," Dwarf Shaman said, sounding revived as he grabbed a horn cup. The wine was weak, but alcohol was alcohol. It was still good for stirring up a dwarf. "Is there nothing you can do to rein her in a bit?"

"We did attempt to instruct her in the more womanly arts. Weaving, music, song, and more besides."

"And did it work?"

"………We spent two thousand years on the project."

"I see..." *And this is what they've got to show for it.* The three of them looked at one another and sighed in unison.

"I still say, though, that she isn't a bad young woman."

"Yes, I know that." Dwarf Shaman's answer was brief, and then he reached out and grabbed a leg off his beetle. He demanded salt even as he chewed on it, sauce flying everywhere as he feasted on the meat.

He burped diligently then swigged more wine, then another burp.

"I admit her inability to be ladylike displeases me, and I do wish sometimes that she would calm down and act her age," the elf said.

Lizard Priest squinted. "Hmph," Dwarf Shaman snorted, as if to say he wasn't entirely happy with this assessment. "As long as she doesn't slow us down, dear Groom, we'll be happy enough to have her."

§

A pounding could be heard, as of falling water, and a white spray seen.

A waterfall? Yes, there was one.

But it was not such as those that fall upon the surface of the earth. Not the kind that are shone upon by the sun.

This was a river that ran in the hollows of the earth, up its waterfall, up the great trunk and onward to heaven.

Go through the great hall and down a flight of stairs, and there was another vast chamber.

It was a great stone cavern carved out by water over many thousands of years, worked into just this shape. The rock had been worked by the unceasing flow into a spectacular limestone cavern. It was startling to see a rain forest that also had stalagmites rising up from the ground, and stalactites dangling like leaves from above.

It was a stone forest. A river flowed through it, complete with waterfall and a deep, dark lake.

That lake gave off a faint emerald glitter.

The water itself, however, was not the source; it was the moss.

The moss, which packed the lake bed, was shimmering.

"Oh... Wow..."

So this was what it meant to be speechless.

Cow Girl trembled at the otherworldly scenery, unable to say anything. The damp but cool underground air blew across her naked, suntanned body wrapped in a towel.

She glanced behind to see the elf serving girl withdrawing with the clothes Cow Girl had taken off.

Cow Girl looked dubiously at Guild Girl, who stood beside her.

"D-do you really think it's okay for us to get in this?"

"They said this place is for washing, so I think it's fine."

Maybe she was used to this sort of thing, because she seemed to have no hesitation about exposing her polished beauty.

Guild Girl took a quick look around then dipped a toe into the water. That special chill of underground spring water sent a shock through her. She gave an involuntary yelp, causing Priestess to giggle.

"It's warmer than the water we used for washing back at the Temple," she said. She slid her delicate legs into the pool, closing her eyes as if savoring the sensation.

"You clerics always seem to be so good at this sort of thing," Guild Girl muttered with something like resentment, after which she slid slowly into the lake.

Cow Girl, loath to be the only one left on shore, screwed up her courage and then all but charged into the water.

"Eee... Y-yikes...!"

She felt the soft moss under her feet. She thought she was about to slip on it but almost immediately found that it held her weight firmly. The water was cold at first, but she soon grew used to it and even found it felt pleasant.

She thought she was going to be okay here.

That encouraged her to submerge herself up to her shoulders; the water supported her, and she swayed gently back and forth in its embrace.

"Ahh..." Cow Girl found herself letting out an easy, relaxed sound, her face turning red. She glanced at the other two girls, whose expressions were much like hers. That helped her relax.

"You're right, it's warmer than well water," she said. "I wonder why."

"I heard a story once that said there's a river of fire that flows beneath the earth," Priestess said. She cocked her head. *I wonder if that's why.* Maybe High Elf Archer or Dwarf Shaman could tell them.

"You adventurers are really something," Cow Girl said. "Always going to places like this."

"Not always," Priestess replied with an ambiguous smile.

Cavern, ruins, ruins, ruins, cavern, cavern, ruins, cavern...

When she thought back over her adventures, she realized that most

©Noboru Kannatuki

of them *had* taken place in caves or ruins. And most of the ruins she had gone to had ended up burned to the ground, or blown up, or inundated with toxic gas...

"...Well, still, not *always*."

She would have to talk to Goblin Slayer about evaluating his actions a little more carefully.

"Lots of people become adventurers hoping to find hidden treasures," Guild Girl offered. She held her hair with one hand to keep it out of the water while she listened to the other girls' conversation. "The trust afforded to some homeless ruins-raider and that accorded an established adventurer is very different."

"Oh yeah, that makes sense." Cow Girl nodded vigorously, droplets of water flying from her short hair. "Sometimes people stop by the farm asking for something to eat, but I'm always kind of scared of random travelers."

And lodging? No way. She waved a hand emphatically.

"Porcelains can be a little scary, too. Er, not so much young traveling priestesses."

"I'm Steel already, anyway," Priestess replied. The slight hint of pride in her voice made Guild Girl smile even more.

The still-young (despite being sixteen) girl put a hand to her modest chest, as if the steel level tag were hanging there even now.

It hadn't been long since she'd passed the promotion interview and risen to the eighth rank.

"Adventurers... Man, adventurers," Cow Girl said, looking at Priestess, too. "I remember how often I thought about adventurers when I was a kid."

"You were pretty keen on them, were you?" Guild Girl asked, cocking her head. A droplet of water tumbled from a stalactite, making tiny waves ripple across the lake's surface.

"Er, who, me? N-not the adventurers as such, no," Cow Girl said, shaking her hand in a way that made more ripples.

"Ahh," Guild Girl said with a nod. "The princesses, then?"

"Don't say that."

"Or maybe the heroes' *brides*?"

"Don't make me say it!"

Cow Girl sunk into the water up to her cheeks as if trying to hide the flush in her face. She sat there silently, blowing bubbles up to the surface, like a little girl.

For a moment, the only sound in the cavern was the rush of the underground river.

Think about it—was it really so unusual?

Boys always wanted to be heroes, or knights, or dragon slayers, or adventurers. Girls, too, had their dreams.

Princesses or shrine maidens, beautiful brides. Perhaps, they hoped, some faerie might one day come to take them home with him.

Though in the end, infatuation was merely infatuation, dreams only dreams...

"But..." Priestess's single word was like a drop of water, and it, too, rippled through the room. "I think being a bride would be nice."

§

"I'm going to get things set up," Goblin Slayer said, hardly bothering to let out a breath. The luggage had all been deposited in their respective rooms.

"Huh?" High Elf Archer exclaimed. She was slumped among a collection of cloth, looking quite at her leisure. Some of the pieces were inverted triangles, others like large bowls; she observed them with a medley of *oohs* and *ahhs*.

"Sorry, I haven't cleaned up yet," she said.

"I was told not to touch them."

High Elf Archer's remark was without malice; Goblin Slayer's, in turn, sounded cold.

He obediently neither touched nor looked at the girls' clothes and underwear. Instead, he brought in the rest of the baggage with his usual silence.

At first High Elf Archer, lounging on a chair, had declared that she would help—and this had been the result.

"Clean it up before everyone gets back."

"...Yeah, sure. I know."

Goblin Slayer didn't even bother to look at her as he spoke, causing High Elf Archer to pout a little. She *was* the one who had made the mess, and she knew it, so she slowly but steadily collected the underwear.

"Man, look at this one. It's huge. I could get my whole head in here."

"Don't show that to me. And don't spread everything all over."

"Don't worry, I'm working on it!" High Elf Archer insisted, but then she rose lightly to her feet.

"What is it?"

"Work is making me thirsty. I thought maybe we could both use a drink."

"I see."

He was only remarking out of courtesy, but she took it as agreement and headed for the kitchen.

She *hmm*ed and reviewed the contents of the shelves (also hollows of the tree).

"Hey, Orcbolg," she said, her ears flicking back, "think I should make some tea for you, too? Just to try."

"If you give it to me, I will have it." He didn't seem to read anything into the offer.

Hmm, High Elf Archer said again, sounding displeased. Soon, she was getting ready to make the tea.

First, she took some herbs and spices, which she had grabbed almost at random, and began mincing them with a large, obsidian knife. Eyeballing the measurements, she put them into cups made from hollowed-out acorns and poured water over the top of them.

The carafe was made of mithril, a unique piece that would keep the water cold almost indefinitely.

Dwarves considered steel to be their servant and mithril their friend, but it would be wrong to imagine the elves didn't know something of metallurgy themselves. After all, that which comes from the folds of the earth is also part of nature. The elf with the shining helmet might have said, "They kindly alter their own forms for us."

Normally, it takes quite some time to make cold-brew tea, but in this land, it took less time than most. Any elf, even if they were not a spell caster, could simply make a polite request, and nature would bend itself to their will.

By the time High Elf Archer had made a couple of lazy circles in the air with her pointer finger, the water in the cups was already tinged with color.

She offered one of the cups to Goblin Slayer, who had settled himself on the floor and was unpacking his own luggage.

"No promises about the taste, mind you."

"Okay," Goblin Slayer said, taking the cup. In the same motion, he gulped it down through the slats in his visor. "As long as it's not poison, I don't mind."

"Gee, I'm flattered."

"I meant only what I said," Goblin Slayer said nonchalantly. "I didn't intend to flatter you."

With another snort, High Elf Archer sat down on the chair, letting her legs dangle. She sipped her tea, ignoring the way the cushion of mushrooms shifted under her.

"Hey, that's pretty good," she said, blinking. Then she grinned a catlike smile. "So what're you up to, Orcbolg?"

Goblin Slayer was sitting firmly on the floor, doing some kind of work.

He had pulled out three strips of cow leather and put them together in a bunch, almost like he was making a rope. High Elf Archer climbed off her chair and looked over his shoulder, watching the complicated motions of his fingers. The restless flitting about was characteristic for her.

"Do you remember the goblin champion?"

"...Yeah."

To Goblin Slayer, the question was unremarkable, but it caused High Elf Archer to frown deeply.

That wasn't a battle she wanted to remember. Their painful defeat in the labyrinth beneath the water town remained an unpleasant memory.

"That was hardly a year ago. How could I forget? Getting that out of my mind is going to take at least a couple of centuries."

"This is a little something I've prepared against encounters like that, or the goblin paladin we faced."

"Hmm..."

Goblin Slayer worked mechanically, weaving the strips together. The three strips in unison looked like they would be difficult to break.

"I might call it a *very* little something. It's just a rope."

"I will attach a heavy rock to one end."

The rope was unusually long. It might be a full ten feet when it was completed.

To High Elf Archer, though, sitting and quietly weaving leather straps together didn't seem very adventurer-ish.

"...I'm impressed you would think to make something so bulky."

"They don't sell it in any store."

"Not really what I meant." High Elf Archer sighed, her words part serious and part sarcastic. Then a second sigh. "If it were me doing it—" She grabbed one of the straps Goblin Slayer had on hand, along with a couple of the slinging gems from Dwarf Shaman's luggage. "I think I'd do it like this!"

"...What do you have there?"

Instead of answering, High Elf Archer put her finger in the middle of the strap and began to spin it. The stone on the end swung in a wide arc, whooshing through the air.

"Hear that noise it makes?"

"Yes. What about it?"

"It's fun!"

"...Hrm."

Goblin Slayer turned his metal helmet, tying a heavy stone securely to the end of his leather braid.

He slid his finger just off the knot, grasping the rope; he gave it a swing to check the heft.

He must have liked the feel, because he set about wrapping the stone up, putting the finishing touches on the device.

"I'm thinking of making several. I've heard of this sort of thing before."

"Neato. I'll take one, then!"

"How about this one I just made?"

"No! A different one!"

"I don't mind."

Maybe it was because High Elf Archer was absorbed in all the fun she was having at that moment. Or maybe, having returned to her own home after so long, she had let down her guard.

Whatever the reason, something happened that would normally have been unthinkable for her.

Ahem.

She completely missed the person standing in the doorway until she heard the cough.

"May I ask what is going on here...?"

The voice sounded musical even when annoyed. Needless to say, its owner had leaf-sharp ears.

It was a woman with golden eyes and hair like the star-scattered heavens. A single look at her made her nobility clear. Her pale body, draped in a dress of silver thread, was graceful and tall.

The bust that pushed out against that clothing, though, gave an impression of abundance.

Sometimes a person was beyond description not because of a failure of words, but because she surpassed the imagination.

The forest princess, her head bedecked in a crown of flowers, wore a willowy expression. High Elf Archer all but jumped to her feet.

"Wh-wh-wh-wh-whaaa?! B-Big Sis?! Why are you here?!"

"Why shouldn't I be? I heard you had come to celebrate with me, so I thought I would say hello..."

"Err, ha-ha... Th-this, I mean, it's not really what it looks like..."

"What a great supply of lewd underwear you've brought."

"*Oh, Sis, you know about underwear?*" High Elf Archer muttered, her words not lost on the sharp ears of her elf sister.

"And what about it?" Sister asked, eliciting a choked sound from High Elf Archer.

"Er, uh, that stuff's not mine—it belongs to my friends, okay?"

"Even worse, then. Going through other people's belongings."

"Awww..."

"For that matter, you—" And once the words had started, they came in a torrent, like an epic poem.

"Your skin is in terrible shape. Your hair is disheveled. Have you forgotten all moderation? Are you looking after yourself properly?

©Noboru Kannatuki

"I know how dangerous adventuring is, and I know how reckless you can be, and are you really okay?

"I asked if you're avoiding weird quests, and then you tell me it's a mistake when you do take up a quest.

"After all, they say in all the world, even demons are second to humans in hatching insidious plans.

"How many times have I told you that you have to listen carefully to people and then think even more carefully before acting?"

At last, the elf with the flower crown, who had conducted even her lecture to her little sister with utmost eloquence and poise, collected herself once more.

"I've been terribly rude."

"..."

Goblin Slayer didn't speak immediately. He turned his steel helmet to the elf, stayed silent a moment more, then finally shook his head and said, "It's all right."

The elf with the flower crown, noticing that her sister had once again begun assiduously organizing the underwear, gave a little sigh.

"And...you," she said, her eyes narrowing and a smile growing on her cheeks and lips, "must be Orcbolg."

"That girl calls me such."

Ah, so it is you. The elf clapped her hands.

"I knew that in person you would not be as you are in any song."

"Songs are songs," Goblin Slayer said, shaking his head. "And I am me."

"Well..." *Tee-hee.* Her laughter was like a tinkling bell. It sounded much like High Elf Archer's. "Thank you for always looking after my sister. I hope she isn't causing you too much trouble?"

"Hmm," Goblin Slayer grunted, his gaze moving behind his visor.

High Elf Archer's ears drooped.

"No," he said finally, with a slow shake of his head. "She is often of help."

This caused the ranger's ears to spring up.

"If you should ever meet another capable ranger or tracker, or a scout or some such, please don't hesitate to cast my sister aside."

"Capability is not the only—"

But Goblin Slayer stopped partway through his sentence.

"Hmm?" High Elf Archer cocked her head. Such behavior was unusual for him. "What's wrong, Orcbolg?"

"Hmm. Nothing."

Hmmm? High Elf Archer inquired, following his gaze.

She found a serving girl—needless to say, another elf—kneeling and waiting.

She was half in shadow, and her hair was grown long on just one side of her head.

"Ah, she's..." The flower-crowned elf princess trailed off as if unable to speak.

"I know."

The casual remark caused the serving girl's shoulders to tremble with surprise.

Goblin Slayer got to his feet and strode boldly over to her.

"Hey, uh, Orcbolg?"

He ignored High Elf Archer's attempt to stop him, only coming to a halt in front of the attendant. Then, without hesitation, he knelt in place so that they were eye to eye.

"I killed them."

The attendant looked at him, her gaze wavering. Goblin Slayer nodded then continued:

"I killed all of them."

Hearing that, a single tear rolled out of the woman's left eye and down her cheek.

A shake of her hair revealed the right side of her face. The grape-like swelling was gone by now.

She had once been an adventurer herself.

§

"Right. He was the one who helped her. As I thought."

A gentle breeze came blowing through, catching High Elf Archer's hair. The breath of the forest. The breath of her home.

She inhaled deeply, filling her small chest with as much of that air as she could. Then she replied, "Orcbolg wasn't alone, you know."

"Yes, I understand that."

One of the doors in the guest room led to a balcony. It was formed by huge branches, connected by vines that wove together to make a place to stand.

Such architecture could only be found among the elves, but what really warranted remark was the scenery.

The elf village was located in an open space amid the sea of trees, like a giant atrium.

From here, everything could be seen at once—here, one could feel the wind that blew through it all.

Her very status as an elf princess had prevented High Elf Archer from knowing they even had these guest rooms until this very moment.

They had left the serving girl with Goblin Slayer; this seemed the best place to pass the time until she stopped crying.

The elf with the flower crown held back hair blown by the wind and turned slowly toward High Elf Archer.

"You saved her. You and your friends."

"I had to do something to show off my good side."

She had left the forest at her own insistence, after all. She gave a triumphant, nasal chuckle.

In response, the elf with the flower crown squinted at her little sister. She rested an elbow on the ivy that served as a railing, leaning against it.

"And now you have," she said. "Is that enough, then?"

"Enough what?"

"*Kuchukahatari.* Adventuring."

High Elf Archer's long ears trembled slightly.

"You undertake great danger for only a modicum of reward, do you not?"

"Er, yeah..."

There was nothing else to say. Adventurers' status as such might be guaranteed by the human king, but it was still a mercenary enterprise.

One delved the depths with weapon in hand, hacking and slashing and getting covered in blood and mud.

Youth and death went hand in hand in this profession.

Since leaving her home, High Elf Archer had thrown herself into all this.

"Then there's the matter of your companions. A lizardman is one thing, but I can't approve of you being around a dwarf day and night.

"Are you not the daughter of an elven chief, even if you don't always act like it?"

High Elf Archer frowned at this little addendum.

She was indeed an elf princess, but here she was doing humans' dirty work. With, as her sister had been at pains to point out, a dwarf in tow.

High Elf Archer knew how a little sister was supposed to act in this situation. She had at least acquired enough restraint in two thousand years not to simply give in to her emotions and whine and complain.

"Surely, there is no—"

"No! There definitely isn't."

Despite her attempts to remain cool, she couldn't help laughing at this.

Yes, ancient love songs contained a few ballads that spoke of love between elves and dwarves, but it was fair to say that such lyrics didn't describe her.

Even as her little sister cackled and waved her hand dismissively, the elf with the flower crown let out a sad sigh.

"...And then there's *him*."

"Orcbolg?"

"Yes."

The other elf nodded, her gaze settling on the horizon. The forest appeared to spread out forever beyond the village. These trees had been growing since the Age of the Gods. This wood.

The leaves shook softly with each gust of wind, and birds could be heard flapping.

There was a flock of pale-pink flamingos. The curtain of night was starting to fall over the forest.

"I thought he would be like the hero in the song," High Elf Archer said, the wind caressing her lips as she smiled softly.

The Goblin King has lost his head to a critical hit most dire!
Blue blazing, Goblin Slayer's steel shimmers in the fire.
Thus, the king's repugnant plan comes to its fitting end,
And lovely princess reaches out to her rescuer, her friend.
But he is Goblin Slayer! In no place does he abide,
But sworn to wander, shall not have another by his side.
'Tis only air within her grasp the grateful maiden finds—
The hero has departed, aye, with never a look behind.

High Elf Archer recited the lyrics with only the wind for accompaniment. It was a song of valor. The story of a hero of the frontier who fought goblins all alone.

The killer of the little devils: Goblin Slayer.

Despite its bold tone, as the wind carried the words away, they seemed immensely sad.

The elf with the flower crown shook her ears as if to clear away the syllables from the air.

"...He certainly looks like nothing of the sort."

"Well, it's just a song." High Elf Archer raised a pale, slim finger, drawing a circle in the air.

A song is a song. And he's himself.

"Still," she said, "I admit the mithril sword is going a little overboard."

The crowned elf cast down her eyes as her little sister giggled. If a man had been present, he would surely have prostrated himself in hopes of taking away her sadness.

A princess of the high elves must be the epitome of beauty at all times and in all things.

"Why are you with such a man?"

"Why? Sister, that's—"

Why am *I with him?*

Hmm. Compelled by the question to consider, High Elf Archer sat down on the railing—another faux pas.

She kicked her legs forward so her body leaned back, causing her sister's eyes to widen once again.

High Elf Archer, however, ignored her. They had been this way for two millennia. Why worry about it now?

I really do wonder, though.

In the beginning, it had been because she'd needed someone to slay goblins. She had grown more interested because he was a kind of human she had never seen before, and then…

"Since all he ever did was fight goblins, I thought it was my business to introduce him to a real adventure for once in his life."

Yes, that seemed like it. And so she had gotten ever more drawn in to goblin slaying and adventuring. She counted off on her fingers, and discovered that she had been on more than ten adventures with him, over the course of more than a year's acquaintance.

"The longer I know him, the less I feel like I can leave him behind. I kind of…never get tired of him? Maybe that's it. That's all."

"…And that is why you continue to go goblin hunting?"

"Just every once in a while."

High Elf Archer suddenly kicked her legs up, flipping backward through the air so that she ended up hanging upside down from the railing like a bat, from whence she stared at her sister. She was grinning like a cat.

"And each time, I make sure he takes the front row on a real adventure."

"You know…," the elf with the flower crown said, her voice shaking as she glanced quickly toward the guest room, "…how this will turn out, don't you?"

High Elf Archer never lost the ambiguous smile on her face. Nor did she speak.

She didn't have to: the despair of an elf who found living a burden needed no explanation.

"Then why…?"

"We each have just one life, Sister," High Elf Archer said, flipping back up through the air. She clapped her hands together to clean off the dust, letting the wind take her hair as she nodded. "Elves and humans both. Dwarves and lizardmen are no different. We're all the same that way. Right?"

"Is it possible you…?"

But before the elf with the flower crown could finish her thought, a great howl exploded as if from the depths of the earth.

The sound, not unlike thunder, caused the flock of flamingos to take to the air in a panic.

The cracking of trees continued, along with a cloud of dust.

"Sister, get down!"

"Hwha?!"

High Elf Archer instantly moved to cover her sister. She instinctively reached behind her back, but her great bow was in the guest room.

She clucked her tongue, but then her ears twitched, and a smile tugged at the edges of her lips.

She raised her hand, and an instant later, the bow dropped into it.

"What happened?"

"Kindly don't throw people's weapons, please."

She didn't even have to turn around.

There would be a man there, in a cheap-looking steel helmet and grimy leather armor, with a sword of a strange length at his hip and a small, round shield tied to his left arm.

Goblin Slayer, in full armor, came out of the room as calm as ever.

"Is it goblins?"

"I don't know."

He tossed her quiver to her, and she quickly tied it at her waist, her ears twitching.

"Please… Look after my sister."

"I will."

Goblin Slayer pulled a sling from his item bag and loaded a stone. He dropped to one knee, covering the other elf's head with his shield.

"Stay down. Crawl back to the room."

"Y-you dare ask me to crawl…?!"

"If there are goblins here, they may have archers with them."

High Elf Archer sneaked a glance at her speechless sister out of the corner of her eye, grinning the whole time, then jumped up on the railing of the balcony.

She kept her balance with no trouble at all, and then she made another jump. She climbed up the trunk of the great tree then out to the edge of one of its massive branches. She was light as only an elf could be, not so much as breaking a twig or disturbing a leaf.

"...Mm... Hmmn?!"

Then her eyes were wide. She saw something that could not be.

It was a massive beast. It trod upon the earth with legs like pillars, and its tail made an audible sound as it cut through the air.

Something like a fan sprouted from its back, and its body, thicker than a wall, was covered in tough skin.

It cleared away the trees with horns like spears, and its back, which looked like a throne, had to be at least fifty feet high.

The beast turned its ropelike neck, opening its great, fanged jaws.

"MOOOKKEEEEELLL!!"

"I see," Goblin Slayer said, looking at the beast from the far side of the balcony as the air shook. "So that is an elephant."

"No, it's not!" High Elf Archer shouted back.

This was the first time in her life she had ever seen this creature. But every elf who was raised in the rain forest knew of it.

"Emera ntuka, mubiel mubiel, nguma monene!" Killer of water monsters, creature with a fan on its back, Great Lord of the Serpents.

In other words...

"Mokele Mubenbe...!!" The One That Stops the Waters.

CHAPTER 4

THE FIGHT WITH THE BEAST

Goblin Slayer and High Elf Archer were coming down through the zelkova tree about the same time their friends were coming up from the root.

They linked up in front of the elf fortification but found themselves instinctively stopping at the sound of crashing trees that could be heard in the distance.

"What in the world's goin' on?!" Dwarf Shaman groaned.

"A monster called something-or-other is on a rampage," Goblin Slayer replied, an explanation that hardly explained anything. Then he looked around. "What about the other two?"

"Oh yes. I thought I would ask them to go back to the room and wait there."

The answer came from Priestess, whose hair and skin were still damp. She must have come from the bathing area in a great hurry. Her cheeks were flushed, and she had a hand to her chest to slow her breathing and pulse.

"It's probably safe there," she added.

"So we missed one another."

Well, fine.

Goblin Slayer came to his conclusion quickly.

There could hardly be a place safer than the inside of an elven bulwark—even if no place could be said to be completely safe. The fact that he couldn't see them would be a difficulty, but there were any number of difficulties here. It would do no good to worry about one more.

"MBEEEEEEENEE!!!!"

The beast's continued bellowing drowned out the shouting of the elves, even as elvish warriors—hunters—jumped from leaf to leaf, quivers of arrows on their backs.

"It appears they're going to do battle," Lizard Priest said, stroking his jaw; he was the only one who looked amused by the entire situation. "I won't ask whether the elves have prowess in battle. At the very least, I doubt they're inexperienced."

War had been the way of the world since the Age of the Gods. However much the elves might have wished for a peaceful and safe place to live, surely they could not have avoided combat. There had to be very few elves who had never stood against the forces of Chaos, bow in hand.

"That's the One That Stops the Waters," High Elf Archer said. "If we shoot it dead and it dams up the river, there'll be real trouble."

She knew the answer. Even as she took up her bow, casually nocking an arrow into it, she seemed to be having difficulty moving. Her ears twitched once, then again, taking in the sounds all around.

"The Lernaean Hydra... That's what you humans call it."

"...?" Priestess looked at her in surprise. "I thought hydras were supposed to have lots of heads."

"That one's still young."

"*Even though it's been around since I was a child,*" High Elf Archer muttered darkly.

"At any rate, it's a creature that demands respect. It's more than we can handle."

I have no idea if we can win. Her words caused Priestess to nod gravely.

"So you're saying we need to stop it from getting any closer somehow, make it go back to the forest."

That would be more than difficult enough, but still...

Priestess, however, clutched her sounding staff tightly in both hands and said with a look of determination, "We'll do the best we can!"

Somebody laughed—a nonchalant, relaxed laugh as if they suddenly found they were enjoying themselves. Lizard Priest spotted the creature in the distance and said jovially, "I never thought I would be blessed with the opportunity to feast upon an ancestor of the great nagas. Most excellent!"

"...Don't eat it, okay?" High Elf Archer looked at him as if unsure whether he was speaking figuratively; Lizard Priest opened his jaws with utmost seriousness. "Milady ranger, let us climb up that monster's neck and jam an arrow in its eye!"

"I told you, we can't kill it!"

"Can't y'shoot it in the foot, or catch a tendon?"

"...Sometimes living things die just from the shock of being shot, right?"

"It's a hydra, not a flea."

"But," Goblin Slayer said quietly, looking away from the encroaching monster, "in either case, we would have to get close enough to fire an arrow."

The creature was already visible past the felled trees.

The great ash-colored monster walked along on its trunk-like legs, its giant tail and neck sweeping trees aside.

It looked like a dragon but wasn't one. It appeared like a lizard but wasn't one!

Lizard Priest could not help letting out a gasp of admiration to see before his very eyes the half-beast, half-divine creature said to accompany the rainbows.

"Oh! Was Brachiosaurus or Brontosaurus, or even Alamosaurus, such as this?" He gave a great animalistic howl as he offered up the emotional prayer to his forelizards. "I never imagined that I should see such a thing in this place...!"

"Look. There, on its back," Goblin Slayer said softly, and they did as he said.

"Hrm...!" It was impossible to say who in the party the grunt came from.

Mokele Mubenbe's back must have been at least fifty feet in the sky. Each time the creature thrashed about, the fanlike protrusions on its back made a crackling sound.

But that was not all.

In between the spines on its back were squirming shadows.

The shadows were clinging to something, waving their arms madly and jabbering.

"Is that a...saddle?"

High Elf Archer blinked, astonished by something that just could not be.

"Goblins?!"

And so it was.

Goblins, clinging to the back of Mokele Mubenbe, filthy spit flying from their mouths as they howled.

High Elf Archer remembered them.

They were the terrible creatures who had attacked them first at the farm, and then yesterday at the river.

"Goblin riders..." Priestess's voice was shivering with this first glimpse of something unbelievable.

It made some kind of sense to see the goblins on the backs of gray wolves. Even horses or donkeys would not have been so terrifying.

But—but—oh yes.

"Are those goblin...*dragoons*...?"

"They do not appear to be holding reins," Goblin Slayer said blandly, simply reporting the facts.

"Indeed," Lizard Priest agreed. "Still, even one who does not know how to ride can spur on a horse... I suppose that's what we have here."

"What do you think about it?"

"The riders do not frighten me in the least. However..." Lizard Priest put a hand to his jaw and rolled his eyes, looking thoughtfully at the saurian monster. "They say that if you wish to stop the general, you must first kill his horse. So I suppose if you wish to stop a horse, you must first kill the general."

"I'm prepared for that." Goblin Slayer glanced briefly overhead, toward the balcony of the room they had been given to stay in. "In any event, I will kill the goblins. There's no reason to let them live."

"Let me handle it!" High Elf Archer said, immediately raising her hand. Her voice was upbeat, but she was staring daggers at Mokele

Mubenbe and the goblins on its back. "Frankly, I'm starting to get a little tired of goblins. Yesterday, today... And in my house, no less!"

Goblin Slayer nodded. Then he gently patted High Elf Archer's shoulder. Her ears twitched.

"We will hold this beast, whatever it's called, here. You two, help me."

"Sure thing," Dwarf Shaman said.

"But of course," Lizard Priest added.

High Elf Archer was still stiff from being patted on the shoulder.

Could Goblin Slayer's judgment at a time like this...? No.

Whenever she had known him to let someone do something over the past year, it had always been based on a firm grasp of the situation. There was a reason they had entrusted this strange, bizarre adventurer with the leadership of their little band.

"Um, what about me...?" Priestess asked hesitantly.

Goblin Slayer's instruction was without hesitation. "Prepare to administer first aid. If killing it is bad, I suppose it should not be injured, either."

And so the plan was set.

High Elf Archer took up her bow and began looking for a chance to launch a surprise attack, while Dwarf Shaman reached into his bag of catalysts. Lizard Priest grabbed some fangs and began praying, while Priestess clung to her staff and supplicated to the Earth Mother.

Goblin Slayer was just setting about his own preparations when...

"Hey, you lot! What are you doing?"

A sharp voice came flying their way. The elf with the shining headpiece, who had been making a circuit of the village, came up to them covered in sweat, looking anxious and excited. Presumably, he had been evacuating the women and children who had been outside.

"Oh, hey, Bro. Look, don't worry." High Elf Archer grinned, entirely at ease. "We're used to this sort of thing."

"But...!"

"This," Goblin Slayer said, cutting him off, "is my work."

With this last quiet declaration, Goblin Slayer drew his sword, turning it with his wrist.

These were goblins they were facing.

Goblins.

The response was obvious.

"Slaying goblins is my work."

§

Trees fell. Howls sounded.

The beast came on, its fangs going everywhere, trying to kill anyone and anything it laid eyes on; it paid no heed at all to the goblins on its back.

If the little devils' objective was to put the spurs to this monster and drive it mad, they had accomplished their mission.

But as if they still thought of the monster as their mount, they continued to hold the reins and spit abuse at it. Not that any amount of blathering from some goblins would change anything.

Mokele Mubenbe was not that kind of creature.

"GOO! GRRB!!"

"MBEEEEMMMBE!!"

It remained, however, a creature that threatened the elvish homeland.

The giant came thundering through the forest, ever closer to the village.

If they ride that thing into the middle of the village…!

But the elves who dashed among the trees, trying to keep an eye on the situation, could not readily do anything about it. They called upon the sprites of the earth and the trees to help them, throwing barriers up in its path. Mokele Mubenbe smashed through them easily, but it was far better than nothing.

Hardly any of the elves loosed an arrow at the god-beast.

Or, they weren't supposed to…

"Hnn—yah…!"

High Elf Archer, moving like a gust of wind, was one of the few exceptions.

She dashed along a branch, swung on a vine, flung herself through space, and then, with an elegant motion, sent a bud-tipped bolt flying.

It sliced through the air but then bounced off one of Mokele Muben-be's back fins with a thump.

"...Grr."

Her foe moved quicker than she had expected.

Those elves who were her elders raised a chorus of outrage toward their impetuous younger sister, but High Elf Archer didn't get distracted by her mistakes. She licked her lips briefly then kicked off the ground, then the bark of a tree, and in an eyeblink, she was picking up speed again.

She caught up to the gray monster with no effort at all, whereupon she leaped up into the branches, grabbing at the moss on the bark.

"I know it's not exactly polite, but... Yah!"

Using a hand and a foot, she sprang forward, maintaining her poise, while with her other hand, she grasped her bow and put an arrow in her mouth. She drew the bowstring back with her teeth and let it loose.

"GOORB?!"

There was a scream.

The bud-tipped arrow had woven neatly past the plates on Mokele Mubenbe's back and pierced one of the goblin riders through the eye. The creature, with the bolt lodged in his right eye, writhed and screeched until he fell off the monster's back and was crushed. All that could be seen underneath Mokele Mubenbe's foot were four limbs.

"It went that way!"

"Hmm!"

It was Lizard Priest who responded to High Elf Archer's somewhat panicked shout. He planted both feet on the earth, spread his arms, and blocked Mokele Mubenbe's path.

A rampaging beast was heading through the forest straight at him, yet not one scale shivered; not one muscle in his tail twitched.

"A fit and glorious opponent this is. Shall we have a combat here and now?"

The lizardman's great jaws opened in a grin, and a wild laugh escaped him.

What honor would be his if he took victory! And if he should die here in battle, at least he would buy time for his friends. It didn't much matter to him which way the dice fell. He had firmed his resolve and would now go forth.

Few lizardmen were blessed with the opportunity to confront an ancestor of the great nagas on behalf of their friends.

Wonderful!

Lizard Priest took a deep breath, filling his lungs with the wet forest air, and thought clearly of death. Like every lizardman, he considered death in battle to be the highest honor, for like all of them, he hoped to become a soul who could proceed boldly to the land of the nagas at the center of the ever-turning wheel of life.

"Iiiiiiiiiiiyyyahhhhhhhhhhhhh!!"

Borrowing the strength of his forefathers, Lizard Priest's own Dragon's Roar flew from his mouth like fire breath. The hot air he expelled from his lungs caused the entire place to quaver and quake as it flew out into the world.

"MOOOOOBMMBE!!" Mokele Mubenbe bellowed in return. It stamped the ground with its rear legs as if issuing a challenge to the lizardman who stood before it, holding its front legs aloft.

It was impossible to say whether such a vast and great creature was actually in any way intimidated by Lizard Priest. But whatever the case, the adventurer had succeeded in arousing the monster's ire at an impertinent challenger.

The upraised front legs came down at Lizard Priest like twin hammers...

"Drink deep, sing loud, let the spirits lead you! Sing loud, step quick, and when to sleep they see you, may a jar of fire wine be in your dreams to greet you!"

The monster reeled and stumbled. Its feet slammed into the earth, throwing up mud, well away from Lizard Priest.

"Hmm! Well. Goodness gracious."

"Call it a draw and let's keep going, Scaly!"

It was the Stupor spell. Dwarf Shaman, who had appeared at Lizard Priest's side without him even noticing, held in one hand the jar of wine that allowed him to use the magic.

They might have been in an elvish village, in the middle of the elves' forest, but the sprites of the spirits still had a deep affinity for dwarves. And for gods.

"MOKEEEEEKEKELE..."

Mokele Mubenbe, which had imbibed no small amount of the spell, shook its head uncertainly.

"Right, all good, Beard-cutter!"

"Good."

Now Goblin Slayer, who had been waiting by the root of the giant tree behind them, sprang into action. He quickly pulled an egg-like object from his pouch, flinging it in a single smooth motion.

"MOLLLLKEEEEEL?!?!?!"

The object hit the monster in the face, waking it up but also causing it to cry out and thrash with pain.

The egg was full of a blinding powder made up of crushed peppers and insects. It was not remotely pleasant to get hit with.

Now unable to see, and still not thinking entirely clearly, Mokele Mubenbe began to flail wildly. Its neck, its horns, its tail, the plates on its back, were everywhere at once, like a localized typhoon. If one were to approach carelessly, one would soon find oneself thrown back.

"So what do we do?" Priestess asked from beside him, her expression tense. She must have been nervous. Goblin Slayer, however, didn't seem bothered by her imploring gaze.

"We have robbed it of its ability to think," he answered calmly. "Now, we finish it off."

He raised a hand over his head.

"Drop it."

"Um, are you sure? Is it okay?"

Above them, Cow Girl looked over the edge of the balcony that jutted out from the great tree, clearly hesitant.

"I do not mind."

Okay. She nodded, not appearing entirely convinced, then grabbed the thing that was sitting on the ground.

It was rather bulky and heavy; even with the muscles she had developed doing farmwork, it took her some effort.

She looked at Guild Girl across from her, thankful that there were two of them.

"Okay, I'll take this side…"

"All right, I've got this one. Just give the word and we'll lift."

"Mm. Okay… Now!!"

The two girls hauled the thing off the ground, then flung it away: it could almost have been described as a bundle of ropes.

Specifically, it was the gaggle of leather straps Goblin Slayer had been working on until just moments before.

It hit the ground with a great ripple, twisting like a living thing.

"Eek!" Priestess couldn't help jumping back, but Goblin Slayer simply grabbed the end of one of the straps.

"You two, stay up there."

A voice came back down at him: *"Are you all right?"* But he waved his hand as if to tell them to stay back then hefted the net onto his back. Lizard Priest took up one of the dangling ends with a noise of considerable interest.

"And what will we do with this?"

"We will throw it," Goblin Slayer said. "And entangle the creature's legs."

"Entanglement? Do you think that will be enough?"

"If it isn't, I will think of something else."

"Very logical."

The two warriors ran nimbly, maintaining distance perfectly.

"Oh-ho," said Dwarf Shaman, jumping back; from her vantage point, High Elf Archer let out an impressed "Huh!"

One step, two, three.

As they closed the last of the distance, Goblin Slayer casually tossed the net.

Of course, Mokele Mubenbe was not so easily taken in. The quasi-divine beast stomped on the net with its giant foot. The shock wave caused the straps to waver.

The bouncing net caught the monster's foot. The ends and edges caught on the trees and became more tangled still.

"Ho!" Observing the situation, Lizard Priest stroked his jaw appreciatively and rolled his eyes. "A fine plan indeed."

"We still don't know."

"But even if we do nothing further, the net should continue to ensnare it."

With its restricted vision, the monster struggled mightily, howling and shaking the ground. But each time it did so, the net became more and more trapped on branches and bushes.

The harder it tried to escape, the more the heavy stones tied to the net slowed its movements...

"MBEMBEMBEMBE?!?!"

Finally, the creature reached its breaking point.

Mokele Mubenbe's massive body, all four limbs now restrained, began to tilt.

And once the motion started, there was no stopping it.

There was nothing for the monster to do but fall over.

Mokele Mubenbe collapsed onto the ground with an earthshaking slam.

"...Y-you brought it down...?" Priestess asked, stunned.

"In the most literal sense, yes."

A cloud of dust filled the air, and the monster's pitiful crying could be heard.

Goblin Slayer shook his head at the young cleric, and she gave a small nod. Then she grasped her sounding staff, closed her eyes, quickly whispered the name of the Earth Mother, and began to pray—for all the dead goblins.

"...Are you satisfied?"

"Yes." She nodded. "I'll go handle first aid!"

"All right."

"I think I might just go with you," Dwarf Shaman said, slapping his belly and causing a ripple in the spirits in his jar. "If that thing looks like it will cause any trouble, I can just cast Stupor on it again."

"I'm sorry to bother you, but I'd appreciate it!"

Priestess went pattering away, followed by the distinctly heavier footsteps of Dwarf Shaman.

Mokele Mubenbe moaned piteously, projecting an air of anxiety, but then came Priestess's healing incantation, "*O Earth Mother, abounding in mercy, lay your revered hand upon this child's wounds*," and the creature's injuries were healed.

The divine will was present. This creature, more god than beast, ought to understand that. Thus, Mokele Mubenbe grew more and more still. Goblin Slayer therefore ignored it and moved brusquely to his next destination.

That was the corpses of the goblins who had been crushed beneath the monster, not that anyone would feel sorry for them.

"...Hmm."

The bodies had become pools of blood and guts and bones, with bits of leather armor mixed in. Although their former weapons were now too broken for him to be certain, it seemed they had been carrying daggers. At the very least, the armaments were not made of stone. They were metal... Steel blades. He was sure someone must be producing them.

"...Where did you learn to spring a trap like that?"

The voice came at him suddenly.

"It is an old method for catching large game," Goblin Slayer replied.

The elf with the shining helmet was there, having arrived as suddenly and silently as the wind. He had one of the huge elvish bows slung across his back, and at his hip a bundle of ropes that appeared to be made from vines.

"You entangle its feet and let the quarry do the rest. To think, you had such a thing prepared ahead of time."

"I had heard talk of this 'elephant' already, after all."

"...I'm sorry?"

The elf bent down next to Goblin Slayer, but Goblin Slayer hardly even looked at him. "Are there other villages deeper in? Including any belonging to non-elves?"

"No, there are no other villages. Even the medicine men who come from the city stop at the borders of the forest. Not that there have been many of them recently..." The elf put a thoughtful hand to his chin. "Once in a while, adventurers travel here seeking special herbs or the pelt of some monster in order to craft something, but... Well, they don't come back out."

"I see," Goblin Slayer said with a nod; he took the knife in his hand and put it in his belt at his hip. "...I see."

"I don't believe I ever got a proper answer."

"My father was the chief huntsman of my village," Goblin Slayer said with a shake of his head, not even looking at the elf. "That's all."

Shortly after, the last rays of the sinking sun disappeared below the horizon. In their place, the twin moons twinkled faintly down on the forest.

§

The meeting went on and on.

Elves had practically endless life spans; how could one of their councils not run long?

People of great age gathered, sat in a circle, and there, beneath the light of the sea sparkles, they discussed the future of the village.

They spoke of the rampage of the god-beast, Mokele Mubenbe. Of the terrible disrespect of entrapping it.

There was the goblin horde that had appeared nearby. Was it not the way of the world for goblins to be numerous?

There was the fact that the goblins had attacked boats and adventurers. The elves would not want the humans to come and make trouble in the forest.

Then what of the fact that the goblins had been riding on the god-beast? Did the little devils possess such courage?

Each proposition invited rebuttal: What if we did this? Why not do that? The suggestions piled up.

Let us be clear: the elves were no fools. Elves are the wisest of races, perhaps more intelligent than any in the four corners of the world. All the more reason, then, that they like to consider every possibility and perspective before acting.

They are aware of the foolishness of the mob mentality, everyone heading mindlessly in the same direction.

Perhaps they should take some special measure against the goblins, but then again, perhaps their fears were unfounded.

It was clear that something nefarious was happening, because at the very least, someone had provided the goblins with resources.

Was it an attack by other Non-Prayer Characters, or perhaps a squabble among the humans?

The answers to such questions often led to unprecedented threat and menace.

Humans threw a rock in the water and saw the ripples, but elves saw where the ripples went. Humans could hardly think ten years into the future, but an elf could easily contemplate a century, a millennium yet to come.

Humans mocked them for this, said it made the elves slow to act, cowardly, even stupid—but this was itself a sign of human arrogance.

And so what amounted to a brainstorming session went on.

High Elf Archer, who had scant patience for such things, excused herself quickly.

Basking in the night air, she gave a great yawn.

There was a branch of the vast tree. She jumped from the balcony of their guest room, walked to the end of it.

She savored the sound of the rustling leaves, letting her thoughts run to the ends of the clouds as she gazed up at the stars and the two moons.

This had to be one of the best places for simply lying back and enjoying all that the world had to offer.

I know what he's going to say anyway, so what's the point of talking?

However the elves' council turned out, she knew full well where Orcbolg would be going. Goblins, goblins, goblins, goblins.

She was the deserter who had fled her forest, the delinquent who in her youth had fired an arrow at the god-beast. She had no obligation to obey the council of elders. Surely. Probably. She thought.

High Elf Archer smiled at the idea, watching a bird that had come flying up even though it was night.

Whereupon…

"Atana." My dear one.

She heard a voice like music, even though not a leaf or branch had been disturbed. The voice was even, not scolding, but High Elf Archer quickly let go of the bird, to whose leg she had tied a small tube.

It flapped away noisily, after which it disappeared into the window of the hall where the council was being held.

"Ettobo ni norokotan nokatamu. Ianachisafu." Climbing in the trees again? You're hopeless.

"Ara, iana yujuretto bonettadasen." Oh? And yet, here you are, dear older sister.

High Elf Archer tilted her head all the way back so as to peek at the other elf and smirked. The rich silver dress covering the generous body filled her upside-down vision. Her sister walked noiselessly along the branch; High Elf Archer righted herself with an easy movement.

"*Onii, etsuka nedigiaku?*" Shouldn't you be at the council?

"*Awachisesakamo, inatagamashijo.*" I'll let the old men handle things.

The elf with the flower crown shook her head elegantly, a melancholy expression on her face.

It was obvious that she, too, had escaped the council. She was the chief's daughter, a princess of the elves, and yet, even she was still too young to be allowed to speak in council.

For the elves, seniority was immutable. All the more reason to watch how mortals behaved before passing judgment upon them.

"…*Iromutsuki?*" Do you mean to go?

"*Oisedianekoettsuo?*" I can hardly ignore the issue, can I?

It wasn't clear whether she meant the goblins, or Goblin Slayer. Even if her sister had ventured to ask, most likely High Elf Archer would have smiled ambiguously and not bothered to answer. Maybe she herself didn't know the answer.

"……*Onuriettakau?*" Do you understand?

That was exactly why the elf with the flower crown had to ask.

She didn't understand what her little sister was thinking, what had driven her to become an adventurer. Even a high elf could not read the mind of another.

"*Hito nio numuuuya, oyoniakijimu.*" Human lives are short.

The branch didn't quiver as she walked, as if she were herself a part of the great tree. As if she were a blossom springing forth from it.

"*Uamisetiku, inuoyukatatamagisofu.*" Like twinkling stars, they soon wink out.

The elf gestured to the star-spattered night sky as she spoke. The glittering heavens were so far away, unreachable. The gateway of the rains. Home of Phlogiston, the burning wind.

The younger sister chuckled at the elder's gesture, which was almost as if she were trying to grasp what could not be reached, and then the younger sister stretched her own hand out toward the sky.

"*Oyonuriettakau, amaseen.*" I understand, Elder Sister.

High Elf Archer made a brief circle in the air with one pale finger.

"So I think...," she said musically, switching to the common tongue.

Why were elves always so conscious of beauty? Was it a mark of grace? Or was it precisely because this girl had fled the forest, unable to be contained within the framework of her people?

"Maybe his life will last another fifty years, sixty, seventy. I don't know. It might end tomorrow." In the moonlight, her smile made her seem so young as to appear cherubic, innocent. "So why not stay with him? I have the time to spare."

It would be like the drinking of a single cup of wine.

Like the passing of a dream.

Were high elves not immortal?

To them, the life of a mortal was like the glittering of a star. They could reach out to it but not touch it. And were they to touch it, the heat of it would scorch them.

"Isn't that what friends are?"

"...Parting will bring you sorrow," the elf with the flower crown said. She gestured at her younger sister as if sweeping away the stars she had collected.

"I don't really think so," High Elf Archer said, averting her eyes just a bit. "It's not such a big deal."

Her tone was nonchalant; the next instant, she kicked her legs perilously toward the sky.

With hardly even enough time to think, her body floated in the air—

"The dwarf told me once."

—but then she grabbed the branch with great dexterity, letting the momentum carry her in an arc. She did a backflip through the sky and landed beside her beloved older sister.

"He said the hangover is part of the fun of drinking."

"...I can see it doesn't matter what I say." The smallest of sighs escaped the elf maiden's lips. She looked at her beloved younger sister like the bird who cries at the moon at night. "You've always been this way. No matter what I say, you never listen to me."

"Oh? And how does that make me different from you? Miss I-Ran-Away-from-the-Council-because-I-Felt-Like-It.

"He-he." High Elf Archer let out a tiny giggle, like the chirping of a bird. Then she squinted like a cat, grinning up at her sister.

"I don't know what you see in such a serious, hard-nosed elf like him."

"...You're hardly one to talk." The older sister pulled her lips back disapprovingly, giving her sister a not-quite-gentle smack on the forehead.

Just as she had when they were little—a thousand or more years ago, when they had been playing as girls.

"Eeyowch," High Elf Archer said, acting dramatically injured. But then she had a thought.

When had it started? When had she and her sister gotten to be about the same height?

When had it started? When had her sister and that cousin come to have such feelings for each other?

When had it started? When had she first wanted to be not the younger sister of her older sister but an elf of her own?

And now her sister was getting married. She would no longer be first and foremost her older sister, but a wife, a ruler.

It hadn't even been several years yet that she had spent traveling, following the leaves down the current of the stream. And yet, it seemed longer than memories from a thousand years ago.

"Whatever you do, return to us safely... Because we will be waiting for you."

"...I will," High Elf Archer replied and then nodded.

§

"...And what exactly are we doing again?"

The elf with the shining headpiece was the picture of annoyance as he lowered himself into his chair with due grace. He had a severe beauty, like a carving of a myth. The night wind picked up his hair, and he brushed it aside again with utmost irritation. The fact that even this simple movement was filled with elegance spoke to the kind of beings that the elves were.

Sitting before him on the balcony under the moonlight were several jars of wine and a plate full of fried potatoes.

"Whaddaya mean, what?" Dwarf Shaman spoke up from among the circle of people, stroking his beard and sounding as if he didn't think the situation needed any explaining. "On the last day of a man's single life, he and the other men get together and drink themselves silly."

"The wedding ceremony is several days away yet, and we are in council to boot."

"The elves wouldn't know a few days from a thousand years, and as for your council, it'll go on whether you're there or not."

"Gods above. You dwarves are insufferably lackadaisical."

"And you elves always miss the forest for the trees—even though you live in one!" *It takes years off your life, not that you'd notice.*

The elf actually appeared somewhat abashed by Dwarf Shaman's jab. He knit his brow in a show of frustration, causing Lizard Priest to roll his eyes.

"Well, one does drink wine before going into battle," Lizard Priest said. "You may consider it our way of rallying your spirits, if you prefer."

"Or perhaps the elves have no such custom?"

The elf with the shining headpiece allowed grudgingly that they did.

"Hence, I do not refuse you, but…do you really mean to go?"

"Of course."

This answer, immediate and sure, naturally came from Goblin Slayer.

The cheap-looking steel helmet, the grimy leather armor, the weapon and shield that the adventurer at the moment had set down—with all this about him, Goblin Slayer nodded.

"This concerns goblins. I will not leave even one of them alive."

"How do you plan to attack them, then?" the elf with the shining helmet asked with considerable interest, running his tongue along his lips to moisten them. "Assuming the goblin nest is in the rain forest…"

"Hmm. By land or by water, I suppose," Goblin Slayer replied, folding his arms and grunting. "What do you make of it?"

"I believe water is our only option. Our lady ranger may be all right, but I should wish to spare our dear cleric the humidity of the rain forest," Lizard Priest answered without hesitation. "The terrain favors our enemy. Rather than tramping among the trees, we would do better, I think, to follow the river."

"The problem is the raft," Goblin Slayer said, thinking back to their journey. "It affords no shelter from arrows. It practically begs to be capsized or sunk."

"Do we not have enough time to make some improvements?"

"The goblins know about this settlement. The sooner we can move against them, the more limited their options will be."

"'Swift attack is better than belated stratagem.' Indeed, indeed."

As they sat with their legs folded, Goblin Slayer and Lizard Priest quickly worked out a plan.

It was entirely typical how, amid the *hmm*ing and *huh*ing, Lizard Priest craned his long neck to look over at Dwarf Shaman.

"Master spell caster, have you any little tricks up your sleeve?"

"Well, let's see now." Dwarf Shaman licked his fingers clean of the potatoes he'd been eating and began digging through his bag of catalysts.

At first glance, it might appear to be a collection of junk; the untutored mind would never imagine that these were magical items.

Dwarf Shaman went through his supply like a card player checking his hand, and a moment later, he gave a deep nod.

"It might be all I can manage t'get the wind sprites to deflect the arrows for us. Unfortunately, they and I don't get along very well." Granted all four of the great elements—earth, water, fire, and wind—were used to forge steel. Even so, the quality of his relationship with wind was another matter.

"If that's all you need, maybe I could ask the sylphs," the elf with the shining headpiece offered, to which Dwarf Shaman slapped his belly and replied that he would be most grateful.

In contrast to the jovial dwarf, however, the elf muttered, "It makes no sense." Goblin Slayer looked at him.

"...If I may say so, I can't quite believe it," the elf said.

"Believe what?" Goblin Slayer asked.

Perhaps the groom-to-be had finally accepted the humble banquet, because he was filling a horn cup with a prodigious amount of wine.

"This is an elf village. Would the little devils really build a nest so near to us?"

He wondered, even when he had seen the riders, had witnessed how they sent the god-beast Mokele Mubenbe on a rampage.

"I just can't bring myself to think that they would do such ill-conceived things," he said.

"Yes," Goblin Slayer replied. "I had the same thought."

"Hrm..."

"Goblins are stupid, but they are not fools. They are cunning. But..."

Here. Dwarf Shaman poured him some wine. Goblin Slayer accepted it then drank it down in a single gulp.

"Do you think the goblins are smart enough to be intimidated by the elves?"

This was what it all came down to.

They didn't think ahead but only tried to get the most out of whatever was immediately in front of them.

If they were attacked by elves, or by adventurers, they might struggle, or they might flee. If not, it meant there was only one truth for them: *The stupid elves are living the easy life, so let's attack them and steal from them and rape them and kill them.*

That was all.

Why? Because the elves always made life so unpleasant for them.

Of course they would kill the elves.

Of course they would rape them.

They would bring everything they had to bear against those who scorned them as weaklings.

"Before you know it, there will be a nest near the village. First, they will steal livestock and crops, tools. Then people. And finally, your village."

"One would never praise goblins, not in the slightest—" Lizard Priest took an appreciative bite out of a round of cheese he had brought in his own luggage, working his great jaws up and down before chasing it with a noisy swallow of wine. "—but the mind can only boggle at their motivation and greed."

"Do you honor their greed?" The elf with the shining headpiece asked, to which Lizard Priest gave a pronounced shake of his head and said, "Of course not."

He swept his tail along the balcony floor then spread his hands wide as if delivering a sermon. "What indeed is this thing we call greed?"

"Well, y'know, Scaly. It's...when you want to eat something delicious, or make love to a woman, or when you're after some money."

"Mm. Appetite is a form of greed, as are our friends, our love, our dreams. Whether a thing is good or bad is a secondary or even tertiary concern."

There was no guarantee that the strong would eat the weak, that the great would one day fall, or that the fittest would survive. Lizard Priest's jaws came up in a reptilian grin.

"To be alive is to desire and hope, to want things; the way of life is for even the smallest insect on a blade of grass to throw himself into living."

"..." The elf with the shining headpiece paused then grunted appreciatively. "I'm not quite sure that applies to elves, though."

"Gods. You're all impossibly slow to act. What, are you too fat to move? Fatter than a dwarf? Hmm?"

"Mortals are simply too hasty."

"That's why it takes you so many centuries to pick a wife, eh?"

"Hrm... Watch your mouth," the elf said crossly. Lizard Priest stuck out his tongue gleefully and poured more wine.

"Here, here, have a cup."

"...Very well."

The elf drained the horn. His cheeks were already starting to glow.

"If you don't mind my saying so—you all know about my sister-in-law, I suppose."

"Yes." Goblin Slayer nodded. "We have known her for a year... A year and a half now."

"I'm marrying her older sister." He reached out, almost annoyed, and took one of the fried potatoes; he stuffed it in his mouth and frowned. "...Too salty."

"I love a bit of saltiness, myself," Lizard Priest said, happily tossing handfuls of the snacks into his jaws.

The elf with the shining headpiece, abandoning his august dignity of moments before, put his elbows on his knees and his chin on his hands.

"The younger sister is who she is, but then, so is the elder. I've had no end of worry, but I don't get the feeling that I'm much liked."

"Hoo, hoo-hoo," Lizard Priest laughed. "Milord Goblin Slayer knows something of being the younger brother. Perhaps he might have some thoughts?"

"Ho," the elf said, a sense of closeness obviously piqued. "He has an elder sister?"

"So I once heard, at any rate."

"...I wonder," Goblin Slayer muttered then took a swig of wine. "I was never anything but trouble for my older sister."

"A brat always causes trouble, that's the way of things," Dwarf Shaman said as he added a generous amount of wine to his empty cup. His bearded face had a soft smile on it. "It's nothing to be ashamed of."

"I don't agree." Goblin Slayer drained another cup, shaking his head gently. "If I hadn't been there, she would probably have left the town."

And that would have been better for everyone. He groaned. Then he emptied another cup.

Dwarf Shaman poured him some more wine, and Goblin Slayer drank that, too.

"I was the one who trapped my sister in the village."

"Speak not such foolishness," the elf with the shining headpiece snorted. "Do we ask the worth of a flower that withers in a year? What is the meaning of the seed that falls in the sand? Can you weigh the life of a rat against that of a dragon?"

"What're ya goin' on about?" Dwarf Shaman said, still happily drinking his wine.

"It is an elvish aphorism," the elf replied, as if bestowing upon them a secret. "Wheresoever and whatsoever one be, no matter how one lives or dies, all is equal. It is a precious thing." He held his pointer finger straight up, making circles in the air. It was an elegant and beautiful gesture. "All things are one in life. Would something as simple as location change how happy one was?"

"I see," Goblin Slayer said, nodding. "...I see."

"I should think so," the elf with the shining headpiece said then breathed in deeply. The night air filled his lungs.

Love is destiny	destiny is death
Even a knight who serves a maiden	will one day fall into death's clutches
Even the prince who befriends a Sky Drake	must leave the woman he fancies behind
The mercenary who loved a cleric	will fall in battle pursuing his dream
And the king who loved the shrine maiden	controls all but the hour of their separation
The end of life	is not the last chapter of an heroic saga
So the adventure called life	will continue to the very end
Friendship and love	life and death
From these things	we cannot escape
Therefore what have we	to fear
Love is destiny	and our destiny is death

Ho. Dwarf Shaman clapped. Lizard Priest rolled his eyes to indicate his profound engagement. The elf, having completed his song, must have felt embarrassed, because he drained his horn of drink.

"That is why I will marry."

"…But the trouble I caused my older sister," Goblin Slayer said dispassionately, "is part of why she never married."

"All the more reason to repay your debt to her."

"Yes," Goblin Slayer said, patting Lizard Priest on the shoulder. He had much to think about, and even more to do. "That is my intention."

Sheesh, they should leave the clerics of the God of Knowledge to do this sort of thing.

In the library in a corner of the temple of the God of Law, a nubile young acolyte pulled a face.

In any event, the books in this library were a breed apart from run-of-the-mill books (as valuable as those were).

Best were old collections of case law, but the shelves were also packed with sealed-up forbidden tomes, magical volumes, and occult texts.

Many sections of the library were blocked off with chains, but all too often, even when she could get at the books, the titles were written in incomprehensible characters.

The real cause of the acolyte's distress, however, was the format of the books themselves.

To put it quite bluntly, they were heavy.

Some had rich leather pages, while others had weighty steel covers, and others still were adorned with decorations...

She had to pull those bulky volumes down from the shelf, lug them over to the lectern, and then put them back when she was done reading. It was real work, and she thought it would be better handled by a cleric of the God of Knowledge, someone who was used to such things.

...Unfortunately, there's no choice in this case.

On this occasion, the text-house of the God of Knowledge had been attacked.

They could hardly ask those girls, battered in heart and body, to take on even more responsibilities.

And above all…

"I'm very sorry. I've put you to such trouble…"

"Oh, not at all! I'm just glad to be of service, even a tiny bit."

The acolyte smiled at the archbishop where she sat in the chair, even though she knew the priestess couldn't see it.

This honored personage came here so excited—how could I do less than this?

Sword Maiden, the woman on whose shoulders rested this entire temple, had changed much in the past year.

For the better, of course.

Until recently, she had simply tried to do too much. It was as if she didn't quite think of herself as human.

And yet, from time to time, the acolyte saw Sword Maiden get a look on her face like a lost little child.

On quiet nights, for example.

As her attendant, the acolyte had seen Sword Maiden rush from her bed to throw herself in beseeching prayer at the altar.

But—why?

"But tell me, ma'am. Has it helped? Have you learned anything?"

"To borrow a phrase," Sword Maiden said, a chuckle escaping her, "not even a tiny bit."

Of late, she had shown such softness, such enjoyment, more and more often.

Over the course of the past year, she had also ceased to go to the altar in the middle of the night.

If it was really all the doing of that strange adventurer, then the acolyte would have to make sure she thanked him.

Although I have to admit, I don't think much of her pouting like a child…

"Hmm…"

Even as she spared a wry smile, Sword Maiden kept reading the book of legal precedent.

Her right hand caressed a clay tablet, while the left ran over the book on the lectern.

She claimed that the subtle differences of texture in paper and ink allowed her to decipher letters. That was surprising enough, but what really impressed the acolyte was that Sword Maiden could understand the letters at all.

Some people chose not to learn the ancient writing systems, because they feared gaining untoward knowledge. They didn't want to stumble upon any maledictions that might be tucked away in the text, or be driven mad by the shock of unimaginable truths that they came into contact with.

But reading and writing being such valuable skills, could any explorer afford to be illiterate?

If you were going to go into battle, you had to know who you were fighting.

That was true even with goblins; how much more so for terrible wizards or evil Dark Gods...

"...Ahh, now... This, I remember."

Sword Maiden's sudden remark brought the acolyte back to herself.

"Does it make sense now, ma'am?"

"Yes. Hee-hee... I wonder what *he* would make of this. I think it might be helpful for him to know."

But I don't suppose he would actually be interested.

She sounded a touch disappointed as she closed the heavy metal cover and let out a small breath.

"I apologize again, but could you bring quill and paper, and ready a pigeon?"

"This isn't another of your love letters, is it?"

The acolyte smirked as she offered this twist of the knife, provoking a "Why, you!" and a puff of the cheeks from Sword Maiden.

"I will be writing to His Majesty and the chief of the elves. I do know how to separate my official and private lives, you know!"

The acolyte nodded obediently as she opened a drawer, pulled out lambskin paper and a pen, and set about preparing a candle and seal.

She could bring the pigeon after the letter was written. She would ask the gods to protect it.

If Sword Maiden said so, then this certainly had to do with the fate of the world.

"I suppose all of creation is still in danger, and there are still many adventures to be had, is that right?"

"Indeed it is. We face a very powerful foe. A terrifying one. The world may yet be destroyed.

"But," Sword Maiden whispered and put a finger to her cheek, her lips softening like fresh petals.

"If *he* can save people, then we must save the world."

CHAPTER 5

JUNGLE CRUISE

The tweet of a bird, *cheep-cheep-cheep*. The sunlight that slashed in through the windows. An atmosphere to be found only in the depths of a forest.

Any one of them would have been enough to rouse Cow Girl from her slumber, but none was what actually woke her.

"Mmn, hggh—ahhh…"

She pushed aside the fur blanket, giving a big stretch. The early morning chill was pleasant on her naked body.

There was no time to savor it, however.

One thing had awakened her from sleep.

Clank, clank. It was the metallic scraping sound that could be heard from the adjoining guest room.

"…Right!" Cow Girl gave herself an invigorating slap on each cheek, then set about stuffing her ample frame into her clothes. She pulled on her underwear in a hurry, fastened the buttons of her shirt, and then…

My pants! What's with my pants…?

She was by no means overweight, but somehow she just couldn't get them on. Her fingers slipped, perhaps because of her haste.

"Ohh, for…!"

She clicked her tongue and decided it wasn't something she usually worried about anyway. Instead, she pushed past the divider that separated her from the living room, wearing just a shirt over her undergarments.

"G-good morning!"

"Hrm…"

As she'd expected, he was there.

He was in his usual cheap-looking steel helmet and grimy leather armor, his sword of a strange length at his hip and his small, round shield on his left arm.

He was also carrying his bag of miscellaneous items; he looked ready to depart on a trip at any time.

She murmured "Umm" or some such as a way of diverting him then hugged her own arm. "…Are you going already?"

"The goblin hideout is almost certainly upstream," he said, nodding crisply. "If they were to put poison in the river, that would be the end."

"Yeah, that'd be bad," Cow Girl said with an ambivalent smile. Her head was full of the weather, and the sun, and her uncle. All going around and around…

"Er, well… Be careful, okay?"

Those were the words that finally made it out of her mouth—those obvious, banal words.

He nodded and replied, "I will."

Then he strode toward the door at a bold pace.

As she watched him go, Cow Girl opened her mouth several times, but each time, she closed it again without saying anything.

"You too…" With his hand on the door, he shook his head slightly. "All of you."

Then there was a sound as the door opened, and another as it shut.

Cow Girl let out a breath. She pressed a hand to her face then ran it through her hair.

Oh, for… The softest of groans escaped her.

Suddenly, there was a rustle of cloth and a voice from behind her.

"…Has he gone?"

"…Yeah." Cow Girl gave a small nod then rubbed her face. Finally, she turned around slowly. "Do you wish you'd had a chance to say good-bye?"

Guild Girl, still in her nightclothes, mumbled, "Not really," and scratched her cheek awkwardly. She offered a weak smile. "I don't… want him to see me before I put my face on."

"Can't say I don't sympathize, but…"

Guild Girl may not have had her makeup on and may not have done her hair. Yet, as far as Cow Girl could tell, she still boasted an unadorned beauty.

Still, she and Cow Girl were about the same age. Cow Girl knew how she felt and was, in fact, painfully aware of it. And yet, even so…

"I like him to be able to see the way I normally look."

"………I envy your courage," Guild Girl said, somehow sad.

Cow Girl tried to distract her with a dismissive wave of her hand. "I just try not to think about it, is all."

Neither of them said what it was they were trying not to think about: That each and every good-bye could be the last.

§

The elf harbor: on a collection of leaves that came out into the river like a bridge, the adventurers were gathered.

"Mm… Hmm…" High Elf Archer squinted like a cat and gave a great yawn; she was still half-asleep. The other adventurers, though, were already busy loading luggage onto the boat.

Elvish boats were elegant teardrop-shaped vessels carved from the silvery roots of the white birch.

"And heave, and ho, and hup, and oh!"

Dwarf Shaman was busy lining up wooden boards along the gunwales as shielding, turning the little bark into a crude warship.

"…Could they not be made a little more…pretty?" the elf with the shining headdress asked, pulling a face.

"'Fraid beggars can't be choosers. We don't have very many of them, and I had to come up with them in a hurry. No time to be concerned about looks." Dwarf Shaman gave an annoyed snort and stroked his white beard. "Not like I'm happy to hang them up this way anyway."

It would have been one thing if they'd had more time, but in a pinch, this was the most that could be managed. The elf must have acknowledged as much, because instead of continuing to complain, he reached out his hand into the wind.

"O sylphs, thou windy maidens fair, grant to me your kiss most rare—bless our ship with breezes fair."

There was a whistling as the wind gusted up in time with the elf's chant and began to blow around the boat.

"I have a certain affinity with the sprites by virtue of being an elf, but I'm still a ranger, a tracker. I ask you not to expect miracles."

"Believe me, I don't," Dwarf Shaman said with a mischievous smile and a glance out the corner of his eye at High Elf Archer. "Everyone is good at some things...and *not* at others."

"...Yawn..." High Elf Archer was still rubbing her eyes, her long ears drooping pitifully. It didn't look like she would be fully awake for a while yet.

"And where's her older sister?" Dwarf Shaman said.

"...It seems the two siblings were up talking until quite late last night."

"Still in the Sandman's grip, eh?"

The elf with the shining headpiece let out a sigh, then furrowed his brow as if his head hurt. "Humans are quite industrious... My new younger sister could stand to learn something from them."

He was looking at the two clerics, who were already aboard the boat and offering their prayers to the gods.

"O Earth Mother, abounding in mercy, please, by your revered hand, guide the soul of we who have left this world..."

"O great sheep who walked the Cretaceous, grant to us a modicum of your long-sung success in battle!"

Priestess was clinging to her sounding staff and imploring the Earth Mother to keep them safe on their adventure.

Lizard Priest was making a strange gesture with his palms together and prevailing upon his ancestors for aid in combat.

Even if these were not requests for miracles proper, there was no question that the gods' protection would be with them.

"Phew..." Finished with her prayers for the time being, Priestess stood up and wiped away her sweat as the boat rocked gently in the current. "I'm not so sure we should beg the gods for favors like this.

We should try on our own until we understand where we are insufficient." Priestess looked like she might topple over at any moment; now a scaled hand supported her, and Lizard Priest nodded.

"I don't suppose it should hurt so very much to ask. Why pray to a god that would not grant you victory even after you had staked all on a tremendous battle, expending your every effort?"

"I think that may be a little beyond what I'm talking about."

One of them was a devout cleric and servant of the Earth Mother.

The other was a lizard priest who venerated his forefathers, the fearsome nagas.

But this difference didn't mean they necessarily had to be at odds.

"Anyway, let's do our best." Priestess nodded to herself, clutching her sounding staff with vigor.

"Are you finished?" Goblin Slayer asked as he emerged from belowdecks.

His arms were full of provisions and sleeping gear, and he ran his gaze along the shields that had been put up against the sides of the ship.

"Oh yes. The shields are up, we've said our prayers, and we have the blessing of the wind as well."

"I see," Goblin Slayer murmured. "Thank you for your help."

"Oh, not at all!"

Priestess had a bright smile on her face; Goblin Slayer nodded at her and then boldly climbed down onto the wharf. The large leaves shuddered slightly under the weight of him and his equipment, and a ripple ran along the surface of the water.

"I'm grateful for your help."

"Think nothing of it," the elf with the shining headpiece answered evenly. "However," he added, "if you wish to thank me, see my younger sister-in-law safely back."

"Very well," Goblin Slayer replied without hesitation. He turned to look at the girl in question, who still appeared dangerously unsteady.

Priestess was trying hard to shush Dwarf Shaman, who was suggesting that a dunk in the river would do the elf some good.

"I accept," Goblin Slayer said.

"Very well," the elf replied. His face relaxed in what might have been relief, but he quickly made his expression taut again. Then he reached into an item pouch at his hip and withdrew a small jar of rich golden honey.

"This is an elixir," he said. "A secret remedy passed down among the elves. It is said to be made with a combination of herbs, varieties of tree sap, and fruit juices, along with a ritual to the spirits. The top was sealed with a kingsfoil leaf, so the elixir can be drunk only once."

Goblin Slayer took the bottle without a word and put it into his own item pouch.

"If I do not come back, please see to the two women."

"I accept."

"And to the goblins as well."

"But of course." The elf nodded and then, after a moment's thought, added somberly, "...She may not be perfect, but she is my younger sister by law now, and I have known her for a long time. Take care of her."

"As long as it is within my power, I will do so."

Even the elf, for all his long life, seemed surprised by Goblin Slayer's response. "You don't take anything lightly, do you?" he said, his expression softening just a little—but he spoke so quietly that only the trees could hear. Then he went on, "The elders have received some kind of news from the water town."

"Oh?"

"...But even I am not yet mature by the reckoning of the high elves. I can't guess what move the elders may be planning to make."

The elfin imagination spanned a vast period of time. The smallest and most seemingly insignificant thing could have ramifications countless years later.

The actions they took here, now, would most likely be the same. The elf with the shining headpiece gritted his teeth. He was to be the next chief, and yet, even he had not been told what the news was.

Not that he couldn't take a guess, of course. But a guess was still a guess. It was not a fact.

So long as he didn't know what the ripples on the surface might form, he could only stay silent.

Goblin Slayer looked at the unspeaking elf and grunted. Then slowly, as if nothing had happened, he opened his mouth.

"Also, be careful of the river."

"You're the ones who will need to be careful," the elf said lightly, feeling a bit odd at the nonchalance of Goblin Slayer's words. "I believe there will be a mist today."

His ears twitched like leaves as he took in the sound of the wind and looked at the pale light of the morning sky.

"Goblins are not the only danger in this forest. At the wrong time, Nature itself can be your enemy. Bear that in mind as you go." *Because after all*... The elf with the shining headpiece and Goblin Slayer looked into the forest. "You will be journeying into darkness."

"Into darkness," Goblin Slayer repeated softly.

The sea of trees that extended to the source of the river harbored an impenetrable blackness.

There was a warm breeze that brought thick, humid air. Like the inside of a goblin nest, Goblin Slayer thought. And that was a fact.

What should he do, then? He considered for the space of an instant then formulated his plan.

"...I have one further request."

"What is it?" the elf looked at him questioningly.

"Prepare another boat."

"I will do it." The elf nodded, making the ritual sign of a promise of his people.

Seeing this, Goblin Slayer said, "By the way," as if he had just thought of something. "I have been wondering. Is it true that elves have no concept of 'cleaning up'?"

"We do," the elf with the shining headpiece replied, looking very weary. "But some *sisters* don't."

"...I see."

§

The fog turned out to be a true blessing.

It blocked out the sun, daubing everything with a white haze, so that even objects only a short distance away were vague and indistinct.

The goblins didn't think of the fog as a blessing; to them, it was only natural. When something good happened to a goblin, he didn't feel gratitude toward anyone or anything. Since goblins were so often tormented, so thoroughly put-upon, it was only right that something decent should happen to them sometimes.

It was no different now.

The goblin who had been told to watch the river flowing through the forest noticed it immediately. He had been slacking off in his work, so he squeaked and squealed when it happened.

It was "nightfall," when the sun behind the veil of mist had only just risen.

Mingled with the river's gurgling current, he heard a creaking sound getting closer.

The goblin guard's ugly eyes got wider; he peered into the fog and listened as hard as he could.

Yes, there it was.

Creak, creak. There was no question: the sound was coming from downstream, from the direction of the elf village.

The elves, who always contemptuously looked down on the goblins, thought they could just come right on up this river!

"GROORB."

When he spotted the slim form of a sailor emerging through the mist, the goblin licked his lips.

If it was a he-elf, they could beat him to death and feast upon him.

If it was a she-elf, they could make her the bearer of their young.

Whichever, he had found them first, so he was entitled to be the first to enjoy them, wasn't he?

He didn't think for one second that the only reason either of these outcomes was possible was exactly because his companions were with him.

"GRORO! GROOBR!!"

The goblin put his fingers in his mouth and produced a not very skillful whistle.

"GROB?!"

"GOORBGROOR!"

The goblins, who had been sleeping, were not pleased to have been roused early. But they, too, snapped awake the moment they caught sight of the elvish boat.

Elves! Adventurers! Prey! Food! Women!

"GORBBR!"

"GOBGOROB!"

As quietly as they could, they whispered their lusts to one another, taking up their equipment and flying to their cherished mounts.

Well, let us not say *cherished.* They didn't care all that much for the wolves they rode.

"GOROB!"

The guard, who now fancied himself the leader, gave an order, and the goblin riders galloped off.

Unlike horses, wolves make no clatter of hooves as they approach. As long as they're muzzled, they don't howl, either. Goblins (except hobgoblins) could conceivably ride horses, but wolves were more convenient.

The goblins beat cruelly at the sides of their mounts, pushing them onward.

"GROOROGGR!!"

First, they would deal with the captain. Then, the oarsman. Then, they would climb aboard and finish the job.

The goblins grinned and laughed, imagining the panicked faces of the elves. The sight of the prideful forest people spilling their guts upon the deck would be delightful indeed.

The dark imaginings made the goblins grasp their weapons that much tighter. They carried crude stone spears and arrows, along with slings. Primitive though the weapons were, they were more than potent enough to take a life.

"GGRO! GRRB!"

The guard yowled calamitously, and the other goblins clicked their tongues. He was getting too full of himself. They would have to correct that later.

"GRORB!"

"GGGROORB!"

Ignoring the yammering guard, the goblins held their weapons at the ready, drew their bowstrings tight.

The guard complained about this with gusto, but when he found that no one was listening to him, he glumly raised his own hand spear.

Spurring on their mounts, the goblins began their attack.

They aimed in the general direction of the creaking boat; there was no leader to coordinate their offensive.

"GORB! GBRROR!"

Nearly half the arrows that came raining down simply splashed into the water.

Some, though, not only the arrows but also the spears and sling-stones, managed to connect with the rower.

"!"

The fiend was dead! That was the collective thought of every goblin there. Some even cheered.

But…

"—?"

Without so much as a quiver or sound, the rower continued to row.

Had the attack not been intense enough? Or had the oarsman, by sheer good luck, avoided fatal injury?

Taken aback, the goblins nonetheless prepared for another attack. But in that instant:

"One…!"

A warrior in grimy leather armor leaped into their midst and slashed the guard's throat.

"GBBOOROB?!"

The monster screamed and crumpled, and Goblin Slayer kicked him out of the way, into the river.

The ensuing splash was the signal.

"Bbffah!"

The signal to *the second ship being pulled behind the first one.*

This ship, whose sides were protected by defensive shields and which had the blessing of the wind sprites, was totally unaffected by the arrows.

High Elf Archer threw off the fur covering that had been concealing the vessel and stood from where she had been hiding behind the armor.

"You stinking, stupid, ugly little—! How dare you come so close to my own home!"

Still on one knee, she brought her great bow to bear in an elegant motion and loosed three bud-tipped arrows simultaneously. They flew through the air with a whistle.

"GOOB?!"

"GROBO?!"

The bolts pierced the eyes and throats of goblin riders, throwing them from their wolves as if they were already drowning. High Elf Archer's impeccable technique was not in the least affected by the swaying of the boat or the fog that obscured her vision.

Her long ears twitched, taking in every sound on the battlefield.

"Orcbolg! They're coming from the right!"

In lieu of an answer, she heard a goblin cry, "GBOR?!" and she nodded in satisfaction.

"I've gotta say, though, preparing a whole second boat just to distract them with the similar sounds seems like a waste of time…"

"True, it needed Dragontooth Sailors and everything," Dwarf Shaman grumbled, drawing his ax and peeking out from behind the shielding for a better look.

The two Dragontooth Warriors, who had been dressed in overclothes and placed on the leading boat, continued to row faithfully even in the face of the attack. Arrows and spears had passed through their largely vacant bodies, or occasionally lodged in a bone.

"Oh, but we have to reduce our speed…" Priestess put her pointer finger to her lips even as she huddled down and clung to her sounding staff. "Goblin Slayer's on the shore and everything."

"Mm. I shall go ashore as well, so please do convince them to slow."

Ready with a Swordclaw in hand, Lizard Priest cried: "Hrrraaaa ahhhahhhh!" and flung himself toward the goblins on the shore, his tail flailing, crushing the neck of the first monster he encountered.

Priestess cried out and grabbed hold of the shielding as the boat rocked with the force of his leap.

"Can't you jump a little more quietly?!" Dwarf Shaman demanded. Then he called to Priestess, "You still aboard?"

"I—I'm okay!"

Priestess and Dwarf Shaman were mainly supposed to stay out of the way, so their job was to deal with any goblins who happened to get onto the boat.

"Huh, don't you worry. I won't let them get…anywhere near us!"

High Elf Archer's posture wavered not an inch as she let loose another three arrows.

Three screams followed. Her archery bordered on magical.

"Nine... Ten!"

"GROOBOO?!"

Goblin Slayer had jumped ahead into the mist, and now he swung his shield to the left, trusting to luck to strike something. The polished and sharpened edge tore through a goblin's face.

He moved again, relying on the scream to guide him, piercing the creature's throat with his sword.

The monster waved its arms, trying to pull the sword out; Goblin Slayer kicked it away and grabbed the dagger from its belt.

He flipped the dagger into a reverse grip as he heard the howling of wolves coming closer. Even as he did so, his left hand searched through his item pouch and came up with a leather strap with stones tied to either end.

"Hmph."

He let the strap fly; it spun, skimming the ground, and from somewhere in the fog came the yelp of a wolf.

"GORB?!"

There followed the sound of something collapsing to the ground, and a goblin's shout.

The bolas had wrapped themselves around the legs of one of the bestial mounts.

Without pausing, Goblin Slayer jumped in that direction, cutting the throat of the goblin who had fallen.

To him, there was scant difference between the darkness of a cave and the limited visibility of the fog.

"Ten and one."

Thus, it was Goblin Slayer who held the advantage when jumping into the maelstrom.

After all, the goblins could hardly tell who was friend and who was foe. A careless swipe of a weapon might strike an ally. Unlike in any cave, it was difficult to rely on numbers to overwhelm the enemy.

Not that any one goblin was especially concerned about what happened to the others, but they did hate to lose a shield that might have protected them.

"…A patrol, or perhaps a random encounter."

"GOROOB?! GROBOR?!"

"So you agree?"

Lizard Priest kicked down one of the riders then grabbed the wolf by the snout and tore open its jaws through sheer strength.

Being in combat made him sound happy, but it was the blood all around that quickened the thinking of the lizardman.

"If this is supposed to be an ambush," Goblin Slayer said, shredding the spine of the rider on the ground and muttering "*Twelve*" as a muffled scream sounded. "They lack offensive power."

As he stood up, he launched his dagger into the fog, provoking a shriek.

"We can't let any of them get home alive."

"Ha-ha-ha-ha! Were we ever going to?"

Lizard Priest swept out with his tail, slamming a goblin behind him against a tree, shattering its spine.

Thirteen. Six, maybe seven remaining. Goblin Slayer grabbed a spear at his feet.

"In that case…"

He raised his shield and advanced, deflecting the poisoned dagger of a goblin hidden in the mist, striking out with his spear.

He could feel it hadn't sunk deep enough. Instantly, he pushed with the polearm to keep the monster from moving then smashed its face with his shield.

The creature fell, its forehead shattered, and Goblin Slayer came with it to crush its throat.

Fourteen. Goblin Slayer extracted his spear from the dead monster.

"…we should finish this before the fog clears."

And that is exactly what they did.

§

"…I wonder if the flowers are blooming?"

The murmur came from Priestess, shortly after the party had defeated the goblin riders.

The only sounds were the rush of water, the creaking of the oar, and five adventurers' shallow breathing.

As they got farther upstream, even the animals that lived in the trees seemed to be holding their breaths.

The sun climbed higher and the mist began to dissipate, but the thick vegetation all around them cast dark shadows. Brightness did not return, and there was something eerie about it all, as if they were entering the depths of a cave.

Maybe that was why Priestess responded to the unexpected and ever more noticeable sweetness in the air the way she did.

Priestess clung to her sounding staff, but High Elf Archer shook her head. "I dunno, but…I've never heard of a flower that smells like this."

"Their territory is close," Goblin Slayer said calmly, keeping his hand on the weapon he had stolen from the goblins. It was a club that appeared to be a shaved-down tree, and it had gruesome dark-red spots here and there. The splatter was from when it had been used to crush the heads of people—and goblins.

Ultimately, more than twenty goblins and their mounts lay dead in the river. They couldn't have left the corpses out in the open; too much chance they would have been discovered by another group. And there was no time to bury them.

Anyway, if the corpses washed downstream, they wouldn't be noticed by the goblins upstream…

And the carnivorous fish in the river would probably get rid of the bodies for them.

This had given Priestess some pause, but Lizard Priest had told her it was a form of burial in its own way.

"The mist is beginning to clear. Perhaps we should be making ready." That same Lizard Priest was now trying to see as far through the fog as he could. With a wave of his hand, he dismissed one of his two Dragontooth Warriors, the one that had been piloting the boat. The skeletal sailor pulled up the oar and sat down, hugging it.

"It would be no small trouble if they were to discover us by the sound of the paddling."

"Oh, should I pray for the Silence miracle…?" Priestess asked.

"Not yet," Goblin Slayer said, shaking his head. "We've already used Dragontooth Warrior twice, and Swordclaw once."

The helmet turned to Lizard Priest as if seeking confirmation, and the cleric gave a great nod.

The party had a total of seven miracles. Now they had four left, and the only magic available to them all belonged to Dwarf Shaman, who could manage another four, as well. The party was blessed with considerable magical resources, but it was still important to keep track of how many miracles and spells were available.

In addition, Silence by itself was no guarantee that they would avoid combat.

"Keep saving your miracles."

"All right." Priestess felt she hadn't been much use in the earlier battle. She nodded unenthusiastically. "...?" Then she blinked, rubbed her eyes, and peeked out between the shields guarding the boat.

"Ho, careful now," said Dwarf Shaman, taking hold of the girl's waist to support her.

"Of course," Priestess said, looking around wide-eyed.

She had seen a slender shadow rising through the mist.

It wasn't a tree. Its silhouette looked far too strange to be vegetation.

Standing alongside the riverbank, the misshapen thing looked almost like the prey of a butcherbird, impaled on twigs...

"...Is that a...totem?!" A gasping cry escaped Priestess's throat.

It was a corpse. The earthly remains of someone who had been pierced through, from between their legs to their mouth.

Being left out in this warm, damp place, they had begun to rot, their juices expanding to the point that now they looked barely human. Judging by the rust-eaten armor, it had been a woman. The corpse had been so badly mutilated by bugs, though, that now it wasn't even clear what race she had originally belonged to.

"Ugh...!" High Elf Archer felt herself about to retch but forced down what threatened to come up.

It was obvious why the goblins had exposed the corpse.

Cruelty.

A bold declaration to the world that this was their territory, and a brutal mockery of any who might dare to impinge upon it.

They simply wanted to see any interlopers terrified, panicked, mad with fear, or at least enraged.

Why else would they put up a trophy like this, an object at the gates that served no defensive purpose?

"Was she skewered alive, or mounted on that stick after death…?" Lizard Priest asked, glancing around as he brought his hands together in prayer. "…At the very least, she has had the good fortune to remain a part of the natural cycle."

The reason for his broad gesture became clear: there was more than one totem.

There was a forest of them.

Corpses impaled on sticks lined the riverbank like trees along a roadside. Some were only bones; on others, the flesh had not yet begun to rot.

Some bore a panoply of fresh scars, while others had swelled almost comically with gas.

Some of the corpses appeared to be merchants, while others bore ornaments that made them seem like adventurers.

How many had been killed?

How many had been made the playthings of the goblins?

"Ergh…" Priestess put a hand to her mouth, and who could blame her? She crouched down, her face pale, while her sounding staff clattered to the deck.

"Hrrrgh…!" Clinging to the side of the boat, she emptied the contents of her stomach into the river. What had finally done it was the realization that the sweet smell she had wondered about was the stink of the rotting corpses.

For a year and a half now, she had witnessed the goblins' cruelty and had become somewhat inured to it, but even she couldn't stand this.

There was a series of splashes as she vomited into the water.

"Here, chew on this. And have a drink of water." Dwarf Shaman rubbed her back gently.

"…Ur…urgh. Th-thank you…" Her voice was faint, her throat burning.

With both hands, she took the herbs and water he held out to her, chewing the leaves gently.

"…So is this what's gonna happen to us if we lose this fight?" High

Elf Archer must have been feeling just as bad as Priestess, because her always-pale skin was now absolutely bloodless. She spat out a curse. "This is no joke."

"I agree," Goblin Slayer said. "It is not a joke."

The cheap-looking metal helmet stared straight ahead.

There, in the mist, a strange shape rose like a mountain.

The thing appeared as a dark shadow in the white fog.

Unexpectedly, a fetid wind came up, pushing the mist away.

"...Huh," High Elf Archer said, her lips still tight but her tone terribly even. "So that's the One That Stops the Waters..."

How to describe this thing?

It was made of great chalk blocks, a temple or a shrine—or perhaps a fortress.

The elegant structure, which had stood since the Age of the Gods, was now worn away, covered in moss and vines. Yet the construct, built to dam the river, hardly seemed like the sort of ruins that goblins would find amenable.

"It was right next door, lass. You really didn't know about it?"

"Hey, this was Mokele Mubenbe's territory." High Elf Archer pursed her lips and flicked her ears as if remonstrating with Dwarf Shaman. "Maybe the old people of the village knew about it, though. Maybe my sister had even heard about it."

"So you really *didn't* know about it," Dwarf Shaman teased, provoking an angry hiss from the elf.

Their argument was just as energetic as ever, and perhaps that was deliberate. After the terrible sight they had just seen, anyone would want to shift the mood.

"What we have to worry about now is the goblin fortress," Goblin Slayer spat, looking around. "Stop the boat. The fog is lifting."

"Aye, aye," Lizard Priest said, gesturing a quick instruction at the Dragontooth Warrior. The skeleton brought the little craft closer to shore.

Goblin Slayer put a hand to the club at his belt and knelt down beside Priestess.

"What do you think?"

"Er... Wh— What do *I* think?" The blood had drained from her face, and she was shaking her head listlessly from side to side. "We have to…do…something…"

"Yes."

"If we…j-just leave this…"

"Yes." His voice was quiet like hers, but not weak. "We will not *just leave* it."

Priestess swallowed heavily. Goblin Slayer saw her hand go to her armor, and he picked up the fallen sounding staff. Priestess gripped it to her chest with both hands, as if in an embrace, then got unsteadily to her feet.

She forced herself to relax her stiff facial muscles and glanced at his visor.

"…Because…they're goblins."

"Yes." He nodded. "They're goblins."

"Hold it, Beard-cutter." Dwarf Shaman heaved himself ashore as the elven boat came soundlessly to the bank. He skillfully tied the boat up, securing it to a nearby tree. "Like you said, the mist's clearing. And it'll be night soon. Sneaking in is going to take some doing."

"In that case—" High Elf Archer tried two or three times to snap her fingers but ended up just clucking her tongue at the pitiful *fp fp* sound she got. "…In that case, I have an idea!"

§

Some time later.

The party crept like a train of shadows under the illumination of the twin moons.

Through the undergrowth, pushing aside leaves and branches, they kept their weight low, moving as quickly as they could.

The only sound among them was the barest whisper of a prayer from Priestess: *"O Earth Mother, abounding in mercy, grant us peace to accept all things…"*

She ran through the absolute silence as fast as she could, sweat pouring down her brow, her hands gripping her sounding staff.

As they got closer, the goblins' levee and fortification loomed up strangely ahead of them.

The way the rocks had been piled and carved was the work of dwarves.

The way the structures had been built without disturbing the trees around them was the doing of the elves.

The preparations against attack must have come from the knowledge of the lizardmen or the humans.

Here and there, a stone had been dislodged by the goblins, besmirching this place.

What could this place have been built for? Priestess wondered suddenly.

A shrine, a temple, a tower, a castle, a levee, a bridge… It seemed to be all these, and yet none of them.

Whatever it was, it was a goblin nest now, and to challenge it would take more than a miracle of the Earth Mother, no matter how merciful she might be.

That was why the adventurers had something else to defend them.

A white mist that seemed to rise up of its own accord, *fssh, fssh*.

It was also intensely hot.

To an extent, that was to be expected—they were in a rain forest, after all—but it was punishingly humid as well. Priestess's vestments had absorbed enough water to grow heavy, and her sweat made her clothes cling to her most unpleasantly. She'd rolled up her sleeves out of necessity but never stopped praying.

There was someone else who hadn't stopped at his work—Dwarf Shaman.

He held a stone, glowing red, in his roughhewn hands. The source of the heat, of the mist, was in that stone—in the salamander who lived within.

Dancing flame, salamander's fame. Grant us a share of the very same.

The fire spirit invoked by the Kindle spell evaporated the water with which the spirits of air were so pregnant. The result was just like being cloaked in mist.

Dwarf Shaman looked suspiciously at High Elf Archer as she gave a triumphant little snort.

She's getting to be as bad as Beard-cutter.

Nonetheless, Lizard Priest came from the South, High Elf Archer was from this very forest, and Dwarf Shaman was quite intimate with fire. The thick heat made their movements quicker, if anything.

Priestess huffed and puffed along, and Goblin Slayer's expression couldn't be seen.

Lizard Priest looked up at an observation tower high above the goblins' fortress. With his heat-detecting eyes, he spotted a goblin with a spear happily taking a nap.

No problems. He nodded at Goblin Slayer, who then led the party forward again.

The gates of the fortress were practically in front of their noses now.

The huge, thick door was characteristically elven, made of ancient, sturdy wood. There was no sign of metal anywhere on it, but its durability was beyond question.

At first, it appeared to be all of a piece, but in the right corner of the massive gate a square outline could be seen. A smaller door within the door, perhaps a sally port.

Goblin Slayer gestured to his companions to wait in the bushes then pulled his club from his belt. High Elf Archer clambered into a tree, her long ears twitching; she reached a branch and sat down without so much as dislodging a single leaf. She put an arrow into her bow and drew it with a hush, while down below, Lizard Priest adjusted his grip on his fang-sword.

As for Priestess and Dwarf Shaman, they continued to intone their miracles and magic respectively. The silence went on, and the fog kept rising.

Priestess's lips briefly formed the words *Be careful*. Goblin Slayer nodded.

When he left the bubble of silence, the hue and cry of life suddenly returned to the forest. Leaves rustled as the wind blew through them. The river gurgled. He could hear his own breath inside his helmet.

"Hmm." He stood for a moment in front of the gate before pounding noisily on it. Then, with an agility that belied the weight of his full body armor, he dug his fingers into the grain of the wood and pulled himself bodily up.

The reaction came just a moment later.

"GROB?"

The sally port opened, and a goblin, most likely a sentry, stuck his face out.

High Elf Archer was prepared to loose her arrow that very instant, but Goblin Slayer didn't move. A second, then a third goblin crowded out of the little door.

The click of High Elf Archer's tongue was muted by Priestess's prayer, so no one heard it.

A fourth monster emerged, and then after waiting exactly five seconds, Goblin Slayer moved.

"GORAB?!"

He jumped down from above, landing squarely on the back of the last goblin to come out. The impact stole the air from the creature's lungs, and he didn't make any more noise.

Goblin Slayer brought his club down.

There was a dry sound of something breaking, and the goblin's skull turned an impossible direction at an equally impossible angle.

Goblin Slayer drew the sword from the twitching corpse's belt. "One."

"GBBR?"

The first goblin, surprised by the sudden shout, started to turn around—

"GORB?!"

A bud-tipped arrow whistled through the night, spearing the creature straight in his right ear and out his left. He collapsed to his knees like a marionette with its strings cut, and an instant later, the second goblin was dead.

Despite their shock at the ambush, the remaining two monsters had begun to act.

But the adventurers were too quick for them.

One goblin turned toward the enemy behind and found his face smashed in with the club.

"Two, and…"

"GRRB…?!" The creature fell backward, clutching his crushed nose; Goblin Slayer immediately jumped on top of him. He had already dropped the club, drawing the stolen blade from his scabbard. He clapped his left hand over the goblin's mouth, and with his right, he mercilessly stabbed into the creature's windpipe then slashed.

"That makes three…"

And that meant one left.

This last goblin was slightly smarter than the others; he at least grasped that two of his companions had been killed. He was taking a deep breath, opening his mouth wide to yell for reinforcements, but before he had time to raise his voice, he found an arrow lodged in his throat.

He toppled forward with the force of the shot.

"…Four."

Goblin Slayer confirmed with his own eyes that all four of the creatures had stopped breathing then quickly glanced inside the sally port. It was dark, but there were still two moons in the sky to provide illumination.

Inside the gate was an open square. There was no sign of goblins nearby.

However indolent goblins might be, though, the absence of the guards would not go unnoticed for long.

Goblin Slayer propped the small door open with a peg then motioned to the bushes.

Priestess let out a long breath and rushed over to him.

"…Are you okay? Are you hurt, or—?"

"No, I am not."

At that, her little chest relaxed, relieved.

Lizard Priest emerged just as quickly, almost crawling along the ground, and Dwarf Shaman trundled after him. Last of all came High Elf Archer, jumping down from the tree and heading for the door so quickly she hardly even left a shadow. It would not be amusing if the one who was supposed to make sure everyone got to their destination safely was herself discovered.

"I'm supposed to be a scout, but I felt like an assassin just now," she said. "So what's next?"

"I don't like it, but we will have to mount a frontal assault." Goblin Slayer wiped his blade on a goblin's rags and returned it to his scabbard. Then he took a hatchet from one of the monsters and thrust it unceremoniously into his belt. "I'm sorry," he said, "but it looks like there will be no time for rest. I need you on the front row."

"Just so, just so," Lizard Priest hissed. "I have never been one to do less than stand out front in battle."

He had one single miracle left. The Dragontooth Warrior had been left to guard the boat, so his Swordclaw and his strength were all they could count on.

But for Lizard Priest, that was enough.

"Got three left, m'self," Dwarf Shaman said, stroking his beard.

"And as for me, uh—" Priestess counted on her fingers. "Two more."

"All right."

That meant six altogether.

That would be a veritable bounty for the average adventuring party. But would it be enough for assaulting this fortress?

They had started with eleven, so they had used up roughly half their supply so far.

"…" Priestess shook her head, trying to clear away a sudden rush of bad thoughts. What had happened on her first adventure didn't have anything to do with this. Not even the dead she had seen on their way here mattered now.

"Um, what should we do about light…?"

"No lights until we're inside."

Goblins could see well in the dark. They needed no fires to get around at night. To enter the courtyard with torches burning would be as good as begging the goblins to come find them.

"Once we get in, we treat it like any other cave," Goblin Slayer said.

"Okay. I'll get some torches ready, then," Priestess replied.

"Please do."

As he spoke, Goblin Slayer drew his dagger.

"Er," Priestess sighed. She pulled a face then let out a resigned breath. "Do we have to…?"

"Yes." Goblin Slayer flipped his knife around in his hand then walked over to the goblin with the smashed face.

High Elf Archer, catching on, quickly patted down her clothing, making sure everything was ready. The blood drained from her face, and her ears drooped pitifully. "…Aw, are you serious?"

"Unless you have a packet of perfume."

"H-hey, I never imagined a trip home would mean g-going goblin hunting..."

"It's part of the job."

Goblin Slayer paid no mind to her excuse as he cut the goblin's belly open. He pulled out the steaming entrails, and Priestess wrapped them in a handkerchief she had produced, her face expressionless.

High Elf Archer backed away with a sort of choking sound; Dwarf Shaman quickly caught her by the hand.

"You've gotta know when to fold 'em."

"It just takes *guts*," Lizard Priest offered from where he had moved to prevent her escape, his eyes rolling in his head.

"Huh—? No, no way, there's gotta be something else we can—!"

"Pipe down."

It was, perhaps, only High Elf Archer's level of experience that saved her from screaming.

§

The adventurers slid along the wall, High Elf Archer at their head as scout.

The tower was in ruins, the gate devastated, nature reclaiming the structure for itself, and there was no shortage of shadows in which to hide.

And by the same token, many shadows in which things might be hidden.

High Elf Archer licked her lips, trying to decide where she could put her feet without disturbing the underbrush. If any goblin sentinels found them, that would mean an alarm, and that would be no fun at all.

"Thanks."

Goodness gracious. High Elf Archer blinked. Orcbolg, thanking her?

Humans were not best equipped to creep through the night with only starlight and misty moons to guide them.

"Humans have it rough pulling something like this, huh?" she said.

"I—I'm sorry...," Priestess replied.

"It's no problem. Don't worry about it." High Elf Archer waved a dismissive hand without turning around. "...Ooh." At that moment, her pointy ears twitched, as if blown by the breeze.

She narrowed her eyes: she was looking at a goblin who lolled around, a spear resting on his shoulder.

There was some distance between them. The adventurers hadn't been noticed yet. But he was coming this way. A sentry.

High Elf Archer drew an arrow from her quiver and put it into her bow.

"What should I do?"

"Shoot."

Her bow twanged almost before he finished speaking. The goblin, pierced through the throat, waved his arms uncomprehendingly as he toppled to the ground. There was a muffled whisper of grass, but that was all. No other guard seemed to have noticed what happened.

High Elf Archer let out the breath she'd been holding and started moving again, Goblin Slayer and the others following behind. She grabbed her arrow out of the goblin corpse as they passed by.

"Ugh..." She scrunched up her face at the black goblin blood, giving the arrow a thorough shake. "I don't want to get any dirtier than I already am..."

"No kidding," Priestess agreed in a truly pitiful voice. High Elf Archer nodded sympathetically.

These two sweet young women were covered from head to toe in unspeakable pollution. It was smelly and sticky, and as much as they were used to it, it still made them a little sick. It was necessary, but never fun.

"Argh, the tip broke off... This is the worst."

"Well now, if this is the worst, then perhaps we will never be discovered." Lizard Priest, crawling forward, raised his head like a snake. "I should think things will be a mite more troublesome when we enter the tower."

His eyes were focused ahead, on the huge wooden gate that barred entry into the tower. It was obviously immensely thick, and it was not the only such door. A whole series of them stood surrounding the structure's outer wall.

"I have heard that royal tombs are sometimes supplied with false entrances," Lizard Priest added. "Perhaps it is of that nature."

"You mean those are all...fake?" Priestess poked her head out to look, taking care not to be noticed by the goblins. The massive, heavy door, standing imposingly in the pale moonlight, hardly appeared anything less than real. "It certainly doesn't look like it..."

"We should be so fortunate that it were mere sculpture," Lizard Priest replied. "If it should be a trap, I hesitate to think what would become of us."

"......"

For a few seconds, Priestess stared silently at the doors among the ruins. Something felt wrong about them, something she couldn't explain. She tried to put her finger on it...

"...Well, I don't think we need to worry so much," she said with a giggle after a moment and pointed a pale, slim finger at the door. "Look how the undergrowth has been trod down there."

"Goodness, indeed...!"

The false door, the brainchild of some ancient elf or the like, had now been rendered pointless by the passing of time and the goblins' stupidity. The goblins unthinkingly used the door in and out, so the bushes by it were indeed trampled flat.

"I guess this leaves us with the same problem we started with," High Elf Archer said irritably. "Goblins."

One or two guards were lolling about, looking bored.

"The quickest way would be to off the guards and steal the key."

"That's if goblins knew how to lock doors," Dwarf Shaman said, brushing an errant leaf out of his beard and letting out a thoughtful breath. "At the very least, we have to take the ones on the right and the left simultaneously if we aren't to be discovered."

"Not a problem," Goblin Slayer said. "I know eight different ways to kill goblins silently."

"Really?" Priestess asked, blinking.

"That was a joke," Goblin Slayer continued, slowly shaking his helmeted head from side to side. "It is many more."

In light of High Elf Archer's assessment that arrows were at a premium, it was decided that Goblin Slayer and Dwarf Shaman would take the offensive. Each of them readied a sling, moved to close distance, and loosed their stones at almost the same time.

The rocks flew through the air, unerringly finding the throat of one goblin and the head of another.

"GRORB?!"

"GBBO?!"

The first collapsed with his windpipe cruelly crushed; the other got unsteadily to his feet, clutching his forehead. Before the creature could cry out, however, Lizard Priest sprang up to him, as if in a dance. His Swordclaw slit the monster's throat before he could make a sound.

Thus, the guards were dispatched without a noise, the silence of the courtyard in front of the gate continuing undisturbed.

"…I learned to use a sling, too, but it doesn't seem to have helped much," Priestess said despondently.

"Don't worry, there's a time and a place for every talent," High Elf Archer said, patting her on the back.

Lizard Priest gave his Swordclaw a great shake to get the blood off then began dragging away the corpses of the goblins. "You must do what you can," he agreed as he stuffed them into some bushes. While High Elf Archer made sure they were covered up, Dwarf Shaman rifled through the goblins' weapons, selecting a hand spear.

He held it up to the moonlight: the iron tip gleamed, plenty sharp. No rust, either.

"You know, for a bunch of goblins in a rotting fortress, they've got pretty fine weapons. Wonder if they nicked this off an adventurer."

"Perhaps there was an arms merchant among those they killed," Goblin Slayer said. "Or perhaps it was already here…"

"Hrm," Dwarf Shaman murmured, shaking his head at Goblin Slayer's musings. "Who can say? It seems antique at a glance, but sometimes products are made to look weathered."

"What are the chances it was forged here?"

"That I can rule out," Dwarf Shaman said confidently. "Fire can't be used here. Can't do any smithing at all without a special spell from the elves."

"…Hrm," Goblin Slayer grunted. "Whatever the case, the one thing we know for certain is that a goblin was carrying it. Did you find a key?"

"Yeah, here," High Elf Archer said, handing it over to him. It was an old key that had been hanging from a goblin's neck a few minutes before. It took the form of a tag with numbers carved in it, strung on a rough, frayed rope.

"Good." Goblin Slayer held it tight, examining it closely. "We enter, then go as far in as we can," he said.

"Is that our, uh, strategy?"

"Yes."

As always, Priestess couldn't help but smile at his behavior. Then she quickly knelt and held her sounding staff. "*O Earth Mother, abounding in mercy*," she intoned, praying for the peace of all the goblins who had died so far, and all those who had been killed by them. "*Please, by your revered hand, guide the souls of those who have left this world.*"

The adventuring party waited until she was finished with her prayer of repose, then they hurried toward the gate.

Goblin Slayer slid the key in the lock, turned it. There was a hollow *clack*.

"It doesn't fit."

That meant it had to go to some other door somewhere else. He clucked his tongue and pulled the key out.

Priestess opened her bag, clearing some space. "Here, I can take that."

"Yes, please."

She took the key, put it away, and let out a breath.

"I guess that makes it my turn," High Elf Archer said, crouching confidently in front of the lock. Her ability to pick such devices, which she claimed to have learned largely to amuse herself, had proven quite valuable to the party.

She used a pick to fumble with the lock, twitching her ears in search of the gentle click that would announce her success. When it came at last, she announced, "Excellent," and puffed out her chest proudly. "It's unlocked."

"Right, now before we open it…," Dwarf Shaman said. He crouched next to her and rooted through his bag of catalysts, pulling out a cloth.

Priestess tilted her head in confusion, asking hesitantly, "What are you doing?"

"Gotta put a little oil on there," Dwarf Shaman winked. "Wouldn't want it creaking, now, would we?"

"Oh, I'll help!"

"I'll take the right, then, and you take the left."

He tossed Priestess a rag dipped in oil, and she got to work. She showed herself to be an excellent cleaner, from long experience with her duties in the Temple. Soon, the door had been carefully oiled, and the adventurers pushed it open with nary a sound.

They slipped through as quietly as shadows then closed the door behind them. The goblins still had not noticed their companions had been killed.

If they had realized it, they would not have mourned or wept but would have thought only of how to punish the adventurers.

CHAPTER 6

HEART OF DARKNESS

"Geez... It r-reeks of mold...," High Elf Archer complained. The nest blended the odors of an ancient ruin with the rotten stench of a typical goblin habitat.

"W-well, it *is* an old building... Here, I'll light a fire," Priestess said. "Hup!" she grunted cutely, as she struck a flint and lit a torch.

They were smack in the middle of the fire-prevention ward the elves had placed on the structure, so the light was limited and weak. Still, it was enough for the entire party to see by. Priestess swept her eyes across the faces of her companions and then she let out a breath of relief.

The passageway on the other side of the gate was intensely claustro-phobic. It wasn't so small as to force them to crawl, but they weren't going to be spreading out to establish a battle line, either. It might be just the right size for goblins, but as for everyone else...

"Ugh, I don't like this!" High Elf Archer said. "A spike trap could wipe us all out at once."

"I rather worry about my ability to continue onward at all," Lizard Priest added.

"Yeah, chances are the dwarf gets stuck!"

Dwarf Shaman looked incensed but wisely didn't give voice to his objection.

"Let's go," Goblin Slayer said curtly, and the party formed up and started walking.

High Elf Archer went in front, Goblin Slayer just behind her, followed by Lizard Priest: they were technically the front row. In back were Priestess, nervously clutching her staff, and Dwarf Shaman, at the tail of the formation.

The constricting passageway went deeper and ever deeper, bending gently left and right along the way. The booming echo they heard must have been the dammed-up water.

I hate narrow tunnels like this, Priestess thought. If goblins came from the front, they couldn't run away. If they came from behind, the party would be equally trapped.

The fetid air. The clinging sense of dread. An odor she knew all too well from somewhere, sometime. Priestess hurriedly looked around, taken by the sense that if she didn't pay close attention, she would lose track of where she was.

"At least we don't have to worry about our footsteps," High Elf Archer said lightly. Maybe that remark was part of why Priestess found herself breathing a sigh of relief. The air in the tunnel suddenly seemed to grow lighter.

"And it doesn't look like we need to worry about them breaking out of a wall behind us," Dwarf Shaman remarked.

"If there are no hidden doors," Goblin Slayer said.

"And if they don't find the corpses outside," Lizard Priest added helpfully.

"Let's keep going," Priestess said in a trembling voice, swallowing audibly. *"Carefully."*

"Yes. Especially considering that… What was it called…?"

"Mokele Mubenbe," High Elf Archer chimed in as she measured her next footstep. "Right?"

"Yes, that," Goblin Slayer continued, nodding. "Something managed to put a saddle on that. We can't let down our guard."

Lizard Priest gripped his Swordclaw tighter, looking around. "You think it was one of the little devils?"

"Would anyone entrust a dragon to goblins, besides a goblin?"

Dwarf Shaman ran his hand gently along the wall of the passageway. "I've known philistines, but goblins set a new low," he said with a resigned shake of his head. "Look at this. There were these drawings right here, and they—"

The illustrations might have depicted the history of the ruins, or perhaps they were a warning to intruders. Whatever the drawings had once been, they were now daubed over and cracked by the antics of the goblins. It suggested the defacement was not a deliberate act of blasphemy on the goblins' part. If they had really been servants of Chaos trying to desecrate the marks of Order, they would have done a more thorough job.

Instead, the scene was shattered here, painted over there, broken in another place, and left alone in still another...

"...Like children who got bored of a toy," Priestess whispered, chilled. And well she should be: it was clear that this act of the destruction of someone else's labors had been done for the sheer fun of it. Priestess knew all too well what that impulse looked like when it was turned upon living beings.

"..."

It might have been dread or anxiety that made her trembling right hand stiffen upon her sounding staff, while the left adjusted her hold on the torch. She repeated the name of the Earth Mother under her breath.

Perhaps that was why she was the first to notice it when it came blowing on the breeze through the ruins, mixed with the sound of water.

"A voice...?" she said suddenly, stopping.

"What's wrong?" Goblin Slayer asked when he noticed. That fact alone brought Priestess a measure of relief. It was a reminder that he was looking out for her. That all of them were.

She realized she was unconsciously comparing the party to *them* and looked down, abashed.

"I just... There was a voice..."

"You heard a voice?"

"From up ahead, I think..."

Goblin Slayer met her uncertain words with a grunt. "Hmm. What do you think?"

"Well, hold on a second. I've been totally focused on this floor…"
High Elf Archer looked up, her ears now standing straight, straining
to pick up any sound.

Fwip, fwip. They fluttered gently.

"…Yeah, I hear it, too. A person's voice. I can't tell if it's a man or a
woman."

"So there's something alive down here besides goblins," Dwarf Shaman said, frowning in surprise. "I suppose we should be happy, but
it'll add to our troubles to rescue them."

"There's no guarantee it is a prisoner," Lizard Priest added, rolling
his eyes and touching the tip of his nose with his tongue.

"But if there is a captive down here…" Priestess raised the torch
as high as she could, as if using it to wave away fear and indecision.
"Then we…we have to help them…!"

"Yes," Goblin Slayer replied without a moment's hesitation. He
double-checked his shield in his left hand, then turned his right wrist
once and adjusted his hold on his sword. "It doesn't change what we
must do. Let's go."

Shortly after, the party arrived at a spiral staircase that stretched
from the very bottom to the very top of the ruins. Countless tunnels
spiderwebbed away from it in every direction.

The echoing voice could be heard from down below—far, far below,
as if sounding from the depths of hell.

§

"…Smells like a goblin nest, all right."

The party decided to work its way down the stairwell, following the
lead of High Elf Archer's senses.

The staircase hugged the stone wall, winding down into the depths.
The steps were narrow, and there was no railing. Each of them placed
a hand on the wall and proceeded slowly, oh so slowly.

"Rather like an anthill, isn't it," Lizard Priest said, observing the
many tunnels that led deeper into the fortress.

"Mmm, they make pretty good towers, don't they?" Dwarf Shaman replied.

The levees and the riverside fortifications had been withstanding battles for at least an eon. They would shortly be attempting to bring it all down with just five adventurers. One could hardly blame them for feeling a little tense.

"Eep!" Priestess squeezed her eyes shut and leaned against the wall as a sudden gust whipped through the atrium. The strength of the wind was bad enough, but it brought a rank stench that hinted at evil things ahead.

"M-maybe we should tie a lifeline to ourselves so—"

"No," Goblin Slayer said, brusquely rejecting Priestess's idea. "We are in single file. We don't know if goblins may come from in front or behind."

"Yes, it could only be dangerous to restrict our own movements further." Lizard Priest, making up the rear of the formation, rolled his eyes in his head and slapped the ground with his tail. "But never fear; if you should fall, just grab on to my tail and keep going."

"I'd really rather not fall, but… Right, I'll do my best." Priestess nodded, making sure she was holding her staff and the torch tightly so as not to drop them.

At that moment, High Elf Archer's ears twitched.

"Goblins?"

"What else could it be?" The whole party stopped dead behind her and readied their weapons. "We've got a light. They'll notice us when we get close."

"We can't let him get away alive."

"Goblin Slayer, sir, what should we do?"

"Whether there's a captive down there or not, we must get to the bottom of this staircase," Goblin Slayer said darkly. "And then, we must come back up."

"You know what they say about labyrinths," Dwarf Shaman chimed in, adopting a singsong tone: "*Going in is easy done, but getting out is never fun.*"

"Mm," Lizard Priest rumbled, nodding.

"We won't be able to avoid combat," Priestess said, "and if we're discovered—"

—what would happen then?

The blood drained from her cheeks, and she suddenly felt her footing become unsteady.

Torn clothes. Fighter's screaming. Shouting voices. The awful sight of the captured elf. The women on skewers.

All of these memories flashed through her mind, quickening her breath. She felt her teeth chattering.

She fought to keep them still and to steady her breathing. She forced her legs, which threatened to go out from under her, to remain upright.

"...I'll try requesting Silence again."

She would use another of her precious miracles. Goblin Slayer did some quick mental calculations.

"If all goes well, we may be able to rest when we reach the bottom," Dwarf Shaman said as he reached into his bag of catalysts, looking vigilantly down the seemingly never-ending stairs. "This place has got to be too big to patrol everywhere at once, even for goblins."

"How many would you say we are dealing with, milord Goblin Slayer, based on what they have stolen?"

"They even have wolves," Goblin Slayer replied. "There's no doubt they're operating on a massive scale."

"Still, surely not enough t'maintain this entire fortification."

"Most likely."

"Well, that settles it." High Elf Archer smiled brightly, reaching out to pat Priestess on the shoulder. "You're up!"

"Right!" Priestess nodded and bit her lip. She knew what would happen if they didn't do this. She gave her head a vigorous shake, sending the memories flying like the hair around her head. Then she took a deep breath.

She put both hands on her staff, connecting her soul to the Earth Mother who dwelt on high.

"What about the corpse?" Lizard Priest inquired.

"Drop it," Goblin Slayer replied immediately, ruthlessly. "There would be nothing unusual about a goblin falling from these stairs."

"Here I go!" Priestess held her staff, relaxing into the warmth of the torch as she offered up the words of her prayer. *"O Earth Mother, abounding in mercy, grant us peace to accept all things."*

Then all sound ceased.

The goblin emerging from the corridor went wide-eyed at the adventuring party that approached with nothing but the light of a torch.

High Elf Archer's arrow pierced his throat before he could call out to his companions. He windmilled his arms as if swimming through the air as he toppled forward; Goblin Slayer gave him a solid kick.

The goblin fell, disappearing into the endless, deep blackness.

As they continued down the stairs, High Elf Archer swiveled her ears. It was hard to be certain what she was hearing. She kept her eyes peeled, trying to spot any goblins that might be coming their way.

There.

She quickly held up three fingers on one hand before drawing an arrow from her quiver, pulling back the bow, and firing.

The bolt flew silently, catching the spear-wielding sentry square in the eye and lodging in his helmet. He spun and toppled from the staircase.

His fellow guard pointed and laughed then cocked his head in surprise at the fact that his voice made no sound. High Elf Archer rushed past him, while just behind her, Goblin Slayer cracked the creature's skull as if he were splitting wood.

The head broke open and brains spilled out. Goblin Slayer sent the second goblin tumbling into the abyss then continued forward.

The third goblin, although flabbergasted at these sudden developments, nonetheless steadied the spear in his hand.

He was faced with a dwarf and a human girl. It only took him an instant to focus on the girl, but he found his path blocked by the palm of the dwarf's hand. Before he knew what was happening, there was a handful of dust in his eyes, and an instant later, Lizard Priest's tail had swept his feet out from under him.

All that was left was the drop.

The corkscrew-shaped tunnel continued on and on. One could feel faint contemplating its scale.

All sound had vanished, and the only thing they could see was the light they carried. They smelled only bubbling water and their own sweat.

Priestess wobbled, attacked by a spell of dizziness. Even as she registered what was happening, she found her unsteady body wrapped in Lizard Priest's supportive tail.

She gave a hurried look back. The lizardman rolled his eyes in his head and touched his tongue to his nose. He seemed to be saying, *Don't worry about it.*

Priestess shook her head, then she faced forward again with the torch and her staff well in hand and began diligently following the back in front of her. Dwarf Shaman had kindly slowed down for her. Goblin Slayer and High Elf Archer remained as vigilant as ever.

I have to keep praying...!

She made a couple of sharp exhalations as she forced all irrelevant thought from her mind and continued offering her supplication to the Earth Mother.

She was just standing behind her companions, praying. She started to doubt if it was really helpful.

But doubt led to death at times like this. And she would not let it overcome her prayer to the gods.

Everyone is here, and I'm with everyone. They protect me, and I protect them.

She took another deep breath.

Even in these dark depths, she had friends beside her, and her soul was in touch with the Earth Mother who abided in heaven.

Surely there was nothing to fear.

§

Bob, bob. Five or six goblin corpses drifted on the surface of the water.

At the bottom of the vast span was a channel of water. Was it the Silence miracle, or sheer distance, that prevented the adventurers from hearing any sound as the goblins struck the surface?

Dammed up and then stored up, what remained of the river water continued to course downstream.

"Perhaps the little devils think to poison the water," Lizard Priest whispered when sound resumed in the world. Considering they had dammed up the river, that would be the natural next step. Downstream lay not only the elf village, but also the water town.

"Goblins being goblins, their leader might be planning something," Dwarf Shaman agreed.

"What's the use, thinking about what goblins think all the time?" High Elf Archer said, frowning in frustration. She gave Goblin Slayer's helmet a couple of good raps. "You'll end up like him."

"I have a sneaking suspicion y'could stand to think a little harder yourself," Dwarf Shaman said. *"This is about your home, after all,"* he added softly, provoking an angry "Come again?!" from the elf. They managed to keep their voices low enough that Lizard Priest didn't feel compelled to intervene.

Goblin Slayer, completely unmoved, pulled a waterskin from his item pouch and uncorked it. He took several swigs through his visor then offered it to Priestess where she crouched nearby. She took it vacantly, her face pale as she desperately tried to collect herself.

"Drink."

"Uh, r-right, thanks…"

"No," Goblin Slayer said, shaking his head. "You helped us."

Priestess held the waterskin in both hands, bringing it to her lips with just a hint of embarrassment. She had the slightest, shiest smile on her face. She wasn't so tense now, and that wasn't a bad thing.

They had gotten over one hurdle. One thing at a time.

She drank noisily, two mouthfuls, three. Then she let out a satisfied breath and put the stopper back in the waterskin.

"Thank you very much," she said, handing it back; he took it silently and returned it to his pouch.

Goblin Slayer used his hatchet to pull one of the bobbing corpses closer, taking the sword from its belt. He put the blade into his own scabbard, put the hatchet in the goblin's belt instead, and then kicked it away again.

"The voice has stopped," he murmured.

High Elf Archer's ears flicked. "Yeah." She nodded. "I wasn't sure one way or the other on the way down, but now I feel like I don't hear it anymore."

"We were too late."

High Elf Archer, catching his meaning, frowned. She quickly checked the state of her bowstring, retied it, then made sure she had some arrows as she got to her feet. "…That's no excuse to dawdle, is it?"

"Indeed, even so," Lizard Priest agreed, giving his Swordclaw a flourish. "We have come here for battle, and our foe quails before us. We have no reason not to press our advantage."

He held out a bumpy, scaled hand to Priestess.

"I'm all right," she said with a brief smile then hefted herself to her feet, supporting herself with her staff. "Oh, the torch…"

"…Mm," Goblin Slayer said, finally turning his head slowly from side to side. "I'll let you handle it."

Priestess secretly let out a sigh to see him once again striding boldly at the head of their line. But shortly thereafter, registering that she had been left in charge of their light, she nodded resolutely.

"Hold this for a moment, please," she said, passing the torch to Dwarf Shaman. Then she took a lantern out of her luggage and transferred the flame to it.

"Well, aren't you well prepared!"

"A lantern is a must on an adventure," she replied, puffing out her chest with just a hint of pride.

The Adventurer's Toolkit was a package that didn't always come in as handy as it looked like it would, but this time it was proving its worth. She closed the shutter to avoid letting out more light than was necessary then tossed the torch in the river with a little "Yah!" There was a hiss and some white smoke, and then the torch was no more.

"…Okay, let's go."

The rest of the party nodded, and then they followed after Goblin Slayer, taking care to make as little noise as possible.

Thankfully, the sound of the river helped to cover them.

Goblin Slayer spoke softly to High Elf Archer in the murk. "How is it in front?"

"They're there." She dropped her hips like a hare about to run, but she kept moving quickly forward. "There seems to be some kind of… big millstone or mortar? Along with five…maybe six of them, enjoying themselves."

"No spells," Goblin Slayer said, shifting his sword in his right hand. "We'll take care of them."

"But…" Lizard Priest licked his nose with his tongue. "How do you mean to attack?"

"Silence again?" High Elf Archer offered, adding to herself *I'd be okay with that* as she drew an arrow.

Goblin Slayer glanced at Priestess, whose face was bloodless, and shook his head. "We will do something else."

"I'm f-fine…!"

"I do not want to use the same tactic twice in a row," he said, reaching into his bag. "Do we have any glue?"

"Right 'ere. Bunches of it. Hang on a second," Dwarf Shaman said, digging into his own bag of catalysts. At length, he nodded and produced several small, sealed bottles.

"Good," Goblin Slayer said immediately. "Everyone, give me your socks."

Priestess pressed a hand to her thigh, suddenly red-faced; High Elf Archer just looked confused. "What do you want with those?" she asked.

"I will use them."

Lizard Priest nodded somberly. "Do you want mine as well?"

"If you have any."

§

The goblin had finished his work and was in high spirits. He'd not often been drunk, but he had the feeling that this was what it felt like.

Stolen alcohol all too rarely made it to him—the bottles had always been drunk dry long before they reached this far down. He had some doubts about whether the boys upstairs were portioning the goods out fairly, but that was goblins for you. They never thought about their other comrades, who would come after them, but each took a little extra for himself, and before you knew it, it was all gone.

But this magnanimous underground goblin would forgive them.

Not because he knew he would have done the same thing if he were on one of the higher floors—nothing so reasonable. He was content to be enraged at the thoughtless bastards up above, quite irrespective of the fact that he would have behaved just like them.

No, the reason he felt so lenient was because working on the lowest floor had its own benefits.

With a casual gesture, the goblin adjusted the decoration hanging from a chain around his neck. Then he sat heavily in a circle of his fellows and reached for the food at the center.

He popped a finger off the rotting arm and tossed it into his mouth. He chewed then took a breath.

Working down here is the worst, he said, trying to sound good even as he complained.

There was a chorus of agreement from the others, then somebody tore off a leg from the meal.

Somebody else, unable to let this pass, raised a fuss and tried to take the leg, until it was finally torn in two, and the aggrieved party had some for himself.

As they chewed their meat, the goblins whined that the higher-ups didn't understand.

One of them plucked a lovely amber-colored eyeball from the meal, commented, *They sure as hell don't,* then swallowed it.

The goblins' complaints got louder and louder, but of course, the work they were asked to do was not all that demanding. It was simply the way of goblins to be convinced that others had it easier than they did.

After a lazy meal, the goblins hefted themselves to their feet. They collectively agreed that a rhea didn't make as good a meal as an elf, and an elf wasn't as tasty as a human.

Now their stomachs were good and full, and it seemed to them that there was nothing else to do but have a little nap until more work needed to be done.

The goblin gave a great yawn, when—

"—?"

Well, now.

What was this rolling up to his feet? An extinguished torch?

What the hell? The goblin looked stupidly at it.

"?!"

A second later, something heavy and wet struck him in the face. He tried to cry out, but another one hit him, this time in the mouth.

He reached up to peel it off, but his hand stuck to it, and he couldn't get free.

"GROBB!!"

"GRB! GBBOROB!!"

As he tumbled to the ground, the other goblins pointed and laughed at him. They had similarly ridiculed the goblins who'd come plummeting from the staircase earlier that day.

"GBOROB?!"

This time, the things smacked the laughing goblins. Two more of them were clawing at their faces, writhing in pain. Three in total.

The other two finally realized that this was not the time for mirth and drew their stolen swords.

One of them put something that looked like an alarm whistle to his lips—

"One."

—and promptly found his throat pierced by a dagger that came flying from the dark. Blood gushed from the wound with a sound not unlike a whistle.

"GOBBRB?!"

Cutting through the sound came an adventurer in grimy armor, rushing at them from downriver. In his right hand was a sword. In his left, a shield. The goblin's eyes were wide. Adventurer! Hate! This was him!

"GBRO! GGBORROB!!"

He forgot all thought of either calling his comrades or helping them but, instead, shuffled in to fight. His sword was a well-honed thing he'd just recently stolen from an adventurer. It was no rusty knife.

"Hmph."

Goblin Slayer, however, caught the blow easily on his shield. Beat it back, in fact. He caught the monster's overeager swing, which lodged in his shield; he backed up then made a sweep.

"GOBBR?!"

The goblin lost his footing and fell heavily then got unsteadily back to his feet.

Immediately after that, he was aware of a *thump*. And then the goblin stopped breathing, without ever knowing why.

He would never have imagined it was because a bud-tipped arrow had lodged itself in the back of his head anyway.

He tumbled forward, his lifeless eyes no longer perceiving what was happening to his companions.

"GOBB... GRB?!"

"GROBBR?!"

The other goblins, having finally peeled the sticky globs away from their faces and mouths, could hardly speak.

An instant later, Lizard Priest's Swordclaw cleaved torso from legs, and Goblin Slayer pierced a throat.

Dispatching five goblins had taken only ten or twenty seconds. That was experience for you.

"Three... And four, and five." Goblin Slayer counted up the corpses then turned back to the darkness. "That was an impressive hit."

"I've been practicing." Priestess pattered out of the dark, holding her sounding staff. A shy expression came over her face at Goblin Slayer's simple praise. Yes, the creature had been distracted by the torch, but she had hit him fair and square, the result of her own hard work.

She picked up the prepared sock the goblin had torn off its face and thrown aside. "...Ugh. I guess I can't use this anymore...," she said disappointedly. There was blood and drool and snot all over it. She could put it through the wash three times and still not want to wear it again.

"Put rocks in our socks, cover them with glue, and then throw them at the goblins?" High Elf Archer, who had also supplied her footwear for the cause, was retrieving her arrow from one of the corpses. "I swear, you have the imagination of a mischievous little boy."

"But it worked," Goblin Slayer said shortly, turning toward the half-eaten body.

It was such a mass of gore that it was impossible even to tell what gender it had been, until he picked up a blue-colored status tag from the mess. It was a man.

"Wonder if he had a family," Dwarf Shaman said, glancing over and taking the bloodstained chip of sapphire. "Or a party... Doubt he was solo."

"Most likely," Goblin Slayer said, turning his head and casting his eye over the tools the goblins had used for their "work."

High Elf Archer poked at one of them with a *what's this* look, before she realized what she was seeing and jumped back. "Eek?!"

It was a millstone—or more accurately, a press. Turning a round handle caused the device to move, applying pressure to whatever was inside it. It was the sort of thing that might be used to get oil from olives, or juice from grapes. So what had the goblins been pressing with it?

The answer was immediately apparent.

"Ergh... Ah...!" Priestess made little gasping sounds and nearly dropped her staff.

In the crevices of the machine could be seen slim hands and feet, still twitching with the last vestiges of life. They belonged to a young woman whose glassy eyes were staring skyward, her tongue lolling out of her mouth.

This made frightfully clear what the goblins had been attempting to press, and how. As a mode of torture, it was crude. As a means of execution, it was beyond sadistic.

No.

Priestess quickly grasped what it all signified.

The pile of battered female armor in the corner.

The polished short sword Goblin Slayer had collected from the goblin.

The sapphire level tag that had been hanging from the neck of one of the corpses.

The muscles in the arm that now hung limp.

All of it showed that the young woman had been an adventurer.

And led to one inescapable conclusion: the goblins had been doing this simply for fun.

"..."

It was a nauseating scene, but although pale, Priestess gulped the bitter fluid back down.

Maybe—unfortunately—she had gotten used to this sort of thing. Maybe it was just something she had to get used to. She didn't know.

As she crouched, praying to the Earth Mother, a thick, sticky liquid plopped against the ground, spoiling her white boots.

The blackish-red substance the goblins had been squeezing out with their device dribbled into a gutter along the floor and, from there, into the river.

"Hmm," Lizard Priest said, rolling his eyes. "If they are putting this into the river, mightn't it be some kind of poison?"

"It very well may." Goblin Slayer crouched and scooped up a small sample of the sticky stuff, rubbing it between his fingers. Though it was only a tiny drop in the massive river, it was probably enough to be fatal to an individual. "It's like they were thinking 'you've all been drinking, living, and bathing with water full of the blood and excrement of your fellows.'"

"Hrr—ghh…" High Elf Archer immediately retched. Priestess was quick to offer her the waterskin, but she replied, "No thanks."

"I suppose, then, that we should consider this a form of curse," Lizard Priest said.

"So you think so, too?" Goblin Slayer breathed. "That…thing…"

"Mokele Mubenbe, you mean?"

"Yes, that." Goblin Slayer nodded. "This must mean that the one who captured it was some kind of spell caster."

"And a goblin…" Priestess shivered.

A dark cave. Collapsed women. And a goblin shaman jabbering upon his throne.

All of it matched up with memories burned into her mind. She gripped her staff tighter.

"…shaman?"

"Whoever it is, he's nothing to sneeze at," Dwarf Shaman muttered, regarding Goblin Slayer and Lizard Priest. "I'm surprised you're both so calm…"

"It is not the way of my people to keep a captive alive for our pleasure, but killing is our vocation." Lizard Priest shook his head slowly from side to side, almost contemplatively. "It is considered proper custom to split open the guts of a superlative warrior and eat their heart."

"Me, I think it'll be a couple of days before I want meat again," Dwarf Shaman groaned.

"That's dwarves for you," High Elf Archer said with a brave laugh.

Goblin Slayer looked at Dwarf Shaman and nodded. Then he

walked over to Priestess with his typical bold stride and looked down at her.

"Goblin Slayer, sir, uh…"

"We will stop here," he said slowly. "When she has been buried, we will rest."

§

They ultimately decided to give the crushed, smashed corpse of the adventurer a burial at sea.

They wrapped the body in a cloth to hide its wounds then set it afloat in the canal leading to the river.

"O Earth Mother, abounding in mercy, please, by your revered hand, guide the soul of one who has left this world."

Priestess's prayer saw the woman's soul to heaven, and Lizard Priest's invocation ensured that she could rejoin the cycle of life.

They didn't expect any patrols to come looking down here at the bottom of the tower (goblins being lazy as they were), so the party found the cleanest spot they could, spread out some blankets, and went to sleep.

Sleep… They would be lucky to get a few hours at most. It might not really restore much of their strength. What was important, though, was that their spell casters would regain the spiritual energy they had expended.

"……" Goblin Slayer leaned against the wall of the torture room, hugging the sword he'd taken. He didn't want to light a fire, partly because of the elven wards on this place, but mostly because he didn't want the smoke to alert anyone to their presence. Instead, the party took what rest they could gathered around the lantern, its shutters closed to keep the light at a minimum.

Lizard Priest sat in the lotus posture, his hands formed into mudras and his eyes closed, as if meditating. Dwarf Shaman had taken a few good swigs of wine then flopped over, rested his head on his hands, and was soon snoring lustily.

Then there was Priestess, her small blanket-clad body huddled in a corner. Even from this distance, her face looked bloodless and pale.

"…Why aren't you asleep?" a voice asked him suddenly.

"I am resting," Goblin Slayer replied casually.

It was High Elf Archer, back from her shift on guard duty, standing in front of him and looking irritated.

Goblin Slayer lifted his helmet slowly, looking up at her. "With one eye open."

"Hey, I can't see how many eyes you've got in there," she replied in annoyance. She put her hands on her hips and snorted, her long ears twitching, then sat down heavily next to him. It was such a natural movement; she didn't look to Goblin Slayer for any kind of permission.

"She didn't look very happy, huh?" High Elf Archer loosened the string on her bow then industriously started retying it.

"I imagine," Goblin Slayer said from beside her. "If we only consider our actions, we are exactly like the goblins."

He was referring strictly to having given the bodies of their companions over to the river.

They had been too late—whether it was by minutes, hours, or days. Otherwise, perhaps one or two of the captured adventurers might still have been alive.

Never, at no time, could this have turned out like what had happened at that temple, with those nuns.

"They perished, and we threw them in the river. It's the same," Goblin Slayer concluded curtly.

High Elf Archer bit her lip for a moment, not quite able to speak, then shook her head in disagreement. "…It's not the same."

Goblin Slayer gave a quiet, annoyed grunt.

"We aren't like the goblins. And if you say we are again, I'm gonna get mad." She glared at him from lidded eyes.

"I might even kick you," she muttered, and she sounded serious.

Goblin Slayer remembered the time, in some ruins somewhere, when she had given him a serious kick. It had been about a year before. He even felt a certain nostalgia for it.

But how much time was that for an elf?

"I see." Goblin Slayer nodded. Then he heaved a deep sigh. "…You are right."

"You better believe I am."

With that, the two of them stopped talking. The idyllic gurgle of running water sounded out of place. But every once in a while, there would come the cackling of goblins from upstairs, reminding them of where they really were.

High Elf Archer's ears fluttered. Goblin Slayer glanced over at her, but she shook her head as if to say it was nothing.

"I see," Goblin Slayer breathed then lapsed once more into silence.

"Hmm?" High Elf Archer said, tilting her head, but his helmet barely moved as he spoke just two words in response.

"I'm sorry."

High Elf Archer found herself blinking.

Did Orcbolg just...apologize?

It was an unusual occurrence. To hide the sudden smile threatening to take over her face, she produced a studied frown and asked brusquely, "...For what?"

"...In the end, I brought up goblins again."

Dummy. High Elf Archer giggled. Like the rushing water, it seemed like a sound too sweet for this place.

"Whaaat? Is *that* what was bothering you?"

There was no answer.

They had only known each other for a year and change, but that was plenty of time in which to get to know someone.

I hit the nail on the head.

High Elf Archer laughed with a sound like a ringing bell then set her great bow gently on the floor beside her. She hugged her knees to her chest and then rested her head on Goblin Slayer's shoulder.

"You know me... I'm not a big fan of goblin slaying."

That simply made sense.

Back before she'd met Orcbolg, even back when she'd been just a Porcelain, she had never gone on a goblin-hunting quest. But the number of such jobs she had undertaken had increased dramatically since she started working with him.

She didn't have any problem with exploring caves. And fighting monsters was all well and good. Rescuing captives, that was great, too.

But this is just different.

Facing goblins with Orcbolg somehow wasn't the same as other adventures. There was no sense of accomplishment. High Elf Archer could hardly even bring herself to call them adventures.

But still.

"My home is at stake."

It was perfectly obvious, but she voiced the thought anyway.

She felt more than saw Goblin Slayer's helmet shift.

High Elf Archer closed her eyes for a moment. The smell of oil and blood. It truly was a terrible stench.

"I'd hate for my sister to get married with goblins lolling around nearby."

"...I see."

"Normally, I'd be the one doing all the complaining... Hey, I mean, not that I'm really upset or anything."

"No," Goblin Slayer said, shaking his head. "It doesn't bother me."

"No?" High Elf Archer cocked her head in surprise. Her ears fluttered.

"No," Goblin Slayer repeated shortly. "Because I don't know how to go about having an adventure."

"*Huh*," High Elf Archer whispered, and Goblin Slayer breathed back, "*It's true.*"

"Okay, well," High Elf Archer started, sounding almost as if she were singing. "How about we say we're square?" She held up a pointer finger and moved it in a circle in the air.

"I think—" Goblin Slayer was about to answer, but then he hesitated. He never quite found the words he wanted, and finally, his answer was as dispassionate as ever. "That's fine."

"Great!" High Elf Archer sprang to her feet. She gave a huge yawn, like a cat, gently stretching her lithe body. She let out a long breath then asked, "So what do we do next?"

Goblin Slayer replied immediately, "We set a trap then head up."

"A trap?" Her eyes glittered, and her ears waved.

"You'll understand very soon." Goblin Slayer made it sound like it would be incredibly bothersome. High Elf Archer just snorted. *Fine, then.*

"But...now we're going back up?"

"We are dealing with goblins who have set themselves up in this building. I have a fair idea of what they must be thinking."

"——?"

"The most important of them will base himself either on the highest or the lowest level."

"Ahh."

Now it made sense. High Elf Archer nodded, smiling. The worst villains liked the tallest places.

"The only problem is that...thing."

"Mokele Mubenbe?" High Elf Archer sighed again. "I can't believe you haven't remembered its name by now."

"...Whoever is capable of controlling that beast is probably a spell caster."

"A spell caster... Hmm."

High Elf Archer crossed her arms, looking very High Elf Archer-ish, but she quickly abandoned contemplation. Thinking about it now wouldn't get them any answers. They could think about it when the time came.

Anyway, it can be a goblin shaman or a goblin whatever, I'm still just gonna shoot it.

"Won't we just figure it out when we get there?"

"That won't do," Goblin Slayer said with a decisive shake of his head.

High Elf Archer shook her own head, as if to say, *You're hopeless.* "Yes, it will. But you're our only front row specialist. Right now, the most important thing is for you to get some sleep, Orcbolg."

"...Yes."

"With *both* eyes closed."

"...I will try."

"I'll wake you up in a bit."

"Thanks."

"Yeah, well, otherwise I won't get to sleep."

"All right."

High Elf Archer gave him a reassuring wave of her hand then grabbed her bow in her fingers. She bounded easily from one of the sleepers to the next, to check on them, then finally sat down in a spot of her own in one corner of the room.

Beside her was Priestess, wrapped up in her blanket. High Elf Archer gave her a gentle pat. The blanket shifted, then shook, then fell still again.

You could pull the covers up as far as you wanted, but you couldn't hide how you were feeling from the senses of an elf.

§

"Man, why couldn't the ancients have installed an elevator?"

Several hours later, after taking care of a few details, the party had begun climbing the staircase.

High Elf Archer had good reason to complain. They had just come down these stairs the day before, and now they were being forced to hike up them again. The change in direction was cold comfort.

"C-careful not to talk so loud...!"

Someone will hear you. Priestess's concern was equally natural, and with nowhere to run, if any goblins appeared, they would be forced to fight.

The party hadn't changed their formation since before breaking to rest (when—yesterday? Her sense of time was fuzzy), but still...

"Well," Dwarf Shaman said, "it's a big fortress. There might be one if we look." He was breathing heavily. It seemed his small frame made the climb most difficult of all for him. He took the jug of wine from his belt and unstoppered it, taking a few swigs and then wiping some droplets from his beard. "But after all the work I've just done, yours truly has no interest in scrounging around for an elevator."

"As well, it may require some key to activate. One with a blue strap, for instance."

"Aarrgh...!" High Elf Archer cried, flapping her ears angrily. Lizard Priest's calm remark made three voices against her. "Orcbolg, say something!"

"If we found one, we would use it, but we have no time to search."

No help there. High Elf Archer, abandoned, simply harrumphed and kept walking up the stairs.

Each and every one of them was totally vigilant. Even Priestess, watching her staff uneasily, kept an eye on their surroundings. She kept throwing little glances behind herself—no doubt a product of her worst memories.

They might come from behind.

They might break through the wall when you least expected it.

Were there any hidden doors? They hadn't missed any, had they?

"Oops...," High Elf Archer said, and Priestess shivered.

"Wh— What's wrong?"

"The stairs are missing."

"Oh..." She could see that High Elf Archer was right. Just ahead of them, the spiral of stairs was interrupted by several broken steps.

They could conceivably jump the gap—but only if they didn't think for a second about what would happen should they fall. They could hear water echoing up from far, far below.

If they could catch themselves on the next stairs down, that would be one thing, but if not, the drop would surely kill them. If they were lucky, it would do so instantaneously. But if not, they might simply break their legs and have to lie there, waiting to die. Either way, it would be the end of their adventure.

Did the goblins go around this gap somehow, or were the rash tests continuing?

"I don't see any guards," Goblin Slayer murmured. "If it were still noon, I would understand, but I don't like this."

"I think the bigger problem is what to do about this staircase," High Elf Archer said, frowning. She stuck up her thumb, trying to eyeball the distance. "I could jump that gap, but I don't think all of us could. Such as the dwarf, the dwarf, or the dwarf."

"Listen, you..."

That was about as far as Dwarf Shaman's response went, though. High Elf Archer crossed her arms and made a thoughtful sound. "Maybe we could string a rope from one side to the other," she said. "We could take the long way around, but we don't have time, do we?"

"That's perfect," Priestess said, nodding. "I'll get some out!" She dug through her bag, quickly producing a grappling hook. The Adventurer's Toolkit. She was very pleased that the set, which she had bought "just in case," was coming in handy. What was more, the greatest comfort of all to her was to know she was making herself useful to the party.

"Do you think this will reach?" she asked.

"Try it," Goblin Slayer said.

Answering "Right," High Elf Archer grabbed the rope and took a light-footed leap. Her agility could have been matched only by a select number of padfoots or dark elves.

She landed on the far side of the gap with a movement reminiscent of a leaping deer, muttering "Whoop" as she carefully maintained her balance. "You just need me to set this, right?"

"Yes." Goblin Slayer nodded and picked up the rope on his side. "So we are to tie this to our belts and jump...?"

"If I miss the other side, I'm gonna have t'use a spell," Dwarf Shaman said, looking into the pit with a disturbed expression. "Much as I hate to have to do it, in light of our strategic needs... What about you, Scaly?"

"Ahh, so long as there are handholds and footholds on the walls, I shall muddle through." Lizard Priest displayed the sharp claws on his hands and feet, twirling his fingers deliberately. "I should rather worry, master spell caster, about our lady Priestess jumping across. Perhaps it would be best if I carried her."

"One at a time, then," Goblin Slayer said. "Will you be all right?"

"Oh yes!" Priestess was the first to take the proffered rope. With a grunt, she tied it carefully and tightly around her narrow hips, then she wedged her sounding staff between the rope and the small of her back so she wouldn't drop it.

"O-okay, please don't d-drop me...!"

"Mm. You're quite light. Here, now..."

Lizard Priest, with Priestess clinging to his back, dug his claws into the rock wall and hefted himself bodily up.

"Eep?!"

"Hold tight, now. *O Velociraptor, see my deeds!*"

What happened next was indeed something to behold. Working the claws of his hands and feet into the cracks among the stones, Lizard Priest began to crawl deftly across the gap.

As impressive as he was, however, he was not quick; if there had been an archer waiting somewhere on the spiral staircase, he would have made an excellent target. Goblin Slayer and High Elf Archer both looked deep into the darkness, keeping their eyes open for just such a threat.

When they arrived on the far side a moment later, Priestess gave Lizard Priest a respectful nod. "S-sorry for the trouble. And thank you…"

"No need to thank me. Indeed, I believe you could do with a little extra meat on your bones."

"I—I'll try…," she said, slightly embarrassed. Lizard Priest grinned confirmation, then he took the rope from her and made the return trip. Next, he came carrying Dwarf Shaman, and after he was satisfied they had all made it across, Goblin Slayer jumped the gap. In his full armor and chain mail, he was without a doubt carrying the most weight among them, but he made it with room to spare.

Still, when he wobbled upon landing, Priestess was quick to put a hand on his arm to steady him. "A-are you okay?"

"Yes," Goblin Slayer said with a nod then added a moment later, "I'm fine."

"Man, I wish *I* coulda gotten carried across," High Elf Archer piped up.

"Ha! Ha! Ha! Well, perhaps there will yet be another chance," Lizard Priest chortled.

"I'm gonna hold you to that!" High Elf Archer said, but then she suddenly stopped. "Hey, look, there it is! There's an elevator!"

"Hmm," Goblin Slayer said with considerable interest as he shuffled over to inspect the device.

It had a pair of double doors that rolled back into the walls, with what appeared to be a control panel just beside them. Just the sort of thing, he realized, that one often found in ruins like this.

"Have the goblins been using it?" he wondered aloud.

"Good question," Dwarf Shaman said. "Can't say for certain…"

"It does appear to be in working order. But… Hmm, what's this?" Lizard Priest, probing the control panel with a clawed finger, discovered a keypad. It contained squares with numbers in them, apparently waiting to be pressed. "So it functions not with a key, but a code."

"Ah!" Priestess, seeing the pad, clapped her hands and began rifling through her luggage.

She came up with the key she had taken from the goblin at the entrance to the fort. It was a gold plate with numbers carved on it and a rope like a necklace.

"How about this? At first, I thought maybe the keys were individually numbered, but…"

"Yeah, goblins would never do bookkeeping like that," High Elf Archer said with a shrug, and Goblin Slayer agreed. So there was no question now.

"Try it."

"Yes, sir!" Holding the gold chip, Priestess carefully entered the three digits on the keypad.

They felt the slightest shiver as something deep and far away groaned, then finally, there was a screech as the machine came to a stop.

The elevator doors opened silently.

"Looks like I had the right idea," Priestess said, brushing a hand across her small chest with a sigh of relief.

The inside of the elevator was a stone box, just like the outside. It wasn't obvious whether the elevator moved magically or mechanically, but…

"At the very least, there is nothing here so simple that the goblins can operate it," Goblin Slayer replied, looking around the interior and using his sword like a pole to poke and prod. "However, I have seen them use buckets in wells."

"That's enough to give me the shivers." *Stop it already.* High Elf Archer waved her hand. She didn't want to imagine the possibility of the device being cut loose while they were riding on it, sending them plummeting to the bottom.

"…Let's go," Priestess urged, decision in her tone, clutching her staff. This in spite of the touch of pallor in her face, an unmistakable tightness in her expression, and the slightest of trembling in her hands. "We have to…stop the goblins…"

That was a declaration that got an immediate response from Goblin Slayer. "Yes."

Priestess's expression softened ever so slightly.

Goblin Slayer looked around at his party.

High Elf Archer was puffing out her modest chest as if to say that of course she was ready.

Dwarf Shaman was searching through his catalysts nonchalantly.

Lizard Priest made a strange palms-together gesture with his hands and rolled his eyes.

Goblin Slayer searched each face then checked his own shield, armor, helmet, and sword.

No problems.

Their plan was in place.

There was only one thing to do.

"We will kill all the goblins."

The adventurers all nodded at one another then climbed into the elevator.

"I'm assuming this thing goes up," High Elf Archer said, "but this could get ugly real fast."

"It could." Goblin Slayer nodded.

The edges of the elf's lips turned up, and she murmured sarcastically, "Hell, it's hell… Yeah, sure."

Then the doors slid soundlessly shut.

CHAPTER 7

CLEANSE THE BLOOD

With a quiet groan, the elevator ferried the adventurers up, up, up.

Unsure of whether they were moving slowly or quickly, the party found itself assailed by a feeling of being pressed into the floor. They fit wherever they could in the small box, standing with equipment at the ready and nervous looks on their faces. There was no guarantee that the goblins would not launch a sneak attack right here in the elevator.

"Hr...?" High Elf Archer suddenly started making worried little noises, "Hmm?" and "Hmm?", and put a hand to her ear. It flicked restlessly, and an uneasy look came over her face.

"...What's this? Heard some goblin footsteps?" Dwarf Shaman asked.

"Hrn, no... Ahh, arrgh...!" She didn't even snap back at him, but kept flicking her ears in irritation.

"Swallow," Goblin Slayer said, not looking up from his inspection of his item pouch in one corner of the elevator.

High Elf Archer gave him a puzzled look. "Say what?"

"It will relieve your ears."

Could he be right? High Elf Archer was doubtful, but she nodded and tried it.

"...Huh, it's true." She smiled and flicked her ears, now pressure-free, up and down.

Priestess, watching, swallowed, too, then blinked in surprise. "Wow. That really helps."

"This fortress did appear to be quite tall," Lizard Priest said, placing a hand on the wall of the elevator as if checking its position. It was hardly enough to make their place in the building obvious, but if they were feeling discomfort in their ears, that told them something on its own.

"It is evidence that we are ascending safely," he said, "and that is well and good."

"But—" Priestess put one slim finger to her lips. "What if it just stops…?"

"Then we open the doors and climb to one of the cross passages," Goblin Slayer said firmly. They were much higher than they had been before; it shouldn't be so hard now.

Priestess and High Elf Archer exchanged a glance at this characteristically unhesitating answer and smiled.

"I need to borrow your rope."

"Oh, here," Priestess said, nodding and handing the rope to him. "I feel like the Adventurer's Toolkit has been a star player for us this time around."

"They aren't kidding when they say to never leave home without it," Dwarf Shaman chuckled; Priestess smiled and nodded. "Uh-huh!"

And with that, conversation ceased. The whir of the elevator echoed, mingling with the rush of water from far below their feet. For a long moment, nobody spoke, but each imagined what they would soon have to face.

"…I'm sorry." The short, quiet words seemed to spill over from High Elf Archer. She shifted as she felt the party's gaze light upon her. "And, thank you. I mean…all of you."

She blushed slightly, smiled shyly. Perhaps she was embarrassed to thank them to their faces like this.

"I invited you here for my sister's wedding, and… Well, now this."

"Ahh, what of it?" Dwarf Shaman replied without a moment's pause. He dug pointedly through his bag of catalysts, not looking at High Elf Archer as he spoke. "I think I like havin' the elves in my debt.

Besides, we're... You know." He gave a tug of his beard then finally managed to come up with the word. "Friends."

"Oh..."

Lizard Priest chuckled quietly when he saw High Elf Archer's eyes widen; he nodded somberly. "We always rely much on you, mistress ranger." He rolled his eyes in a gesture dripping with humor. "Surely, this is the least we can do."

"And, uh," Priestess clapped her hands quietly, a soft smile coming over her face. "Goblin Slayer would have jumped at this quest anyway, from the moment he heard the word *goblins*."

"Hrm?" the armored adventurer grunted, but Priestess turned a carefree smile on him and asked, "Am I wrong?"

"...No," he said, slowly shaking his cheap-looking helmet. "We must kill all the goblins."

"...Gods," High Elf Archer said, her shoulders slumping as she let out a breath. A smile crept onto her face. "It's just been a year or so. Who knew you could get so close so fast?"

"Well, see if you're still thinkin' about us in a hundred years."

"Silly dwarf," High Elf Archer giggled. She stuck out one long, slim finger, drawing a circle in the air. "Of course I won't forget you."

Right. She gave herself an invigorating smack on both cheeks. Then she took up her bow, checking the string; she pulled a bud-tipped arrow from her quiver and set it. She looked up at the ceiling, and with a flick of her ears, her face became serious. "I hear wind. Footsteps. Chattering. Probably either the roof or a passageway. There's a lot of them."

"I would like to simply cut them down." Goblin Slayer drew his sword, rotating his wrist slowly before assuming a fighting posture. "What do you think?"

"I think it may be time for what you might call a classical maneuver," Lizard Priest said with a wink. Then he nodded and offered a strategy. "I have a suggestion. Milord Goblin Slayer, you shall be at the front, with master spell caster and myself on the flanks. Our lady Priestess shall stand behind mistress ranger."

"R-right!"

The tail of the formation.

Goblins from behind. Ripping and tearing. Gibbering, striking. A dagger buried in her gut.

"...!" Priestess shook her head vigorously to clear away the images that flashed through her mind.

"That position is the safest from enemy attack, so you've no need to worry." Lizard Priest nodded at Priestess, who was biting her lip nervously.

"So all I have to do is keep an eye out and provide support, right?" High Elf Archer said.

"'All'? It is most crucial."

"Yeah, I get it," she replied, puffing out her chest.

"Sheesh. You remember I'm a magic user, don't you?" Dwarf Shaman grumbled as he shifted his bag of catalysts squarely onto his shoulders and drew out his hand ax. As a spell caster, he didn't wear much in the way of armor, yet he still had a certain air of a warrior ready for battle.

Goblin Slayer's helmet turned briefly in his direction, and he murmured, "But we are counting on you."

"Y'damn well are. I'll show you what dwarf men are made of."

"Ha-ha-ha-ha-ha-ha! We of the lizard tribe are all warriors anyway."

As the men bantered, the women shared a roll of their eyes.

Finally, the elevator came to a stop with a crash.

"Are you up to this?" From behind the metal visor, Priestess could feel a pair of eyes settle on her.

Being vigilant and being nervous were different things. Just like warming up and having blood rush to your head.

She took a long breath in then let it out slowly. She put a hand to her chest. Another deep breath.

"...I'm all right. I can do this."

"When the doors open, we run. Get ready," Goblin Slayer said brusquely. He faced forward. He didn't have to see his companions to know they were all nodding.

"What about spell casters?" High Elf Archer whispered, checking the state of her bowstring. "They must have some."

"If we spot any, we will prioritize them," Goblin Slayer said. "That's all we can do."

"I hate fighting spell casters," Dwarf Shaman added. "As ironic as that sounds."

"They may use spells that inflict status ailments, but so long as even one of us is still safe, that person can bring the party back," Goblin Slayer said calmly. "So long as we are not all destroyed, we have a wide range of options."

"And if we *are* all destroyed..." Priestess's voice shook, and the metal face turned toward her.

"Don't."

As a command, it was impossible, and Priestess looked at him in surprise. But then she gave a small smile, even laughed. Even if she had to force herself a little bit.

"...Well, if you say so. I'll do my best not to let us all die."

"Good." Goblin Slayer nodded. "Don't use spells. Miracles only."

"Mm."

"Yes, sir!"

The two clerics nodded their assent, then each prayed to their own gods in their own ways, asking for miracles.

"O sickle wings of Velociraptor, rip and tear, fly and hunt."

"O Earth Mother, abounding in mercy, by the power of the land grant safety to we who are weak."

Finally, the doors opened...

"Go!"

They started running.

§

The goblin shaman looked out over his sleepy-eyed subordinates and nodded in satisfaction.

Each and every one of them wore glittering chest plates or held spears or swords.

This shaman was the recipient of tremendous good fortune. By sheer chance, he had been granted magic, then had risen to control a horde, and had even come into possession of a fortress. Through magic, he had befuddled the mind of the dragon (that it didn't fall asleep was unexpected) and set it loose upon the elves.

He was perfectly confident that all this had been the result of his own blindingly brilliant abilities, but in reality it had been largely luck.

"GORBB! GOBROBBRBOGB!!"

How he loved to see his stupid, idiotic brethren bowing and scraping before him. His superiority was born of his constant sermons proclaiming that he would lead them all to a new heaven and a new earth. At that moment, it was as if he could feel even the river raging far below.

"GORROB! GOROOROOB!"

In the pale darkness before dawn, the far side of the horizon was turning a light purple. The damp, warm wind from the trees felt very good to the goblins.

"GBBORB!!"

All was in readiness, the goblin shaman howled. They would show those condescending, high-and-mighty bug-eaters, he proclaimed. He was oblivious to the rather bug-sized concerns of his own speech.

"GORB!"

"GBBRO!!"

Yes, yes! the ignorant masses shouted. The goblin shaman looked out over them and raised the staff he held. It was his favorite staff, topped with the skull of an adventurer he'd killed. That girl had possessed such a fine skull.

"GOOBRGGOG!"

The curse he had come up with (he was sure he had come up with it; he never questioned his inspiration) was complete. Let the elves, and the humans downstream, drink the blood and feces of their own companions. Let them eat the merchants and the hunters and the adventurers. That would show them.

The goblin shaman was perfectly confident his curse had worked. That was why he now exhorted his goblins to strike down the elves, to rape and kill and destroy.

If it didn't work, it didn't work—and it would be the fault of his idiotic followers, who were too stupid to carry out his plans. If he didn't have to suffer under incompetent help, things would go very well indeed.

A goblin never forgets an injury done.

Certainly not by the elves, who for generations had mocked the goblins. Nor by Sword Maiden, who a decade before had ranged herself against the Dark Gods.

The goblins forgot everything they might themselves have done to earn resentment; they only hated.

Not just things that had been done to them, either, but even things they had only heard about.

That was why the shaman was resolved. He would trample the elves, torture them, get their beautiful princess with his child in front of the decapitated head of her husband.

Then they would pillage the water town, burn it to the ground, and he would slam himself into Sword Maiden until she couldn't stand up again.

Such was his wish, his fantasy, yet it was nothing more than the effluent of his greed.

But what did goblins have except their avarice? Hatred, self-preservation, and what else?

A goblin shaman was still a goblin.

"GOROBOOGOBOR!!"

He raised his staff and bellowed. *Now! Pour forth!*

The blessing of his war cry was interrupted by a gentle *bong* that seemed out of place.

What was that?

A second later, the doors sunk in the walls, the ones that had never opened, slid apart...

"Start with...one!"

§

The first thing Goblin Slayer did as he came charging in was to strike a goblin with his shield.

It seemed like there were at least a hundred goblins on the circular roof. Maybe that was just an illusion. But several dozen, at least. And the adventurers flew like arrows into the middle of them.

"GOROB?!"

He struck one uncomprehending goblin as it stood gibbering, then he slid to the left, slamming his sword into the throat of an approaching monster.

"GOROBOOBGR?!" The creature thrashed and hacked before drowning in his own blood.

Goblin Slayer pulled his sword back and gave the fresh corpse a kick. Then he swung around and launched the sword at a goblin belatedly trying to ready a sling behind him.

"GROOB?!"

"Two."

He didn't spare another glance at the toppled goblin but reached out for the corpse he had kicked away. He picked up a hatchet, gave it a swing. Not bad.

"O great sheep who walked the Cretaceous, grant to us a modicum of your long-sung success in battle!"

To Goblin Slayer's left, Lizard Priest howled like a bird of prey and swung the Swordclaw he held with both hands. Claw, claw, fang, tail. He grabbed the goblin that Goblin Slayer had slammed with his shield. With so many enemies, there was no time to think, and Lizard Priest trusted to his warrior's instincts, crying out like an animal.

"Eeeeeahhhhh!!"

"Here I am, thinking if I ever see another goblin it'll be too soon," Dwarf Shaman muttered from the right flank, "and Scaly sounds like he's having the time of his life." Even so, he was able to wield his ax with effective, well-judged strikes.

Although by his own admission he was not a soldier first, he had a little bit of breathing room. Goblin Slayer and his sword had already cleared away some of the opposing forces. What was more, the divine protection granted by Priestess's prayer safeguarded them from the goblins' attacks. Dwarf Shaman, not a front row specialist, was immensely grateful for that.

"Over there!" called High Elf Archer from beside the dwarf as he stood, feet firmly planted to swing his ax. She loosed three arrows, skewering three enemies, her ears moving all the while in search of more.

As for what she had just seen: one particular goblin huddling deep within the horde.

"He's got a staff! And it doesn't look good!"

"A shaman?" Goblin Slayer buried the hatchet in the brains of his sixth goblin. He let go of the weapon, which fell to the ground along with the corpse, and drew a sword from the slain enemy's belt. He used the momentum to hack off the head of another nearby goblin.

"Seven. Can you hit him?"

"It won't be easy!" High Elf Archer said, yet she was already putting an arrow to her bow. "But I'll try!"

Priestess, running hard behind, watched the entire scene with a sense of unreality.

The enemy were so many, and they, the adventurers, were so few. The last time she had confronted such a vast horde was—

Never.

Priestess, standing behind the others and breathing as deeply as she could, was startled by the realization.

The goblins pressed in before her. Memory struck her like a bolt of lightning.

The fight with the goblin lord. That time, she had worked with Goblin Slayer to defeat the enemy leader.

During the harvest festival attack, the goblins had split up, so no one engagement had been very large.

The frozen fortress had been a fighting withdrawal. They hadn't tried to cut their way through the mass.

Now they were flying into the heart of the horde. The sound of weapons rang around her. Screams. Death rattles. The stink of blood and guts.

We're gonna get rid of some goblins!

Run! Hurry!

…ill…e…

The scream seemed to echo in her memory until it filled her mind completely. Priestess could hear her own teeth chattering. She had done this so many times already, so why did her feet stop now? Why did her breath catch?

"Ergh... Ah...!"

A pebble flew past, grazing her cheek. She felt heat and pain lance along the side of her face. There was a sticky feeling of blood welling up.

She stopped praying, and the effect of Protection began to fade.

"...!"

She suddenly noticed a warm, damp feeling between her legs, and she bit her lip.

Why did she have to be last in line?

What did they want from her?

She knew now; she was too experienced not to.

She clasped her sounding staff in desperate fingers, raised it up, and cried out her supplication to the gods in heaven.

"O Earth Mother, abounding in mercy, grant your sacred light to we who are lost in darkness!!"

There was a veritable explosion of sunlight.

"GOBOGBO?!"

"GOOBR?! GOBOGR?!"

The goblins screamed and thrashed as the Earth Mother's sacred light blazed upon their hideous faces. Some of them tumbled from the roof as they covered their faces and tried to run, while others expired, trampled under the feet of their comrades.

Priestess caught her breath at the piteous scene but continued to offer up Holy Light with all the strength she could muster. It illuminated the adventurers from behind so that they suffered no ill effects from it.

"Yes—you're mine...!"

"GOBBRG?!"

An arrow flew, guided by High Elf Archer's unsurpassed skill. It wove through the horde like a living thing, lodging itself in the goblin shaman's shoulder.

"GORBBBR...!!"

At almost the same instant, a spell billowed from the staff the shaman had been hiding behind his soldiers.

"ODUUUAAARUKKKKKUPIRUUUUS!!"

A cloud of sweet-smelling, light-purple smoke roiled up on the roof.

"Hrk... Crap...!" High Elf Archer stumbled and dropped to one knee, while the goblins caught up in the cloud similarly collapsed around her.

"This has to be Sleep Cloud...!" Dwarf Shaman exclaimed, clapping a hand to his mouth.

"Grr... We must...focus!" Lizard Priest tried to rouse High Elf Archer, but his own movements were becoming visibly slower.

It's like being underwater, Priestess thought dimly. Her eyelids were growing heavy, and her staff was the only thing keeping her upright.

It had been so much fun, all of them playing together in the water on their vacation.

The world swung back and forth, left, right; everything tilted as she found she could no longer stand up.

Maybe it's...all right now.

Her consciousness wavered, just for an instant. But that was all it took for Protection to disappear completely.

With vision grown dangerously dark, she saw High Elf Archer on her knees, and beyond her, someone's back. The goblins who had been kept at bay by the spell now poured in, trying to drag him down.

"Ah..."

High Elf Archer was pulled to the ground. Her clothes were torn. She waved an arm languidly.

A club came down on Dwarf Shaman's shoulder. His grip slackened and he dropped his ax, which clattered to the floor.

A goblin jumped on Lizard Priest's neck. The dagger in its hand worked between the scales.

"...Urg..."

Goblin Slayer's shoulder— A sword—

Blood.

"Goblin Slayer, sir..."

Her voice was so quiet. But it was enough.

"...! Guh..."

She took a breath. That was the first thing. Fill that small chest with air then let it out.

"HHHHRAAAAAHHHHHHHH…!!"

She'd had no idea she was capable of such a monumental shout until it sprang forth from her throat.

"Everyone…! Goblin…Slayer…sir…!"

There was no answer.

She shook her sounding staff.

"Goblin Slayer, sir!!"

No answer.

"…!!"

Priestess gritted her teeth and struggled to maintain consciousness; she could see a goblin shifting and shuffling in the far reaches of her vision. She could see him holding his staff, laughing maniacally despite the blood dribbling from his shoulder.

The blood ran down his arm, splattering against the ground in time with the shaman's footsteps.

Impure.

It was nothing more than an intuition. There was no prompting from the Earth Mother in heaven. No, it was simply the answer she arrived at out of her own experience, her experience as a weak sixteen-year-old girl adventuring with the man called Goblin Slayer.

Her answer to what she could do. What she should do.

"O Earth Mother, abounding in mercy, please, by your revered hand, cleanse us of our corruption!!"

And then a miracle happened.

"GORB?!"

By the time he noticed the change, it was too late. The goblin shaman's blood had been turned to pure water.

"GOBOGGBOGOBOOGOGOBOGOOG?!?!?!"

The goblin shaman howled as if his insides were being shredded. Priestess thought she felt her very soul rocked by the awful bellow, but it brought her back to herself.

"Er—ah—ahh…?!"

Her connection to the world above vanished like a cut string, and the world of sound came rushing back into her ears.

This divine act, Purify, must never be used in this way again.

"Ah, ahh…?!"

Something seemed to impact upon her very soul, rattling every fiber of her being.

She had done something awful.

The honored Earth Mother, the fount of all compassion and mercy, had accepted this connection with her soul, and she—

"Aaaaarrrrghhh…!"

Priestess let out an agonized scream at what she had done.

Her sounding staff made a hollow sound as it rolled along the roof where she had dropped it.

The bloodlust vanished as if it had dropped off into the abyss. Priestess was left with a hand pressed vacantly to her chest, only now realizing that tears were pouring from her eyes.

"Agh—ahhhhhhhh…!"

But two words reached her ears as she stood weeping like a child.

"Well done."

Two words.

"Ah…"

Just the two.

That was all it took to put strength back into legs she had been sure were going to collapse.

"…Y-yes, sir…!"

"All right."

Goblin Slayer was, in a word, a mess. A dagger had been jammed into a chink in his armor, tearing the chain mail beneath. He was scuffed from being hit.

He pulled the dagger from his shoulder; when he saw the sticky liquid slathered on its blade, he gave a cluck of his tongue. Pulling a bottle with a string tied around it from his item pouch, he drank its contents. Then a second bottle.

An elixir. An antidote.

Once he was done, he pitched the empty bottles at the nearest goblin.

"GOOBOG?!"

Then he turned around, using the shield on his left arm to slaughter the goblin crouching by High Elf Archer.

"GROBO?!"

"Twenty-one. Get up!"

"Hrgh, ah… Or… Orcbolg…?"

She got unsteadily to her feet. She was in a terrible state. Drenched in blood, wounded, covered in goblin brains, and her clothes shredded.

But she was alive.

That was enough.

"Drink," Goblin Slayer instructed, handing her a potion with his left hand. "And use this!" he shouted to Dwarf Shaman, tossing him the sword in his right.

"I sh-shall!" He caught the hilt in a backhand grip, raised it, and then brought it down, splitting open a goblin's stomach with it.

"GOBOGOOBOG?!"

"Now I see why you like these things, Beard-cutter!"

He kicked away the gutted creature and swung at the next enemy. His right arm hung limply at his side, but he was capable enough of fighting. The sword in his left hand slashed another goblin.

When Lizard Priest regained his consciousness, his strength was unparalleled. "Hrraghh…!"

He grabbed the goblin attempting to sink a dagger into his neck and flung the creature to the floor.

"GOBORO?!"

The monster's spine adopted an unnatural angle; the goblin twitched once and then lay still.

Before the creature had expired, Lizard Priest was already lashing out with claws and claws and fangs and tail. He screeched and slashed, almost literally blowing the goblins away.

"They nearly pulled one over on us there…!" He wiped the goblin blood from his chin with his sleeve and let out a great whooshing breath. "Milord Goblin Slayer, I shall resume the attack!"

"Please do," Goblin Slayer said as he took Priestess's arm where she was slumped down.

"Oh… Goblin Slayer…sir…"

She took him in dimly. A crack ran along his helmet, there were gouges in his leather armor, and the stench of blood was stronger than usual. But that shining red eye looked straight at her from between the slats of the visor.

"You did well."

"...Oh, y-yes, sir...!" She wiped the tears from the corners of her eyes and collected the cap and staff she had dropped in the melee.

This wasn't over yet. There were still so many goblins. The battle had to go on.

"Gorgosaurus, beautiful though wounded, may I partake in the healing in your body!"

Lizard Priest's prayer surrounded the party with warm light, restoring their energy. It was the Refresh miracle. Ah, how great is the blessing of the nagas!

As he checked the state of his injuries, Goblin Slayer drove his sword into the throat of a nearby goblin.

"GOROBORO?!"

"Twenty and two. Press ahead, run... Can you run?"

"Yeah, I'm good... Geez, this thing is bitter," High Elf Archer complained as Goblin Slayer kicked aside his latest writhing, blood-spurting victim.

She clucked as she tried to pull the remains of her shirt over her chest, then she tossed away the empty bottle and gave Priestess a wink. "C'mon, let's go!"

"Right! I can... I can move, too... I will move!" She forced herself to speak as forcefully as she could. She gave a flourish of her staff to keep the goblins behind them at bay.

"Master spell caster, are you quite ready?"

"Never been readier. I worked hard to save these spells for this!"

And with these shouts from Lizard Priest and Dwarf Shaman, the party moved forward... No.

"GOROB!!"

"GRO! GRB!"

Rather, that is to say, they found themselves cornered at the tower's edge. Just a few steps ahead, they could see a sheer drop down into a veritable ocean of trees. The goblins had recovered from the confusion of Purify and now cackled as they came closer.

They would get that elf on her knees again and make her theirs. They would tear that little girl with her little ploys into little pieces.

Kill the men. Rape and kill the women. It had been stupid of their compatriots to get themselves murdered, but still, the goblins wanted revenge. For the goblins, the death of their fellows was nothing more than a reason to affirm their own greed.

The monsters advanced, weapons clutched in hand, crotches bulging, lust glinting in their eyes.

Goblin Slayer was calm in the face of the encroaching horde.

"Jump!!"

One after another, the adventurers flung themselves into space. The air that rushed upward at them cleansed itself of humidity, cooling their battle-heated bodies.

The first signs of dawn were tracing their way along the horizon, casting light upon the sky, the trees.

Eventually, though, gravity would have its way with the party, crushing them against the ground.

"GBBRB!"

"GROGGB! GORRBGROB!!"

As the goblins yammered and mocked, Dwarf Shaman gave an incongruous grin. His fat, stubby fingers flashed in the air, tracing complicated sigils, and then he shouted: *"Come out, you gnomes, and let it go! Here it comes, look out below! Turn those buckets upside-down—empty all upon the ground!"*

The speed of their descent immediately slowed. It had been worth it to save up this Falling Control spell.

The party floated gently in the sky as if resting on a giant, invisible hand. Now they had nothing to fear from the ground.

"Eep, eep, eep...!" Priestess pressed a hand to the hem of her dress as the wind threatened to blow it up. High Elf Archer smiled in relief. The grim, drawn expression Priestess had been wearing until moments earlier didn't suit that girl. High Elf Archer didn't want that for her.

I knew goblin slaying was nasty.

She reached out a hand, and Priestess took it.

"Oh..."

"You okay?"

"I—I'm very sorry…!"

"Ahh, don't mention it. Hey, dwarf, you actually did it!"

"Was there ever any doubt?" Dwarf Shaman chortled. He smiled with his eyes, pleased to see High Elf Archer so happy with his work, then pulled the wine jug from his belt and took a swig.

The rising sun, the first rays of dawn, the morning light, the wind, the forest, the whole world. Was there anything that could make wine taste better than this?

"I would say this went rather well," Lizard Priest remarked, relaxing his whole body until he was spread-eagled. He looked so relaxed—but his eyes still focused up at the goblins. He could see them clearly, pointing and gibbering to one another. "Though I admit, I wondered, for a moment."

"Yes," Goblin Slayer said, also looking up. "This is the best way to get rid of goblins."

§

"G… B…"

The goblin shaman's consciousness chose that moment to return to him.

The sound of the river seemed so loud. His head was spinning; it was like there was a ringing in his ears. It was hard to breathe, and his vision was constricted. Wheezing and rasping, he managed to use his staff to drag himself to his feet.

He didn't understand why some of his blood had become water, why his breath no longer seemed to transit through his body quite right. He looked around and saw the other goblins clustered at the edge of the roof, chattering excitedly.

"GOBOOGB…!"

What a lot of jackasses. Had they no impulse to help the one who guided them, or at least show him proper reverence? The goblin shaman was incensed, conveniently forgetting that a moment earlier, he had been using these same creatures as shields.

And on top of that, it looked like the adventurers had escaped. Useless louts.

"GORB! GROBOOGOBOGR!!" The shaman exclaimed, waving his staff.

Several goblins looked over. "GBBGROB?!"

The shaman was not so much pleased that some had responded as enraged that some hadn't.

Good help was impossible to find.

If he could get his hands on that elf, or that human girl, or perhaps the princess from the forest, he could use her to rebuild his horde. As the most important creature around, he would take the choicest females and make them bear his own young. Didn't he have the right?

"GROROB...?"

What, though, was the sound of water he was hearing?

"GROROBOROGBORO?!?!?!"

A second later, the goblin shaman's body was hefted into the air by the torrent of water that poured from the open gates of the elevator. Launched into the sky by the flash flood, he spent the last seconds of his life in total confusion. He went to his grave never knowing that Tunnel had been used to punch a hole in the breakwater. Nor that water pressure had caused the geyser to rise up from the lowest to the highest level of the tower.

Goblins, it must be assumed, would never have imagined that water might go up as well as down.

If the builders of the fortress could have witnessed the scene, they would have rejoiced at the doom of the Non-Prayer Characters.

It was precisely the way the goblins had dammed up the water that had caused it to build up until it could explode.

The shaman went up, up with the water then came down, down and splattered his brains on the ground. And even that trace, the last evidence he had ever existed, was instantly washed away by the deluge.

A fitting end.

§

Droplets showered from the geyser as if a sudden squall had come through, the water sparkling in the sunlight. A few goblins also came tumbling down, pushed over the edge of the tower, but the fall was more than long enough to finish them off.

"Are... Are you sure about this?" High Elf Archer asked dubiously, shaking her head and sending water flying from her soaked hair.

Goblin Slayer let out a long breath. "The tunnel will shortly shrink and then close. I don't believe the building will collapse."

"Not what I was asking," High Elf Archer said, her ears slicking in annoyance. "I meant all the water left inside."

"As far as that goes," Goblin Slayer said calmly, "all we can do is ask the elves to come deal with it later."

High Elf Archer harrumphed and fell silent, earning a laugh from Dwarf Shaman. "So there'll be a wedding when we get back?" He was drifting gently through the air, sipping his wine and enjoying the sunrise. Indeed, it was he who held them in this spot. If he let his concentration lapse for even a second, they would all fall to their deaths.

High Elf Archer looked at him incredulously, but he ignored her. "Planning to get married yourself yet?" he asked.

"Not for at least another millennium."

"Think anyone's going to want a three-thousand-year-old bride?"

"What did you just say to me?!" High Elf Archer growled.

They might have been floating in midair, but the tone of their argument was familiar, and Lizard Priest rolled his eyes in amusement. "Upon that dawn when I become a naga, might I welcome you as a naga's bride?"

"I'm sure I don't know what you mean." High Elf Archer's long ears didn't miss Lizard Priest's joking remark. She was smiling like a cat who'd discovered a new toy. "What's this—a confession of love? For real?"

"Mmm. I suppose we won't know for at least a thousand years."

Priestess watched the three friends banter, not paying too much attention. High Elf Archer had let go of her hand, and no one else took it instead. It was just her, floating in the sky, holding her cap down with one hand and her skirt with the other.

She let out a soft but audible breath, and Goblin Slayer's helmet turned in her direction. "Are you tired?"

"Oh, uh, no!" she said quickly, waving her hand. "Not at all…"

But then— But still—

The hand she was waving drooped limply. Not quite sure what to say, she said, quietly, the first thing that came to mind. "…Well, maybe a little."

"I see."

In the end, could she really live with…with the way she'd used Purify?

It wasn't right. There's no question…

Purify was intended to make water clean. It was wrong to use it to take the life of another living being, even a goblin.

Yet, the Earth Mother had answered her prayer because it was a plea to save other living beings.

That was why the goddess, in all her compassion, had granted her imprimatur for what Priestess had done.

Just this one time.

What a thing to do.

But…

Even so, I prayed, and she caused a miracle for me.

How was Priestess to interpret that, how to understand it?

A year before, when she was attempting her first adventure, it had been all things she didn't understand.

And now? She still understood just two things.

That she was and would be still an adventurer.

And that Goblin Slayer always had and always would kill all the goblins.

And I…

Could she go on believing in the Earth Mother?

Did she deserve to have miracles bestowed upon her by the goddess?

She didn't know. There was no way to know.

Had she grown and matured at all over the past year? Maybe just a little…?

"Look," came a murmured command.

"Huh...?" Priestess quickly looked up, taken by surprise.

The sun was blindingly bright; she found herself blinking away tears.

The lightening sky stretched out over an infinity of green. And hanging there, as if to bind the two together...

"It's a rainbow."

"Rrrraagghhhh!!" the girl cried, leaping up into the air, and the deep dark of the underworld was illuminated as by the radiance of the sun.

The place truly was as unto hell itself. A third of the place was scorched, blackened land, and the other two-thirds was packed solid with demons. Towering above her head, ready to tear the board of this world apart, were Rock Eaters, giant bug monsters easily mistaken for massive centipedes.

But the girl, high in the air, only curled up the corners of her lips in a cute but unexpected smile.

"Daaaawn *STRIKE*!!"

Sun explosion!

The sacred blade in her hand released a flash of emerald light, ruthlessly scything down the monsters all around. The horde of Rock Eaters, leaning eagerly forward for a bite of the young woman, was torn apart in the blink of an eye. Blood and fluids that might have stained the girl's black hair were burned away by the heat of the emerald flash.

The girl had refused to so much as flinch in the face of all hell's demons, and indeed, she stood unscathed.

The hero spun in the air, landing lightly on a rocky outcropping with fist upraised, as she shouted, "It's your doom, hellions, your doom!" Then she leveled her holy sword at the monsters, weaving a complex sigil with her left hand. *"Carbunculus…Crescunt…Iacta!!"*

A sphere of flame formed with a roar and went flying, followed by a second, then a third. As charred demon corpses soared through the air, the hero exclaimed, "I'm happy to keep dishing it out—how much longer do you need?!"

"Just…a little longer, I think!"

The answering voice came from within the mass of demons.

The hero gripped her sacred blade with both hands, striking a fighting pose as if to say that any who dared come near would be cut down.

And in fact, that was exactly what happened to any who dared.

The demons shifted, trying to find an advantageous position, but an instant later, their heads went flying. No true, experienced warrior would let a good attack of opportunity go to waste. She ducked away from her enemies' assaults so fast that you would miss it if you blinked, then she thrust her sword through an oncoming opponent. Her fighting was brutal, utilitarian—but that demonstrated exactly how skilled she was.

She was protecting a mage—a woman carrying a large staff and concentrating hard. The woman, Sage, now opened one of her eyes, looking at the rocks high above them.

"…The flow of the water above us has changed. It seems our opponent's magic circle has been broken."

"Huh. I wonder if there are some other adventurers up there." The hero fried a few of the smaller monsters with another spell then jumped in among them.

The gates of hell are nearly open.

Such had been the warning left to them, carved into a clay tablet by mages who had lived nearly in the Age of the Gods.

These wizards had been researching the Gate spell, but they had made a terrible mistake. They had opened a Gate to a place that should have been left closed forever: hell itself. They had immediately sealed it shut, but it was only a matter of time until it opened again. They had predicted the very year and day when it would do so…

And it happened to be right when I was around. Is that good luck or bad for me?

The hero ran straight ahead, never looking back.

She had tried studying, but she was under no illusions that she could ever really grasp the deep logic of the world. She had sat reading thick books of principles and rules, but they only made her head hurt.

Hence, it would be up to Sage to seal the Gate shut. She herself complained that she had not yet reached the apogee, yet she was so stalwart...

"Maybe the elves...?"

"I wonder. They do drag their feet—maybe that's why their hands are so fast."

"...Elves can wind up striking a fatal blow at a time and place you never expect."

"For all my learning, I'll never understand them," Sage murmured, and the hero knew Sage had learned more than any of them.

As for herself, she just swung her sword and let the weapon do the spell-weaving.

The hero was taken once more by the absolute conviction that every corner of this world was amazing. And not because she was strong or because she was a hero. Absolutely not. Could a simple fact like that change the value of the world?

She had friends, a hometown, favorite things. The sky was stunning, and she could even see a rainbow.

"Hah, it's all good! There's one way to solve this problem—slice these guys up!"

All the more reason she couldn't let these monsters have it.

She booted aside a lesser demon and found herself face-to-face with a bizarre spider creature. The gigantic monster was obviously a leader among the demons.

It was a fearsome beast; its metal legs could easily run her through.

The cynical observer might say that it was her job to fight opponents like that because she was the hero.

Pfft. Hardly.

She donned a wild smile, showing all her teeth. She looked like a shark after its prey.

Sage would have the Gate shut in a moment. Until then, she would fight to keep the world from these monsters; she wouldn't cede it to them even for an instant.

If she and her friends were the only ones who knew why she fought for the world, that was enough.

"Here—we—goooooo!!"

The hero leaped in, bellowing and landing what was (if she might say so) a critical hit.

CHAPTER 8

A MIDSUMMER NIGHT'S DREAM

"Now then, I request both of you to speak the words of the covenant," intoned an elf with his head bowed somberly before a dais. He was an elven elder, many long years old and yet still young.

Fireflies or some such luminescent insect floated around, providing light for the great hall full of elves and adventurers. They sat cross-legged on the ground. Food and fruits were served on leaf-plates, wine in large nuts. The dais the crowd focused on was actually an upraised tree root.

Upon it stood the bride and groom, dressed in garments of sheer silk and flowers, shimmering with the wings of butterflies and dragonflies. They shared a shy glance then gently took each other's hands.

"*Usamiakitowotoku riinomochinneie inoyurunahowo chihionokahisatawa!*" the elf with the shining helmet said proudly.

His bride replied, looking at the ground and blushing, "*Usamiakitowotoku oshiroyuinawoto isototowo chihonokahisatawa.*"

Their words, almost musical, drifted up to the great tree, which shook its branches in response, leaves hovering in the night.

Fssh, fssh. The forest was laughing. The trees were singing. *May your lives be blessed. May the span of your days be full of happiness.*

"You have heard the jubilation of the forest?" the priest asked, stepping forward gracefully. The man and the woman looked at each other happily and nodded.

"Mm."

"Yes, we did."

"Then offer the response." The priest passed them a large bow and an arrow. The bow was of yew wood and the arrow bud-tipped, made especially for this day. The elf with the shining headpiece took the bow, and the princess with the flower crown the arrow.

The priest bowed deeply and retreated; the two elves drew near to each other, almost in an embrace, and readied the bow.

The wife nocked the arrow into the bow the husband held up, and then together, they drew the string.

They aimed at the heavens, at the night sky where the moons and stars glittered.

The leaves that formed the ceiling of the hall, everyone saw, had opened the path in one spot, a small passage. Beyond, the night sky flashed and twinkled like a box of jewels. If the stars were indeed the eyes of the gods, there could be no greater blessing in all the world.

The arrow flew from the bowstring with a musical twang. The bud-tipped arrow shot into the sky like a shooting star in reverse, and they didn't see it come down.

Wherever the arrow landed, a new tree would emerge, and grow, one day to become a member of the forest.

"The covenant is hereby completed!" the priest announced.

The forest, and the people of the forest, and the gods had all together acknowledged this marriage and blessed it.

"This eve shall be long remembered as the Night of the Rainbow-Clad Moon!"

The whole crowd of elves broke out in cheering and applause.

Love is destiny	destiny is death
Even a knight who serves a maiden	will one day fall into death's clutches
Even the prince who befriends a Sky Drake	must leave the woman he fancies behind

The mercenary who loved a cleric	will fall in battle pursuing his dream
And the king who loved the shrine maiden	controls all but the hour of their separation
The end of life	is not the last chapter of an heroic saga
So the adventure called life	will continue to the very end
Friendship and love	life and death
From these things	we cannot escape
Therefore what have we	to fear
Love is destiny	and our destiny is death

Then the elves produced harps and drums, and everyone took up a lively song.

The people of the forest have always loved music and dancing, and they enjoy whatever is pleasant. Their lives are too long to simply kill time to pass the days. They may be old of heart, they may take the very long view, but many are the days on the elf calendar that serve as a pretext for celebration.

A wedding was a perfect example: they celebrated both the union of two young elves, and the fact that there would be one less day with nothing happening.

What day is there in this world that is not special? All people were special; this night was special. A hundred years from now, it would still be special and would remain so for all eternity.

Even Dwarf Shaman was surrounded by young (albeit all older than him) elves.

"So what did you do when you fell into the goblins' trap?"

"Er, ahem. Well, me and Long-Ears—I mean, the princess there, we ginned up this hole full of poison gas…"

"This indescribable eyeball monster sounds positively terrifying!"

"Well, ah, you know. It was more…well, *strange*. And it made a very odd noise."

"It sounds like our princess has been real trouble for you. I'm so—"

"Oh— Oh, don't be. Look, she certainly has her moments…"

These youngsters were well aware of the ancient antagonism between their people and the dwarves, but more than likely, this was the first time any of them had ever seen a dwarf up close. Let alone an adventuring one!

Surrounded by elves on every side, Dwarf Shaman's head was practically spinning as he was pelted with requests for stories of adventure and more besides. And the wine the elves served was too weak for him; he couldn't even get properly drunk on it. At last, he raised his stubby arms and shouted, "Heyyy, Scaly! Give me a hand over here!"

And what was Lizard Priest up to when Dwarf Shaman summoned him? He was in a corner of the banquet hall, smacking his lips delightedly. He wolfed down some steamed insects, chugged wine by the cupful, and as soon as he held an orange in his hand, it vanished wholesale into his mouth.

A crowd of elfwives stood watching him eat with astonishment.

"Come now," Lizard Priest said. "I'm no herbivore, but I'm happy to eat whatever—ah, what seems to be the matter, master spell caster?"

"I can't handle this many of 'em all by my lonesome!"

"Well, then." Lizard Priest heaved himself to his feet and shuffled his way among the elves to reinforce his companion. He plopped down in the circle with the elves and the dwarf and announced, "Say, my forest friends. Perhaps you'd like to hear the tale of the lizard hero, a creature with great black scales who could summon storms."

"Oh yeah, I know him!" one of the somewhat older elves said, raising a hand. "I've met him."

Lizard Priest rolled his eyes. "Ha-ha-ha-ha. Then you will enjoy learning the differences between the history of a thousand and a hundred years ago, and the legend that has been told since then."

*   *   *

Just when the first drop fell on the first leaf, to declare the coming of the season of rain

King Jigagei Urogilv, King Red Cloud, and Maaka Waata, Sweet Wind, were joined

After the laying of their egg, the pleasure-woman Hehaka Saba, Black Deer, became with child

The child of destiny, who would be abandoned, who would crawl from a shattered shell

With scales of shadow: one day to breathe blue flame; a child of destiny, to be revered by even his brother naga

The name of he who would one day sink his teeth into the throat of the Demon Lord was Ehena Ulno, Stormbringer...

The elves *ooh*ed and *ahh*ed at the unique way lizardmen sang, with the voice rumbling from deep in the throat. Even the new couple upon the dais were impressed, though they were more restrained in their appreciation than the others. The groom was holding the hand of the bride, and she was looking at the ground, red up to her ears.

"Man, Sis is *actually* embarrassed!" High Elf Archer laughed from her place beside a knot that got plenty of night breeze. Slim and pale, she was clad in a sparkling dress of translucent white cloth. Silk, perhaps. Elves were experts when it came to the handling of insects.

Smiling, a wine cup in her hand and the night breeze caressing her hair, she almost seemed to be floating. Goblin Slayer had heard a word, *wallflower*, that he thought was somehow appropriate for her.

"Don't you want to join them?" he asked, coming over to her from the banquet.

"Hmm?"

This was the same elf who had exploded at the elders the moment she got home while demanding to know why they hadn't told her. Now, with a flush of alcohol in her cheeks and a quizzical look on her face, she seemed an entirely different person.

Goblin Slayer's mind flashed to the fairy stories he'd heard as a child as he continued, "...This is your home."

High Elf Archer seemed to catch his meaning. "Aww, it's fine, really," she said with a wave of her hand, taking a demure sip of her wine. "For us… To put it in human terms, it's like I was only away for a few days."

"Is that so?"

"Besides, Sis promised to write me a letter when things settle down." *Wouldn't want to intrude on the happy young couple, right?* High Elf Archer puffed out her modest chest almost boastfully.

Come to think of it.

A scene from the water town flashed through her mind. She remembered him writing a letter.

"How about you write a letter yourself?" she said thoughtfully. This man never went anywhere but the farm and the Guild and various caves, always muttering about goblins. "You never go home, do you?"

"I can't imagine anyone would read it." He almost sounded like he was laughing. The helmet turned gently left and right. "…I'm not a very good younger brother. Not me."

"You really think so?" High Elf Archer arched an eyebrow then made a circle in the air with one white finger. "I think you're doing well, you know? I mean, you made Silver, didn't you?"

"Is that so?" Goblin Slayer repeated then nodded. "Is that so…?"

"You *really* need to expand your vocabulary, Orcbolg," High Elf Archer giggled. Then she stepped away from the window with a movement like she was dancing.

"You're going?"

"Girls have their own pleasures."

"I…," Goblin Slayer whispered.

High Elf Archer stopped when she heard him. She looked back questioningly, but Goblin Slayer stood silently by himself.

She decided to wait. Elves had nothing but time.

After a moment, he seemed to have finally found the words. "I am glad your sister was able to marry."

They were the flattest, most unremarkable, most disinterested words of congratulations she'd ever heard. Yet High Elf Archer's eyes widened and her ears flicked.

"…Thanks."

She found herself feeling oddly embarrassed and rushed toward

©Noboru Kannatuki

the bustle of the party. She had never expected Orcbolg to say such a thing. She didn't think he was capable of it.

Her footsteps felt lighter than air, but her sharp eyes would never miss her quarry.

She reached out her arm with an agility only an elf possessed, entwining it with another slim limb.

"Oh…"

It was the arm of Priestess, who had been leaning vacantly against the wall. The elves had offered her a dress and clothing, but she had refused, saying her vestments were her proper attire.

"C'mon, what's the matter? You look unhappy."

"No…," Priestess said, glancing down, her face drawn. "Not… Not really."

"You're a terrible liar."

"Aww…"

An instant later, High Elf Archer's finger was an inch from Priestess's nose. "Look, better to talk about anything at all than to keep everything bottled up inside. This is a time for celebration."

"Um…" Priestess felt tears beading at the corners of her eyes as she focused on that finger just in front of her nose. "Okay… That prayer earlier…what did it mean?"

"Oh, that?" High Elf Archer laughed. "Nothing really important. Just a promise to be together always."

I take this person to wife and vow to be with her into eternity.

I take this person as my husband and vow to cleave to him forever.

"'Course, that's 'always' in elf terms." High Elf Archer winked then tugged on Priestess's sleeve. "Hey, say a prayer."

"A prayer? Me?"

"Yeah. To your Earth Mother. We elves owe her something, too, you know."

The very request pained Priestess.

I…

Was she even still fit to pray to the goddess? She had offered supplication at every moment since her youngest days, and even in her battles with goblins, she had stopped short of crossing that final line.

But at the fortress, she had finally done it: she had used a miracle of the Earth Mother to directly harm another being.

It had been a goblin, of course. One of the little devils. She knew full well what would have happened to her if the creature hadn't been defeated.

She had taken life indirectly before. Why should she regret killing now?

But that... It wasn't right...

Thus, why the Earth Mother had become angry and had rebuked Priestess.

"...Okay." Priestess bit her lip so hard she drew blood, but she clutched her sounding staff and knelt.

Even if I'm no longer worthy of love...

Even then, she dearly hoped her prayer for the happiness of her friends who were here, the happiness of her friend's sister, and that sister's spouse, would nonetheless be heard. A selfish wish it was, she knew. But nonetheless...

She closed her eyes and began to pray. *"O Earth Mother, abounding in mercy, by your revered hand may all their paths bear good fruit..."*

Then she let out a soft "Oh" of surprise. Her soul, connected to the gods in heaven, felt a vast, warm hand upon it, comforting it.

The sensation only lasted for instant, not even as long as when she prayed for a miracle, but she hadn't imagined it. For a second, Priestess looked startled and confused, but her face soon split into a smile.

"My prayer reached the goddess..."

"Great! So Sis is all covered."

"She sure is," Priestess replied, then she rubbed her eyes with her sleeve.

"Okay then, let's go!"

"Huh? Ah— Wha...?!" Priestess found High Elf Archer had a grip on her sleeve once more, but this time she was dragging her off somewhere. "Wh-what's the matter?"

"You'll know it when you see it... Oh, there they are. Hey, you two, c'mon over here!"

Apologizing and bowing her head quickly as she stepped around and over food, Priestess followed behind High Elf Archer.

Priestess didn't know how she had done it amid the crowd and cacophony of the banquet, but she had managed to find Guild Girl and Cow Girl, both dressed to the nines. Each was wearing one of the light dresses the elves had prepared, and (perhaps thanks to the wine) they seemed to be in high spirits.

They were wearing almost the same dress as High Elf Archer, but it only served to highlight how much more well-endowed they were than she. That brought a moment of annoyance to the archer's face, but she was soon smiling again. Give it a century or so, and she would be just like her older sister—probably. She hoped.

"Gosh, this is all making me pretty nervous. I've never been to a party like this before..." Cow Girl scratched her cheek, feeling shy.

"Just fake it till you make it," Guild Girl calmly advised her. She tipped her cup toward the other woman as if to say there was nothing to be ashamed of with *those* proportions.

"Well, look who's a social butterfly," High Elf Archer said, impressed, receiving a pointed laugh from Guild Girl in return.

"I learned manners at home," she said. "And public servants have to deal with functions like this sometimes, too."

"Huh," High Elf Archer said then took Cow Girl's and Guild Girl's hands. "Well, whatever. Let's head up to the front, girls!"

Then she practically dragged them, farther and farther forward, toward the dais. The three women behind her struggled to keep up and remain halfway dignified.

"Hey, what's going on?" Cow Girl asked.

"It's something the men don't have anything to do w... Well, maybe a little something. Anyway, just wait and see."

Cow Girl glanced around and found that all the elf women were similarly making their way to the front of the room. She had no idea how old any of them were, of course, but they all looked just about High Elf Archer's age.

"Ahh," Guild Girl said, the pieces falling into place. "A parting gift from the bride?"

"Oh, I know that tradition," Priestess said as she struggled to straighten out her clothing, even as she was pulled along. "They say the person who catches it will be the next to get married… I think. I've helped with the occasional ceremony."

"There are some customs everyone shares," High Elf Archer said with a knowing look and twitched her ears. "If we have a chance to get it, why not take it?"

"Wow…," Cow Girl breathed.

Marriage…

The idea seemed so far removed from her and yet not really that far at all.

Cow Girl looked up at the joyful bride on the dais, squinting as if the woman emitted a blinding light.

All around Cow Girl, excited elf girls waited eagerly.

Then, finally, she looked over to the far wall, where a man in slightly odd armor was standing.

A little giggle escaped her, and she noticed her heart was pounding for some reason. Her eyes met Guild Girl's, and the other woman was wearing the same expression.

Cow Girl shrugged. Better do things the fair way.

There, just in front of her, she could see the priestess, who was interested but unable to take that step. Cow Girl reached out and touched Priestess's back. When the girl looked back at her, surprised, Cow Girl gave a friendly wave.

"Times like this, you just have to go for it," she said.

"Oh, uh, r-right!"

The flower-crowned princess of the forest—no, by now, she was queen, a woman who had become a wife—rose to her feet.

"Love is destiny, and our destiny is death," she said melodically, and then, holding her husband's hand, she pulled the colorful crown of flowers from her head. She hugged it to her generous bosom and recited, "So let the next love and romance be unto these maidens who shall die!"

With that prayer, she tossed the crown into the air, and the night wind carried it.

The crown was the bond between love and romance. The bequest of a jubilant bride.

It made a perfect arc through the air, coming down among the young women...

There was a great cheer.

§

Three days and three nights of celebration later, the adventurers returned to the frontier town.

Although quite a bit of time had passed since then, High Elf Archer had still received no letter.

That had to mean the elves were still celebrating to this day......

AFTERWORD

Hullo, Kumo Kagyu here!

Volume 7 of *Goblin Slayer* features a story in which goblins show up in the elf forest, so they get slain.

Anyway, we're at Volume 7—*Volume 7*! It's got terror, battle, revenge, hope, counterattack, and finally, homecoming and realization.

Things end on a bit of a fairy-tale-like note in this book, and maybe I should've done the same with the previous one.

Anyway, I put my all into writing it, so I hope you enjoyed the story regardless.

Recently, I've been spending a lot of time in dungeons and with dragons, with big angel battles, running through shadows and generally being Getting-Better-at-Shooting-Arrows Man.

And each time, I think to myself, tabletop RPGs really are the best.

And *Goblin Slayer* is going to be a TRPG itself! Go me. Whatever else happens for the rest of my life, I'll always be able to hold my head high and tell people, "My work got turned into a TRPG!"

I hope to become one of those old people who, when they see youngsters in search of tabletop gaming, grin like a shark and proffer a rulebook.

*   *   *

With *Goblin Slayer*, I pretty much just took things that were interesting to me and stuffed them all in there. I wrote it for some hypothetical person somewhere in the world who liked the same things I did.

It turns out there was a whole crowd of those people, and that makes me absolutely overjoyed. Thanks to all their support, the series is going to get an anime. That's incredible!

A manga, a drama CD, a side story, a side story manga, a TRPG, and another manga. And on top of all that, an anime. Seriously, when am I going to wake up?

I assume *Goblin Slayer* will become an anime about slaying goblins. It's going to be great! Probably!

My gratitude goes out to more people than I could possibly include in this space.

Kannatuki, thank you for another volume of wonderful illustrations!

Kurose, every month I find myself squealing over your awesome manga adaptation.

To all my readers, including all those who have supported me since my days as a web novelist, thank you so much for your encouragement.

To the site admins, I really appreciate you having me. Thank you very much.

To all my gaming buddies and creative friends, thanks as always…!

And to the editorial staff and everyone else involved in making this book happen, thank you very, very much!

Happily, I plan for Volume 8 to be about a trip to the royal capital. Goblins that need slaying are going to appear in the deepest labyrinth.

I'll continue to give everything I have to writing, so I hope you'll keep reading.

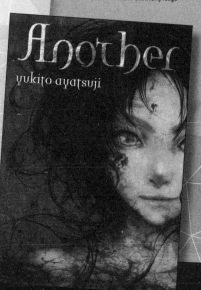